D0095169

10/12

Martha Brockenbrough

DEVINE
INTERVENTION

ARTHUR A. LEVINE BOOKS
AN IMPRINT OF SCHOLASTIC INC.

All rights reserved. Published by Arthur.A. Levine Books,
an imprint of Scholastic Inc.,
Publishers since 1920. SCHOLASTIC, the LANTERN LOGO,
and associated logos are trademarks
and/or registered trademarks of Scholastic Inc.

Library of Congress Cataloging-in-Publication Data

Brockenbrough, Martha.
Devine intervention / Martha Brockenbrough. — 1st ed.
p. cm.
Summary: To graduate from heaven's soul rehabilitation program for wayward
teenagers, guardian angel Jerome must keep sixteen-year-old Heidi safe, but
when he accidentally lets her down, he has only twenty-four hours before
her soul dissolves forever.
ISBN 978-0-545-38213-7 (hardcover : alk. paper) [1. Guardian angels — Fiction.
2. Angels — Fiction. 3. Dead—Fiction.] I. Title.
PZ7.B7826Br 2012
[E] — dc23
2011039768

10 9 8 7 6 5 4 3 2 1   12 13 14 15 16
Printed in the U.S.A.   23

First edition, June 2012

To Adam, Lucy, and Alice, always.

THE GUARDIAN ANGEL'S HANDBOOK: SOUL REHAB EDITION

CONGRATULATIONS!

You have been selected for membership in SRPNT, the Soul Rehabilitation Program for Nefarious Teens (Deceased). This bold endeavor addresses the growing problem of crowding in the lower levels of Hell. Since its inception, SRPNT has saved hundreds of lost souls, making it one of Heaven's most cost-effective interventions.[1]

But you're not here because you care about costs! Let us not mince words! You're here because:

1. You are dead;
2. You were a troublemaker in your earthly form; and
3. Your only alternative is an eternity spent in one of the nine layers of Hell.

This is your last chance to save yourself from Perdition.[2] How well you tend the soul in your care will determine your fate.

Good luck and Godspeed![3]

---

1 If you think it's terribly expensive to warehouse a person in prison, try locking up a soul for eternity.

2 We know you're not much for big words. Guess what? Soul rehab is all about increasing your vocabulary. There's more to language than four-letter words. So get used to big ones like *Perdition*, which means everlasting punishment that sinners like you endure after death. It also refers to the physical location of Hell. It comes from the Latin *perdere*, which means "put to destruction." So don't be fooled by our glowing heads and handsome robes. Beneath our attractive exteriors lurks a pure love for God that is not only bright but also lethal to the wicked.

3 We're just kidding about that Godspeed part. If you attempted that, you'd burn to a cinder in seconds.

The Guardian Angel's Handbook: Soul Rehab Edition

Chapter 1, Subsection ii:
The Ten Commandments for the Dead

I. THOU SHALT NOT COMPLAIN ABOUT BEING DEAD.

CHAPTER ONE

Jerome

ONE MONDAY MORNING, a couple years before my cousin Mike shot me in the forehead with an arrow, my eighth-grade homeroom teacher brought two cartons of raw eggs to school.

"Who can tell me what these are?" Mrs. Domino said. She was wearing her second-hottest skirt, the one with the cherries on it. Score.

I shot my hand up because that was an easy question, and if I answered something right at the beginning of the week, I could go the other four days without opening my mouth except to breathe.

"Jerome?" she said.

"Those are eggs."

I put my palm out so Trip Wexler, who sat next to me, could give me some skin.

"I am sorry, that is incorrect," Mrs. Domino said. Then Trip Wexler left me hanging.

She called on Darcy Parker, who was all, "Those are our egg babies? We get to take them home? And look after them for a week? You told us about them last Wednesday? In health?"

Darcy looked right at me when she answered, like she was getting extra points because I'd messed up again, but here's what I think. Someone who is an encyclopedia with a decent set of legs doesn't need to answer a question with a question.

"Very good, Darcy," Mrs. Domino said. She turned and sort of swished to her desk, and I tried not to stare directly at her behind, which was tough because it was pretty much at eye level and ever since that one time I'd seen her on a weekend at a car show when she was wearing jeans and a flannel shirt tied at the waist, I was thinking of her more in a Bible sense than a schoolbook sense. I looked at Trip Wexler's shoes instead, which helped because he had drawn pictures on them of the Devil with nunchuks.

Mrs. Domino picked up a stack of assignments and gave one to each of us, and when she got to my desk, I dropped mine on the floor. I was hoping she'd pick it up, because, *gold mine!* But she didn't. She just gave me a look. I slid down in my desk until I was low enough to reach my assignment, only I couldn't sink far enough, so I had to slide back up and then get out of my chair and bend over myself.

The sheet had all the rules of the egg-baby drill, but I just skipped to the cartoon on the bottom, which is how I found out about the prize for keeping our eggs alive: two free passes to the Uptown Cinerama.

I was all, "Sweet!" because the new Schwarzenegger movie was opening soon and there was no way my dad was going to give me money to watch, even though, back then, it was the coolest movie ever on account of the special effects. Everybody would be talking about it. My plan was to take Mike, and maybe the two of us could scrape up enough change out from under the floor mats of his mom's Honda and maybe also from her purse to get popcorn and Coke and Reese's Pieces too. It would be epical.

Mrs. Domino clicked back up to her desk and picked up the first carton. She opened it and held up an egg.

"Each of these eggs has a number on it. When you return your eggs on Friday, we will be able to see who succeeded and who failed. If you lose or drop your egg, please — don't even think about trying to sneak a new one in. I can tell the difference between my handwriting and yours. Part of this assignment is integrity, so I expect you to exercise some."

I wasn't sure what she meant by that even though she was looking at me when she said it. Jordan Muscovy tried to exercise his egg by tossing it over his shoulder and catching it behind his back. It cracked and oozed goo all over the checkerboard floor.

He was all, "Can I have another? I wasn't ready."

"Nope. There are no second chances with babies," she said. Her lips went all tight around the *babies* word and I remembered she was on a waiting list to adopt one from China. She used to talk about it a lot, but not so much anymore. While she finished chewing out Jordan, she kept putting eggs in the hands of other kids. "Maybe you'll remember that next time someone entrusts you with something so fragile. Now go get Mr. Moder, please."

Jordan leaned back in his chair and crossed his arms over his chest and glared for a minute before he got up to find the janitor. He kicked the garbage can on his way out and it clanged over, and everybody in the room knew he'd get detention. Other kids were a lot more careful after that. Darcy stuck her egg in a pink pencil box she pulled out of her backpack. She took the pencils out and put in a bunch of Kleenex. She had everything in that pack. She was a Slurpee machine and a porn display away from being 7-Eleven.

Mrs. Domino ran out of eggs right before she got to my desk, so she had to go back for the second carton. I took a break from staring at her skirt and looked out the windows, which were so fogged up with eighth-grader breath, it seemed cloudier outside than it really was.

She finally put an egg in my hand. It was coolish and heavier than I thought it would be, and the shell had sandy-feeling little bumps on its fat end.

"Number thirteen," she said. "Good luck."

Like I'd need luck! I was totally going to win without. I put the egg in the pocket of my hoodie and decided to call him Thirteen, which would be an awesome name for an actual baby, or for a band if you combined it with another word like *chain saw*. Chain Saw 13. Rockin'.

Mrs. Domino handed out the rest of the eggs and reminded us to store ours in the fridge at night so they wouldn't get all rotten. Someone asked if we could boil the eggs or if that was cheating.

"Would you boil a baby?" she said.

I thought about saying I wouldn't put a baby in the fridge either. But one more note in my file and it was detention for me too, and I didn't want to be in a room with Jordan because I valued my life.

After school, Mike came over and we were hanging out in the front yard under the oak tree. I almost forgot Thirteen was in my pocket, which would've been a disaster because we were tossing a football back and forth. I for sure would've smashed him because Mike was the kind of guy who threw really hard at your stomach. But I remembered in time and put my egg on a pile of crunchy leaves instead.

Mike nodded at it. "Snack or egg baby?"

Mike was two years ahead of me, and he remembered a lot about school, but never useful things like what to say to the lunch ladies to get bonus Tater Tots.

"Egg baby," I said, trying to look the right amount of cool and bored. The trick is to keep your mouth open a little.

"I remember when we had to do that."

"You keep your egg alive all week?" My face was sweating warm, and the cool air felt good. Smelled good too, like wet apples or pumpkins. I caught the ball, and my body slipped into position . . . fingers on my left hand tight but not too tight, making the perfect L around the belly of the ball, twisting my shoulders as I brought it back.

Sometimes, I can still feel what it was like to throw a ball, a million complicated moves you couldn't think about without screwing up. You just had to believe you could do it and let go, your throwing hand curving forward like the sun does across the sky, your shoulders rotating like a planet across your body as you step into the pass. Maybe that's how God felt creating the universe, making everything spin in all sorts of ways just before letting it go and watching what happened.

I once tried to explain that idea to Mike.

"Are you kidding?" he said. "Or drunk?"

"Yeah, duh. Obviously. Both."

I never mentioned it again, but I was onto something. I know it. There's something major in the way you can launch a ball into someone else's orbit like it's your own crazy moon.

Mike chucked the ball back and it smacked right into my hands, so hard my finger bones rang. "My egg baby lasted about two seconds. I threw it at a car right after school got out. It was totally sweet. I pegged a minivan full of Cub Scouts, and their mom pulled over and started yelling at me and I pretended like I didn't speak good English and offered to sell her my pants for twenty bucks. Let's do that with your egg too."

I looked down at Thirteen and realized how much I didn't want to chuck him at a minivan. He was my egg. Mine.

"No way, man." I moved my right leg so I could put more mustard on the pass. "I'm gonna take care of him all week. The prize is movie tickets. Me and you are gonna see *Terminator 2*."

"Right on," Mike said. He bobbled the ball and it bounced off to the left. He looked annoyed that he had to run after it, which is probably why he drilled my gut with a tight spiral. "What's the plan for this weekend?"

We put the football down and talked about maybe sneaking into a laser Floyd show and trying to meet older girls. This cat came up to us and was all crawling in our laps and bumping its head on our chins, which is when Mike said, "You can make a bomb out of laundry soap and cat litter." That was the same cat that later got my soul into all the trouble and I wished a thousand times I'd told it to scram way back then.

But I didn't. I just said "cool" to the idea of a cat litter bomb.

After a while of tossing other ideas back and forth at each other, it got too cold to be outside, and the sun was mostly down, so we went in. I put Thirteen in the fridge, and Mike and me watched TV until my dad came home, and Mike said he had to make like a nose and run. It took me a couple seconds to get the joke, but when I did, I laughed until my stomach muscles cramped.

❦

Thirteen and I had a good week together. I took him to school and sat him on my desk so he'd have a good view of things. I skipped my appointment at the orthodontist on account of I didn't want to scar him for life. And I could tell he really liked it when I cranked the tunes in my room, especially the Lynyrd Skynyrd. If you look at an egg or anything long enough, it will let you know what it's feeling. That is a fact.

Then on Thursday night, our last night together, the night before I was going to win the tickets, I went into the kitchen to make myself a ketchup and pickle sandwich on white bread and found Thirteen in the sink. Or what was left of him, namely, his shell. It was broken into two big pieces, with a couple of little chips hanging down around his middle. I went up to my pop's La-Z-Boy, where he was sitting with a plate on his stomach, chewing on something.

"Did you eat my egg?" I didn't even need to ask because I saw the yellow goo smeared on the plate. Alls I could think of was that it was Thirteen's heart.

"What do you mean, your egg?" He swallowed. "You mean the one in the fridge?" Pop was watching the news about the war in the desert, so he didn't even look at my face when he was talking. He hadn't changed out of his coveralls, but his work boots were off and I could see part of his big toe through a hole in his sock.

"It was the only egg in the fridge," I said.

"Well, I made a Doug McMuffin out of him." Doug is my pop's actual name and Doug McMuffins are his version of the McDonald's thing.

"But it was my egg."

"Don't blame it on me, buddy. If it's in the fridge, it's food, and it's fair game. That's your rule, by the way. The one you made after you ate all my kielbasa. 'Your' egg was in the fridge next to the beers and cheese. Anyone woulda thought it was up for grabs." Pop had a string of cheddar hanging from his whiskers and I wished he'd use his sleeve or a napkin or something to wipe it off. He changed the channel to sports, and cheering noises came out of the TV set.

"He had a number on him. It was for school."

"Sorry, kiddo. Didn't know. Not the end of the world. Nobody died or nothing. You can tell your teacher he was delicious." He flashed me half a smile and rubbed his eyes with the thumb and forefinger of one hand. Then he stuck the plate out for me to clear.

Afterward, I took my sandwich into my room and ate it on my bed, even though the bread had gotten soggy. I looked up at the ceiling, where I'd taped a Schwarzenegger poster that I'd swiped from the mall. I shouldn't have left Thirteen in the fridge all by himself. Duh. I should've put him in a box, or taped a note on him, like Darcy would've done. I should've known Pop would eat him. Anybody else would've figured that one out. But it was too late for me. It was too late for Thirteen. There are no second chances with egg babies.

At school the next day, I didn't tell Mrs. Domino it was my pop who ate my egg baby. Even with how things were at home, I have a rule about not ratting because I don't do that to family, no matter what. So I told her I did it, and that it tasted excellent. Because if you're going to get in trouble anyway, you might as well go out in a blaze of glory. That has always been my style. Which explains a lot about the thing that happened later with Heidi.

THE GUARDIAN ANGEL'S HANDBOOK: SOUL REHAB EDITION

Chapter 1, Subsection ii:
The Ten Commandments for the Dead

I. THOU SHALT NOT COMPLAIN ABOUT BEING DEAD.

II. THOU SHALT NOT ENGAGE IN DISCOURSE WITH THE LIVING.

CHAPTER TWO

Heidi

WHEN HEIDI DEVINE was five years old, she was eating lunch with Megan, her new best friend. The sandwich sat on a melamine plate the color of an egg yolk, and Megan grinned at her from across the table, with the tail of a Goldfish cracker protruding ever so slightly from her left nostril. Heidi, her legs dangling from the kitchen chair, couldn't believe it. Goldfish crackers were her favorite. Why waste one up your nose? She had no reason at that time to suspect there was anything wrong with the sandwich.

"Eat your lunch, girls," Mrs. Lin said. "If you do a good job, afterward you can have some Ugli fruit."

The promise of ugly fruit wasn't what made Heidi eat, though she was curious. Would it be furry? Have crooked teeth and purple skin? A tail? No, she ate the sandwich because she was excited to be having lunch at Megan's house. Also, the voice told her to eat it, and at that time, she did whatever the voice said.

You can probably eat it in three bites. I once ate a hot dog in two and I choked a little, but you've got a good-size mouth, and if you really try, you can polish that thing off and we can get a load of this ugly fruit Megan's mom is talking about. I bet it's the color of lizard poop.

Heidi nodded and covered her mouth with her hand so she wouldn't be tempted to reply aloud. The night before, she and Rory had been playing LEGOs in the family room. Or, more precisely, Heidi had been building Rapunzel's tower, and Rory had been knocking it down with his airplane fist, because he was three and that is what three-year-olds do.

Her parents were still at the dinner table, and over the clatter of tumbling LEGOs, she heard her name.

"Don't you think Heidi's too old for imaginary friends, Warren? The other kids are going to think she's strange."

Rory threw a LEGO at the wall, so Heidi couldn't hear her dad's reply.

Then her mother's voice. "But the doctor said —"

"Doctors don't know everything."

"Fine." Her mom sounded angry. Had Heidi done something bad? "I'll deal with it myself." Silverware clinked against dishes, and a blush heated Heidi's face out to her ears. She tried to snap a LEGO onto the green base to rebuild her tower, but she couldn't make it fit.

The voice in her head was making her parents fight. It would make other kids think she was weird. So she resolved not to talk about him anymore, even though she used to tell everyone about Jerome. And why not? She thought everyone heard a voice like that, just as she thought everyone's tuna salad sandwiches tasted like the ones her mom made. She even liked having Jerome there, usually.

There was this one time when she was about three years old and still slept in a crib . . . she woke up in the middle of the night with a sore throat and fever. She had strep throat — not that she knew it at the time. She just knew she hurt all over. Her throat felt like a scraped knee, and her skin hurt to touch. When she tried to call for her mom, her voice came out as a useless squeak. So she lay in her crib, hugging her stuffed bunny, despairing.

That's when Jerome started singing a song she hadn't heard before. It was different from the music she usually listened to. There were no rainbows, stars, or wiggly worms in the song, and maybe because she was at a low point in her life, the song went straight to her soul and stayed there. The song, she learned later, was called "Freebird," and Jerome was just finishing up the last words when her mother came to get her.

She scooped Heidi up and pressed her against her chest.

"Oh, poor baby," she said. "You have a fever."

She carried Heidi into the bathroom and flicked on the light. Heidi closed her eyes against the brightness, listening to the creak of the medicine cabinet, the crackle of cellophane coming off a new box of medicine. Her mom tipped a plastic cup of it to Heidi's lips. The liquid tasted sweet and strange, and afterward, her mouth was sticky, but her throat started feeling better right away, and she was almost asleep before her mom tucked her under the flannel comforter on her parents' bed, where she slept between them for the rest of the night.

The next morning, Heidi went to the doctor's office, still wearing her footy pajamas. She said "aaah," endured a swabbing with a giant Q-tip, and was sent home with a lollipop in her favorite flavor — red — along with a bottle of powdered medicine. Jerome sang songs in her head about candy and sugar all the way home.

Then her mom put her in front of the TV set with a sippy cup of apple juice.

"Who's Jerome?" she said. She'd squatted down and put a gentle hand on Heidi's knee. Even as young as she was, Heidi could read the concern in her mom's face. "You were talking about him last night. A lot."

"He's my friend," Heidi said. She sucked up some apple juice. "He sang to me."

"Where did you meet him?" Her mom tucked a strand of Heidi's hair behind her ear.

"I don't know." Heidi looked at her feet. She could tell it wasn't the answer her mom hoped for. "Can I have more juice?"

Her mom nodded, took her cup, and headed for the kitchen. "Where did he sing to you?"

"In my room."

Her mom stopped walking and turned to face Heidi. "In your room?"

"Yes," Heidi said, watching Elmo recite a poem to his goldfish. "Last night. Every night."

"There was no one in your room last night, honey." Her voice sounded reassuring. She opened the fridge, swished the juice into the cup, and snapped on the lid.

Tell her I'm your imaginary friend.

"He's my imanigary friend," Heidi said.

"Ohhhh." Her mother handed her the cup of juice. "Imaginary. That's a big word for you, Heidi. Good girl. Now finish your juice and let's get you dressed for the day."

Tell her you want to wear your conductor overalls.

"I want to wear my conductor overalls."

"Those again?" Her mother wiped the countertops.

Say "damn straight."

"Damn straight."

"Heidi, I don't know where you learned that language, but it's not okay."

Holy smokes, that hurt. But it was worth it.

"What are holy smokes?" Heidi asked.

Her mother marched over and clicked off the TV. "Enough of this," she said. "It's time to get you dressed."

⁂

So, making a special effort to conceal her invisible friend, Heidi lifted the sandwich. She sniffed it. It didn't seem quite what she expected. Megan, meanwhile, took the bread off the top of her sandwich and sprinkled the tuna with Goldfish.

"It's yummier this way. Try it."

Heidi shook her head. That wasn't what she was used to.

"Okeydokey," Megan said.

Heidi took a huge bite of the sandwich. She gagged.

17

You're not choking, are you? If you're choking, reach around and thump yourself on the back. I'd do it for you, but . . .

She shook her head. She wasn't choking. It was the tuna. It tasted terrible — pasty and sweet like the cat food her grandmother served Mrs. Kitty. Also, there was celery in it. Celery! Why would anyone want crunchy tuna fish?

She wanted to spit out the sandwich, but she didn't want to hurt Megan's feelings or miss her chance to see ugly fruit. She took a huge gulp of milk. Her mouth was so full she thought she might drown. But then she swallowed. She was done.

Heidi, did you see that? Megan took the cracker out of her nose and put it in her sandwich. Then she ate it. What a sicko!

"Uh," Heidi said.

"What?" Megan had a mouthful of sandwich.

"I'm full," Heidi said. She pushed her plate away.

Mrs. Lin swooped in, holding what looked like a dented grapefruit. "Heidi, you've only had one bite of your sandwich. Don't you want some Ugli fruit?"

That's ugly fruit? I've seen worse. Once, my cousin Mike made me eat this apple that was all bruised up. It looked like it had gone fifteen rounds with an angry caterpillar. Now that was ugly fruit.

"No, thanks," Heidi said.

She'd had enough strange food for one day, and her mind was still snagged on what had happened the night before, when she'd heard her parents talking about the voice in her head. There was something wrong with her, something that would make people not like her. Maybe that was why she hadn't liked Mrs. Lin's tuna sandwiches. Megan loved them, so it was probably all Heidi's fault how bad it tasted.

Her stomach clenched. No one could know about any of this. She forced as much sandwich down her throat as she could, and slipped the rest in the front pocket of her jeans, where it left a damp circle and a funny smell, even after they'd gone through the wash.

Over the years, Heidi carried the secret inside her, and it behaved like a jungle plant, climbing and spreading everywhere it could find room. There were some difficult times, like the night Tammy Frohlich had a slumber party in seventh grade.

Five of them attended the party: Tammy, Heidi, Megan, Piper, and Hallie. Or six, if you count Jerome. Megan and Heidi lay on Tammy's hot-pink shag rug, just a little bit on the outs, even then. Everyone else danced and played air guitar and pounded out drum solos on Tammy's queen-size bed, which was covered with a zebra-print duvet. The whole thing struck Heidi as impossibly cool, from the size of the bed to the existence of such a thing as a duvet. Heidi came from a world of twin beds and blankets. Overhead, Tammy even had a disco ball.

Then "Freebird" came on, part of a classic rock playlist they were listening to ironically. Everyone laughed because it ranks as one of the cheesiest anthems ever. Piper sang along to the lyrics, prompting loud complaints from Jerome.

Nobody sings on top of Ronnie Van Zant. That's criminal.

Lodged where they were in Heidi's soul, the opening chords made her eyes sting. Heidi breathed deeply and focused on the lyrics. She could feel herself in them, especially in the line about being a bird you cannot change. While the song itself is about a guy who doesn't want to be tied down, it's also about being fundamentally broken, unfixable. That was her. She was the bird with the fatal flaw.

Overhead, the spinning disco ball cast a constellation of light on the ceiling, across the walls, and over their bodies. Spinning stars and painful words and all those voices — it was more than she could take all at once.

She started to cry, just a little, and Piper was on her like mold on bread. She clicked off the music, stopped singing, hopped off the bed, and loomed over Heidi in her adorable pajamas. "Oh my GOD, you guys! Heidi's *crying.*"

"No, she's not," Megan said. She sat up so fast her glasses slid down her nose.

Heidi wiped her eyes and said, "It's the lights," at the same time Megan said, "She's allergic to dust," which made it clear to everyone in the room that Heidi actually was crying, in violation of one of the unwritten rules of slumber parties.

"This is the stupidest song in the world and it's making you cry," Piper said. She flopped down on the bed. "You're hilarious, Heidi. God."

"If it's such a stupid song," Megan said, "then why do you know all the words?"

That was the last of Tammy's slumber parties that Heidi and Megan were invited to. Jerome remained in Heidi's head, talking to her when she was at school, when she was folding her underpants and putting them away, and of course when she was making the big decision about what to name the terrier puppy she got in eighth grade.

Come on, Heidi. Corn is a funny name for a dog. Corn Dog. *Get it?*

In the one time she was able to ignore Jerome completely, she named the dog Jiminy instead.

Jerome also talked to her when she was doing her art. At first, he used to tell her what to draw. Things like a shark eating an alligator eating a dog eating a baby. But then he figured out it wasn't her style. So he offered encouragement, which she loved. There were maybe a couple of hours a day he was quiet, as though he'd gone to sleep or something. Those were the hours her head felt like it was open to the sky, quiet and clean, and it gave her a little taste of how it must feel to have a life that's really yours, how it must feel to be normal, undamaged goods.

One night during her freshman year, she couldn't sleep. She decided to look up her problem on the Internet and see if it had a name.

It did.

Auditory hallucinations. The heartening news was that one in ten people hear them. She wasn't totally alone in this. But even her case was abnormal. Most people hear either a happy voice or a sinister one — an angel or a devil in their heads. Jerome was a lot more complicated. He was sometimes comforting, but mostly just funny and gross, or funny and gross simultaneously. He had a joke about an Irish zookeeper and a gorilla that made her want to laugh and throw up every time she heard it.

21

But knowing that Jerome was an atypical hallucination wasn't the worst part. Nor was the part of the website that told her how serious her problem was, which she read aloud to make sure she understood:

"When auditory hallucinations are associated with a psychiatric illness, when they manifest frequently, and when they lead a patient to confuse reality with illusion, they can pose a severe disruption in a person's life."

What are you reading? I don't know what any of those words mean. Reading blows. Let's go to that website that shows the funny animal videos because the one with the turtle and the strawberry —

"I'm not reading anything," she said. "I'm just — leave me alone." Her reply was more proof that she'd confused reality with the imaginary. She was mentally ill. Sick. Crazy. Disturbed. Any number of words that coated her stomach with ice. *Disrupted* felt like too mild a word to describe what Jerome had done to her life. But even that wasn't the worst part.

Rather, it was that, deep down, no matter how he shamed and complicated her, she didn't really want him to leave. She loved the quiet parts of her day. But there was something about his voice, his way of seeing things, and just the weight of him in her head that she also loved. When the silence ended and his chatter returned, she invariably felt a flood of relief. He was back. She wasn't alone. Even if everyone else in her life left her, she had someone. And she wanted to stay that way — even if it meant she was beyond saving.

The Guardian Angel's Handbook: Soul Rehab Edition

At SRPNT, we take an innovative, three-step approach to rehabilitating wayward souls: memorization, group discussion, and practical application.

First, memorize the Ten Commandments for the Dead (page 29). Feel free to use whichever technique is most effective for you. One of our wards wrote a catchy ten commandments rap. He graduated to Heaven in just six months!

Next, bring a *positive attitude* and a *willingness to learn* to your group counseling sessions. Candidates for soul rehabilitation have mandatory small-group discussions facilitated by our expert counselors. These begin promptly at nine o'clock each morning.

We've assigned you an infant soul to nurture and protect. Treat this soul as you would your own. We call this the Golden Rule™, and in shepherding another soul safely through the mortal plane, you will demonstrate your readiness for graduation.

Our seraphim-to-wayward-soul ratio is the best in the business because it is the *only* such program in existence. So take advantage! Pour your heart into the process. Your immortal[4] soul will thank you later!

---

4 Souls are mostly immortal. Under certain conditions, they can dissipate into the cosmos, which is why you should read this handbook with care and attention.

Though this should go without saying, we know the likes of you well enough that we shall commit it to print: A failure to protect your soul shall result in expulsion to the appropriate level of Hell (see page 87 of your manual for a description of Hell's nine levels).

CHAPTER THREE

Jerome

WHEN I FIRST got to Heaven, or at least the part they let me visit, I was sitting on a hard chair in a room that reminded me of a principal's office. I kept shifting in my seat, but this was normal for me on account of how I was born with a tail. Just a little one. Lots of people have them and no matter what Mike said, it didn't mean I was the son of the Devil. I was the son of Doug, and chairs were uncomfortable. That was it. Even so, I used to check my forehead in the mirror every so often to see if I was sprouting horns.

Two guys with glowing heads and choir robes were in the room with me. Grown-ups. Smiling, but that lippy way old people do before they drop the trouble bomb in your lap. The one behind the desk had a mustache the size of a harmonica. The other one, a bald guy, stood next to him.

I felt fuzzy-headed, like I was dreaming, so it didn't strike me as impossible or anything that one minute Mike was aiming an arrow at the orange on my head, saying, "I wish we could make a movie of this," and the next I was getting busted at a school I didn't go to by two guys I'd never met, in an office decorated with framed posters that said things like BELIEVE and DETERMINATION and MAKE IT HAPPEN, with pictures of flying whales, three-legged kittens, and people lifting monster trucks off of toddlers. Worse, the background music was classic rock songs covered by a church choir, which ought to be illegal.

Out the window was an extra-green grassy field where a lot of old people were doing something that looked completely wrong. A couple of them had linked elbows and were moving around in a really fast circle. Two more were holding on to the edges of their robe things and snapping them back and forth, and the rest had pulled their robes up real high so they wouldn't trip on the bottoms while they were playing leapfrog. You don't normally see that much leg from old people, so it was hard not to gawk a little. Also, I wasn't totally sure it was happening outside my imagination, especially on account of the sky was so blue it looked like the stuff Mr. Moder used to clean toilets.

"What's up with them?" I said, once I found my voice. "Are they on something?"

"They are frolicking," said the bald one with the dark skin and shiny head. "Would you care to join them someday?"

He stood and walked behind my chair and put his hands on my shoulders and made like he was enjoying the view. A little breeze from his robe brushed against the back of my neck and I shuddered. My dad called that a rabbit running over your grave.

The angels introduced themselves. The one with the lip broom was Gabe. The chrome dome was Xavier.

Gabe started in on me. "There is hope for frolicking, Jerome. There is hope for *you*. But only if you want it. You must believe, and you must show determination to make it happen. So we ask again, do you want to be saved?"

If it meant I had to frolic, then the answer was no. But I knew it wasn't the one they wanted to hear, so I dodged the question and sort of went, "Derrrrr. Nice posters," and then I wiped a little slobber off my chin.

The choir music got real loud then, and let me tell you, "Highway to Hell" isn't anywhere near as good without the guitar.

Xavier said, "It is possible his mind is not fully recomposed, Gabe."

"I think this could be as good as it gets," Gabe said.

They looked at each other and shrugged, and let the air be empty except for the singers. Then Xavier did a little wave with his hand, which turned down the music. He made his voice go all trumpety and announced, "Jerome, thou shalt be a guardian angel in training, and thus shalt thou redeem thyself for thine earthly misdeeds."

I sat up straighter and was all, *You are shitting me*, which is when I found out about the swearing sensors in my skull. If you say that word, or pretty much any of the other swears normal people use all the time, you get a

27

brain shock so bad you could cook bacon on your forehead. Every once in a while I forget, but mostly nowadays I use words like *Chevy* instead. And *flask, motherflasker, apple, jack apple,* and *apple hole*. Among other things.

After my head stopped sizzling, Gabe touched his fingertips together, church-and-steeple style.

"Do you know why you're here?"

I shook my head. That was a huge mistake on account of the arrow, which was still stuck halfway between my eyebrows and hairline.

"Throughout your life, Jerome, you have made a series of errors. Mostly forgivable things. But when taken in their entirety, especially in light of the unfortunate incident with the cat —"

He stopped, either to take a breath or to watch me turn all white and come close to passing out, which is always what happened when I thought about what I'd done that day.

He made the sign of the cross, cleared his throat, and started again. "You are at a crossroads." I figured he didn't mean that literally, on account of we were still in an office.

I nodded gently, so as to not disturb the arrow.

Xavier cut in. "Thou shalt complete our program, or thou shalt descend into the fiery depths of Hell."

Gabe unsteepled his fingers and did this whammy thing with them and showed me, on a big, floating screen, what Hell actually looks like. There are nine rings of punishment stacked on top of each other like used tires. They're Death Star huge, though. Depending on the kind of bad you are, you get sent to one of the tires. For example, there's Level I: Everlasting Standardized Testing for the Ungrateful, and Level II: Ballroom Dancing with the Elderly, which is for Jerks.

The camera zoomed in on each level, one at a time, and through the tiny windows I watched people take their punishments. On Level II, they fancy-danced around the room even though they totally looked like they needed to sit. Every time someone tried, though, a fork of lightning would whip up from the floor and jolt them right back up and smoke would curl out of their ears and hair. Most of the people there were old, but not all. Some of the younger ones were guys about Mike's age.

Each level got worse, all the way to Level IX, where people who were violent in body and spirit turned into maggots and were set loose in the world to eat rotting food before getting eaten themselves, or turned into flies and crushed. Then their souls dropped back to Hell and started all over again as maggots. If I'd ever seen a nature show that bad when I was alive, I would've turned off the TV forever and, just to be sure, put the remote control on the train tracks for a fatal crushing.

The video cut to a part that showed how in the olden days, every angel watched over a human, but then the population got out of hand, and angels started demanding the right to enjoy their deaths without having to do stuff. Pretty soon, the rehab angels were the only guardians left, and there was only enough of us for one in ten people or so to have one.

That made us special. We had a second chance to become good people and get into Heaven. Not exactly what I wanted, which was to not be dead. But it wasn't like I had a choice in the matter.

"Thou shalt have a soul to tend," Xavier said after the video ended. "One carefully chosen for you. Consider thyself blessed to have her."

That's when I first saw a picture of Heidi.

She was a baby then, about the size of a loaf of bread, and I was all, *Sweet! She lives in a crib!* They gave me a handbook that was supposed to have all the rules and stuff for guarding our souls and getting into Heaven. I didn't bother reading it. What was the point? I'd be out of rehab before she got out of diapers. How much work could a baby be? Also, her mom was hot, so I didn't mind hanging around one bit.

I stashed the book in one of my hiding places and pretty much forgot all about it for the next sixteen years, a decision I regretted about five thousand times when that thing happened out at the pond.

CHAPTER FOUR

Heidi

HEIDI KNEW she should have avoided *Talentpalooza!!* altogether. Reason One was the unnecessary punctuation in the name. Reason Two: Tammy Frohlich had organized it. But Megan had begged her to enter, telling Heidi it would be good for her reputation and their friendship if they did a really amazing dance number onstage, like something out of *Dancing with the Stars* but without the traditional moves and same-sex partner restraints, which made Reasons Three and Four.

The more times Megan talked about it, the more Heidi got used to the idea, which stopped sounding like the worst one in the world and instead merely sounded like a mildly embarrassing way to spend two minutes and forty-seven seconds of her life. It seemed a small price to pay to make Megan happy.

But that was before she saw her costume, a formfitting tuxedo made out of black-and-white spandex. "You dance the male role," Megan said. "It makes more sense. You're so tall and muscular."

You look like a . . . Jerome paused.

Like a deranged penguin, Heidi thought.

And that was only from the front. She didn't have the guts to check the rear view in the three-way mirror at the costume shop, not only because the mirror was right by the place where the Goth kids were trying on studded collars, but also because she was still in mild shock that the shop actually stocked a penguin suit that fit her six-foot frame. She tried not to think about who'd rented it previously, what reason anyone might have to wear a stretch tuxedo, and whether they'd worn underpants.

When *Talentpalooza!!* finally arrived, Megan and Heidi made their way out of the echoing hallway and into the semi-darkened auditorium. Heidi wore her mother's trench coat over her costume so she could minimize the amount of time she'd be seen in public dressed like a mutant bird.

Don't do it. Don't go onstage. Don't do it. Don't. Don't. Don't.

Megan's voice filled Heidi's other ear.

"We have to do this, Heidi, if only to take high school back from the people who rule it. They are Satan's minions. They make high school hell. We must defeat them."

Heidi pressed her palm against her forehead. So many voices. Jerome in one ear, Megan in the other. And then there were the machine-gun giggles of people who'd seen Megan's costume. She'd chosen something called Fantasia in Spangles, and it was decorated with enough sequins to cause temporary blindness and/or seizures in anyone who looked at it directly. This did not bode well for Heidi. If Megan's costume was funny, Heidi's was full-on hilarious.

They found two seats near the stage, just in front of Sully Peterson. The back of Heidi's neck warmed, a side effect, no doubt, of sitting in front of the hottest guy in school. For five years, Heidi had studied him, had memorized his jawline, the color of his eyes, the way his hair curled up at the edges. She detected the slightest aroma of leather and sweat, a comforting smell despite the situation.

"Shut up, you two," he said.

Heidi sat up a little straighter. He'd said "you two." He'd noticed her. After all these years, he'd noticed her. Her body went into blush overdrive, and she was glad his seat was behind hers, or she might have melted his puffy quilted vest, the one from the catalog that was banned back in middle school for "inappropriate pairings of classic poetry with images of shirtless minors," according to the letter the principal sent home. The catalog had only gotten racier in the following years, and guys like Sully dressed exclusively in their clothes, looking like Greek gods taking vacations in the Hamptons so they might seduce petite, flaxen-haired heiresses in foamy seaside encounters, a scenario she'd internalized as her personal ideal while reading a romance novel one Saturday morning in the public library.

In the novel, you could tell an immortal by his glow, and Sully definitely was putting out at least sixty watts. He also looked like he had the hand strength to rip open a bodice, not that Heidi actually owned anything more delicate than a sports bra. She simply wanted to worship at his altar. Was that so wrong? Okay, and she would not have objected if he pressed his lips against hers and pronounced them ambrosial. It didn't seem like too much to ask. In her head, when that magical moment happened, she planned to say, "You may drink of them, sir." She hoped it wouldn't sound so goofy in real life. Also, she hoped that ambrosia was something you drank, and not some sort of Jell-O salad like the kind they served in the cafeteria on the fourth Wednesday of each month.

Megan had no problem talking with Sully. "I'll be quiet when I'm dead, Peterson."

Heidi sank in her chair. That was not the perfect conversation starter. She wished she could make like a real-life penguin and dive below a shelf of floating ice in the peaceful frozen darkness somewhere a million miles away.

"Sorry, Heidi, but I had to do that," Megan whispered. "He's a douche box."

"Douche *bag*."

"No, *box*. I'm trying to start a new insult franchise. Put *box* on the end of almost any word and it's an insult. Sully box. Pudding box. See? Foul. Anyway. High school is hell. Truly. Consider the evidence: Morning PE classes on a good hair day. The smell on the bus after they let the middle school borrow it for a field trip. Jockstraps in the lost-and-found outside the office, because how does that happen? HOW?"

Megan stopped talking when the vice principal, Mr. Chomsky, stepped onstage into a spotlight that bounced white light off his glossy scalp. He cleared his throat, tapped the microphone, winced when it squealed, and announced: "Good morning, ladies and gentlemen. It is so nice to see your bright and shining faces today."

Students all around them groaned. Someone a few seats to Heidi's left yelled, "*Talentpalooza!!* sucks!"

She could not have agreed more. And that was *before* everything happened.

Mr. Chomsky raised his index finger in the air until there was silence. "There is a car in the parking lot with its lights on, a black Jeep." He read the license number from a square of paper. Sully cursed.

Go *with.* Jerome again. *His guardian isn't watching. And it's safer than making a fool of yourself in front of the whole school. He might even offer to squeeze your milk cartons behind the bleachers.*

Heidi might have actually gone until Jerome had to mention the part about her milk cartons and the bleachers. Why did he have to take it there? To the milk cartons part. She was indifferent to bleachers.

Then it was time for Tammy to perform. She bounced up onstage wearing a short white dress that showed off her tiny, perfectly pointed knees and slim ankles. Heidi figured she could fit a Tammy comfortably in her left thigh. To make matters worse, Tammy sang like an angel, performing a song she'd written herself, called "Adopt a Million Orphans." That alone justified the two exclamation points in *Talentpalooza!!*

Soon enough, though, Tammy sealed off the glories of her windpipe and stood drenched in the spotlight and the applause that rained from the heavens. Two rows in front of Heidi and Megan, Piper and Hallie jumped up and down hugging each other, something that takes varsity-cheerleader levels of coordination. Heidi hummed a little "Freebird" in her head, but even that didn't help. She started to pray. If there were a god, she wouldn't have to follow an act that good.

When the clapping faded and Tammy floated offstage, Mr. Chomsky bent in to the microphone again. He read off the name of the next act. She couldn't quite make it out because Jerome was talking.

Sure you wanna do this? If I were you, I'd run.

Mr. Chomsky cleared his throat and repeated himself. Megan squealed and bounced up. She grabbed Heidi's hand. "We're going to kill up there!"

Heidi's legs engaged, but they felt like wet logs. She thumped into the aisle, holding her trench coat tightly around her ribs. It wouldn't come off until the last possible second, she resolved. She trudged to the stage, where the light was so bright she couldn't see past the first row of faces.

Megan whispered something between clenched teeth.

"What?"

"The coat! Take it off!"

Heidi untied the belt and unfastened the buttons. Her fingers shook. Outerwear hadn't given her this much trouble since preschool.

"Take it off!" a boy's voice said from the back row. He was rewarded with laughter and applause.

Finally, Heidi triumphed over all the buttons. "Can I keep it like this?"

Megan reached up, pulled the coat off Heidi's shoulders,

and flung it to the corner of the stage. She nodded at the A/V crew, and the music kicked in. A tango.

I can't watch. I'm outta here.

As Jerome went quiet, the world went loud. There was so much noise — the music, the laughter, the blood pounding in her ears. She couldn't remember any of the steps, so Megan pulled her along, doing her best to lead while looking like she wasn't.

"Dee-vine! Dee-vine!" The chants started, then the clapping, timed with the beats of her name but slightly off tempo from the song. If there had been any rhythm in Heidi, it flew away like a startled bird. Around the edges of the auditorium, people — teachers, probably — swooped in to stop the clapping. But it was too late.

They finished the song. Or more accurately, the song ended. Megan looked at Heidi and shrugged. "At least people enjoyed it. And you were very light on my feet."

Heidi bent to pick up her trench coat, trying to make it swift and ladylike. That's when she felt the sudden flutter of unraveling stitches and the unwelcome breeze on her rear. She'd mooned the entire school. And she could forget about the damage deposit on the costume.

The audience roared, and she regretted her choice of underwear, a cross between granny panties and elvish battle armor, because she'd wanted something that would hold her belly tight while she tangoed. Heidi hoped no one had taken pictures, or worse, video. All she could do was put on her coat and slip off the edge of the stage, where Jerome's voice once again found her ears.

It's not exactly Hell, Heidi. But it's pretty close.

In the grand scheme of humiliations, Megan told her afterward, what had happened onstage during the talent show was trivial. The sort of thing people would forget five minutes later. Or maybe a day. Definitely by the end of winter break.

"It might even make you popular," she said as they sat down later that day to eat lunch. Megan peeled the foil off her blueberry yogurt container and swiped it against her tongue. "Especially if people thought you were being ironic. I saw how that worked once on *The View*."

Heidi's face and ears reddened. *The View.* Honestly. Heidi took another bite of her chili and looked toward the recycling can so she wouldn't have to make eye contact.

"Wait," Megan said. She touched Heidi's wrist lightly with her fingertips. "I didn't mean it that way. You know I don't have a speech filter." She took another bite of yogurt and let it ooze from her mouth. "See? Oh, and my mom predicted I'd hurt your feelings today. Admit it: Her psychic powers are unreal."

Heidi managed a small smile.

"Your mom's psychic powers are unreal."

"You'd better have meant that figuratively."

Megan sat with her back to the window, wearing her new coat that looked like something from the Oscar the Grouch pimp collection. Behind her, an unreliable sky trembled with snow-filled clouds. The rest of the kids in school bustled behind Heidi. She felt their body heat, and every so often, a gust of air scented with chili Fritos and cinnamon rolls blasted over her.

Megan wiped her chin with a crumpled napkin. "Anyway, you were fine up there. Most people probably didn't notice. And by tomorrow, people will be talking about other things."

Don't fall for that, Heidi. You were epical today. And not in the good way, like, say, a Frank Zappa solo from Shut Up 'n Play Yer Guitar. *But it's all right. You can make up for it if you do good in your game tonight.*

Heidi pressed her fingertips into her temples, wishing Jerome would leave her alone for a while. He had to remind her about basketball, one more thing she was doing because people expected her to play when they saw how tall she was. Her parents were convinced she could get a college scholarship if only she'd try. But she was mediocre at best. Her heart wasn't in the game.

Heidi slipped a Pigma Micron pen out of her pocket and smoothed her napkin flat. She moved her pen over the napkin's surface, trying to capture a decent portrait of Megan.

"Lemme see," Megan said. She reached for the napkin.

"No, it sucks."

She crumpled it and held it in her fist. The problem with trying to draw people was that she didn't know what to focus on and it felt rude to stare. Typically, she drew tiny towns, cities with skyscrapers, metropolises with floating buildings, exotic villages with gilded minarets, old-fashioned hamlets with leaning three-story half-timber buildings. You had to look hard to see any people in them, but they were there, silhouetted in windows, obscured in shadows, living out their tiny lives. Her school notebooks and binders, and at one point even her jeans, were covered in these sketches, and more than once, she'd lost an entire class period to daydreaming about what it would be like to live in one of those places, to be somewhere else living in some other body.

Her mother had tried to get her to stop drawing countless times.

"You have to stop wrecking your pants," she'd say. "We're not made of money. It makes you look grubby to have all that scribbling on your thighs."

But Heidi couldn't stop, especially after she'd discovered the wonder of the Pigma Micron during her freshman year. With it, she wasn't just drawing. She was becoming the lines, dancing on whatever surface she'd chosen, drinking in the blackness of the ink until she was nothing but what she unspooled from her imagination. It was the only time she ever felt like her hands and mind and body and soul were all working together on the same thing.

That year, she'd made a sketch a day, keeping them in a stack in the family room. One day while she was at school, the stack disappeared. She asked her mom, who was organizing the spice cabinet, if she'd seen it.

"What, those sketches?" She clicked a jar of pepper and one of paprika down on the counter. "I recycled them. I'm sorry. We just have so much art from you, Heidi. You can't save it all. And I have to say, I know you like your drawings, but it's time to realize you don't have time for that anymore. Doodling is taking time away from the things you need to be doing, like thinking about where you want to go to college and what you want to do with your life. The art — it just isn't practical."

"Come on." Megan interrupted Heidi's memory. "Just let me look."

Heidi slid the napkin toward her and took another bite of chili. She forgot to blow on it and scorched the roof of her mouth.

"Hey, not bad, but you forgot something crucial," Megan said. She drew an extravagant handlebar mustache on Heidi's portrait. "Did I ever tell you about my cousin?"

"The one who goes to Brown?"

"No. That cousin is pretty much a perfect specimen of humanity. He's even hotter than Vincent Lionheart, and I would marry him if I lived in one of the twenty-five states where that sort of thing is legal. My *other* cousin. The one who sings on cruise ships."

Heidi smiled at the mention of Vincent Lionheart. She'd just bought Megan's Christmas present, a limited-edition deluxe action figure of the movie vampire Megan had coveted ever since they saw him at Undead Con. He even had hand-painted facial features, a houndstooth blazer, and miniature lace-up wing tips.

"I don't think you've talked about that cousin."

She hasn't. I'd remember that.

"She once messed up really bad at her high school talent show," Megan said. "She and her best friend were doing their two-headed farm-girl act. They were inside a pair of giant overalls together —"

If I was a farmer, I'd be an egg farmer because everyone there gets laid.

Heidi shushed Jerome.

"No, it's a good story," Megan said. "I promise."

"No, not you. I was . . . never mind."

"Were you having another one of your Earth-to-Heidi moments?" Megan said. "You have that look on your face again."

The look was slack-mouthed and vacant, like she'd just come back from getting a cavity filled. Heidi tried to tighten up her expression. "That doesn't sound that embarrassing. Not like what I did."

"Just wait." Megan scraped the sides of her yogurt tub. "So Robin and her friend were in their overalls together, singing 'I Feel Pretty' from *West Side Story*. And they did mean for it to be funny, because, when you get right down to it, there's no way a two-headed farm girl is going to rate as pretty, unless the word is followed immediately by *freaky*."

"So what happened?"

"It was going really well. Everyone in the audience was cracking up. My cousin was laughing. Her friend was laughing. The laughter got bigger and bigger. It was like a rampaging elephant. Unstoppable."

"That sounds like a good thing."

"Not when you've hydrated like a camel," Megan said. "Gatorade, water, chocolate milk. She even had a Frappuccino for breakfast, and you know what all that caffeine does."

"Why didn't she use the restroom beforehand?"

"Because the stupid principal had decided a couple days earlier to take all the doors off the bathroom stalls because people kept writing graffiti on them. 'Taking faculty names and phone numbers in vain,' he called it. So no one was peeing at school, because there is no shame more humiliating than a public tinkle."

Try using a urinal sometime. At a hockey game.

"Uch, I'm eating here," she said, as much to Jerome as to Megan. Not that it mattered.

"So when everyone at school was loving the act, my cousin got the giggle fits."

"No."

"Yes," Megan said. "And she sprang a leak."

"Was it a lot? Could people tell?"

"Well, any pee on stage is too much. That's a truth universally acknowledged. But this was huge."

"You're making this up."

"Nope." Megan mined the bottom of her yogurt container. "The school yearbook photographer was there. They printed the photo. It took up most of a page. For the rest of her life, she'll have to see how she looked doing a surprise whiz. They even packaged it with a pun headline. 'Tinkle, Tinkle, Little Star.' "

That was the worst — to be mocked with a pun. Tammy was the yearbook editor. She'd almost certainly assigned a photographer to *Talentpalooza!!* Heidi tried not to think about it.

"But she got the last laugh," Megan said. "Now she really is a star."

"On a cruise ship, though."

"Captive audience," Megan said. "If they can't leave you, they have to love you."

Just like you love me, right?

Heidi put her spoon down and shoved the remains of her chili away. "I just want this week to end. If I didn't have to play basketball tonight, I would totally go home fake-sick right now."

Megan nodded and started clearing the wreckage of her lunch: the yogurt tub, the peelings of an orange and a banana, and the wrapper from a Slim Jim she'd bought at the 7-Eleven across from school because her mother didn't let her eat nitrates.

Heidi arranged her dishes on her tray. She stood, and someone clipped her hard from behind. Her dishes slid to the floor in slow motion, spattering her with secondhand chili and tepid water. Then they shattered, and time sped up, and she turned to look at everyone else in the cafeteria, even though she knew that was unwise. For the second time in one day, people applauded, the slow kind they called sarcasticlaps. In the corner, someone was dancing a tango.

"I'm going to revise my earlier statement," Megan said, turning Heidi away from her audience. "The bright side is that winter vacation starts tomorrow morning. By the time we get back to school, no one's going to remember this. And on the other bright side, it just proves the point I was making earlier about high school and Hell. Welcome to the nightmare."

CHAPTER FIVE

Jerome

ONE OF THE first people I met in rehab was Howard. His soul, Sully, was a baby too, the big fat kind that crashes around in a diaper, pulling furniture over. Heidi never did that kind of stuff. She was also big, and also wore a diaper. But there was no crashing around. She was all ladylike, and for a while, I hoped it would be enough to get me out of rehab.

But I guess deep down I knew I was never getting out.

They paired me and Howard up a lot on account of our souls were around the same age. Part of me wonders if that's what made her think that douche box Sully was worth thinking about for more than two seconds. I knew all about her crush on him. Anyone within a mile could see it like it was written on her forehead. He was out of her league looks-wise, and she was out of his in every other way. But there was another reason they paired us up — a reason I learned about real early on in soul rehab.

We'd both killed cats. But mine was an accident. Me and Mike were drunk on Jägermeister. He was sixteen and I was fourteen, just out of Mrs. Domino's class. It was one of those hot summer days that make you do stupid things because you're pretty sure the day is never going to end, no matter how you fill the hours, and that life is always going to be the same sweaty mess. We wanted to see if this cat that was hanging around us would keep landing on its feet if we dropped it off higher and higher things, giving it a good hard flip each time. It was wrong. I knew it. But I didn't know what it would be like to live with something like that.

And forget about dying with something like that on my soul.

The cat stopped moving after we dropped it off the roof. It closed its eyes and gave one last creaky meow and it just lay there and I thought I was gonna be sick. All the blood rushed out of my fingers and they felt freezing even though it was almost a hundred degrees out. Mike got a shovel and we took turns digging a hole and I couldn't even feel my hands as I was scooping the dirt. It was a deep hole, way bigger than we needed, and we put the cat in and covered it up, all without saying a single word to each other.

Later, the cat's owner put flyers on all the telephone poles in the neighborhood, and they stayed up there till the rain washed them down that fall. I memorized the phone number and thought about calling it, but what would I say?

We never told anyone what we'd done, but there isn't hiding anything like that when it matters, and when the weight of your life is being measured and you come up worth less than a pound of hamburger meat.

During one of my first group sessions, Xavier split me and Howard off from the rest so we didn't have to confess doing such horrible things in front of everyone else. He told us we could be each other's partners in penance. I wasn't sure what it meant, but I'm pretty sure he didn't want Howard to get off on my story.

Howard had all these questions for me, like *Did blood come out its ears?* and *Did you ever dig it up again, just to see the bones? And this one . . . Were you watching at the very second it died? What happened in that moment its soul left its body? That's what I wanted to see when I killed my cat. That moment in time. But I didn't know then that souls live on, and now what I really want to see is what happens if a soul is extinguished, you know? Does it disappear? Leave a pile of dust? Smell like burning rubber? Scream for mercy? Wouldn't it be awesome to find out?*

I didn't want to be like that Howard guy, but there was no getting around the fact that we were both killers. That made us the same. Still, it didn't make me want to spend any more time with him than I had to.

He cornered me by the craft table the afternoon Heidi stink-bombed the talent show. We were in the place where group meets, a sort of rec room with fluorescent overheads that buzz so much you feel like you're surrounded by flies. The carpets are the color of dust, cookie crumbs, and old bruises, and no one cares if you spill because it never shows. They keep it like that to make us want to go to Heaven more.

We spend part of our time in group at an activity station, like crafts, or board games, or whatever, and part sitting in a semicircle talking about our feelings and what we learned while looking out for our souls. We weren't required to share, so I never did. But we had to show up, or else.

Howard stood between me and the table, leaning into my space with his arms crossed, and I could smell pizza rolls on him even stronger than the open pots of craft paste behind him. It looked like they were setting up for our annual Snowman Gratitude art project, which was a fun thing for a kindergartner, but not so much for someone who'd been seventeen for sixteen years in a row, especially since we'd been banned from giving the snowmen boobs on account of they are not mammals.

"Jerome," he said, trying to make his voice go all low and manly. "Nice work this morning."

He had the hairiest knuckles I'd seen since I went to the zoo in third grade and lost a staring contest with a gorilla.

"You weren't even there," I told him. "Your guy left the lights on in his car. So shut it."

"Got an offer for you," he said. He stepped a little closer and I leaned backward so I wouldn't have to touch his plaid shirt. "I'm gonna trade you souls. My guy's easy. You just gotta make sure he doesn't choke on French fries or skateboard without a helmet."

"If he's so easy, why are you still here?"

Howard squinted and cracked his knuckles, and for a second I thought I was going to lose a staring contest with his fist. Even though we can't touch earthly things on account of we're on a heavenly plane, guardian angels can bust each other's faces just like the living do. We can maybe even hurt each other worse because we're going bare soul to bare soul with nothing in between.

"Don't you ever get sick of spending all your time with one person?" he said. "Don't you want to see what might happen if you tried another soul on for size?"

I didn't like the look in his eye or the sound of his voice when he said that. "Shove it."

"Suit yourself," he said. He flicked the collar of my jacket. Nobody touches my jacket. My dad gave it to me, said he never wanted to wear it again but that he didn't care if I did.

Xavier came in and asked for a volunteer with the chairs, and I stepped forward even though I never do that sort of thing. At first, my hands were shaking, which made the chairs plonk against each other, but eventually I relaxed and unfolded the seats like a pro. I passed them to Xavier, who arranged them in a C shape. When we were done, Xavier clapped his hands together real loud. He has his hands hooked up to a celestial amp, so it was like two metal doors banging shut. People headed for their seats.

During sharing, Howard told Xavier what had happened to Heidi at the talent thing. He even brought a show-and-tell video from the Internet and played it on one of his gadgets. One of Sully's friends had taken it and put it online after the assembly, and he sent a link to everyone in school, and then it made it around the world before lunch because at the 2:57 mark, you could see a flash of her behind when her penguin suit split in two. Some guy in Uruguay even put a marriage proposal in the viewer comments, which I found out about later because Heidi's little brother, Rory, had translated the words on his computer and texted them to her when she was in math, where she cried on her precalculus problem set.

"Maybe Jerome's human should get a more suitable guardian angel," Howard said, looking all innocent-like. "I could watch over her. I could even do two souls at once, you know, if you're gonna send Jerome down."

I wanted to go angry rock star and trash him like he was a hotel room. I had this vision of myself, all slo-mo, where I brought my foot back and swung it under his chair and connected on the metal with this sweet, sweet *thwack*, and then I watched him pinwheel backward into space. The other guys all leaned forward in their chairs. I don't breathe anymore, but it felt like all the air left the room, and the hairs on my arms and head and stuff stood up like they were trying to follow. I curled my fingers into my palms and dug in my nails. The pain was good, so I held on to it and decided that, for now, it was enough.

"She has a name," I said. "Heidi."

I thought Xavier might fling me to Hell right then and there, but he surprised me, which is sometimes the thing with him. He put his palms together and tilted his head. "Heidi suffered an embarrassment, to be sure. But embarrassment is not the end of the world. And in fact, it can build character. Her spirit will rebound, stronger than ever."

Howard smiled and said, "Of course, Xavier. You're right, as always," but I could feel the anger rising off his skin, and I realized that if he wanted Heidi so bad, he probably had some sick reason for why.

Xavier moved on to some of the other guys, asking them about their spiritual journeys, and he wrote their feelings down in his notebook, and then pretty soon group was over. I did this thing we call the shoop, where your molecules slide through the molecules of the universe in a high-speed burst of color and sound. It's a little like sticking your head out of the car on the freeway, only you're going faster than a rocket, so it's a good thing you're already dead.

I was back with Heidi in study hall. I wanted to say something to her to make her feel better, but I couldn't really think of the right thing, so I just hummed a little "Freebird" and hoped she knew she wasn't alone.

The study hall is the worst room at Heidi's school, and that includes the JV boys' locker room. They've set it up in the dungeon of the library, where it's always cold and smells like mushrooms, and the dividers between the desks are covered in so much handwriting, they look hairy. It's not too crowded on Friday afternoons, and she was at the desk in the corner behind the pole, the one people sit at only if they are doing something they don't want anyone to see.

Usually, two people at a time use that desk, if you catch my drift, but Heidi was there alone. She had one of her drawings and was bent over it with her pen, which could make lines practically as thin as a spiderweb. She bought it herself with money she earned taking care of the neighbor's dog, which, if you ask me, was a rip-off because that dog is a lethal weapon in at least seven countries. Dogs can see the dead, and whenever he sees me, he barks so much it feels like my soul is going to vibrate into a heap of shavings.

When she first started making her pictures a few years ago, I used to try to give her ideas for what to draw, mostly of awesome animals, but she was all, "I draw cityscapes. Now shush so I can concentrate."

"What about Godzilla? He busted up cities."

"No living things," she said. "They're too hard." But she was smiling.

"Mechagodzilla? He was mostly robot."

"Jerome!"

Later, when she'd gotten really good at it, I used to wish for more.

There was this one time she was drawing a broken-down street in the bad section of her town, all full of storefronts with handwritten signs advertising cheap stuff no one wants. The one nice building on the block is a church, or used to be. A fat, rusting chain sealed off its door and a FOR SALE sign was stuck by the parking strip out front. I watched her work on that drawing, seeing everything so terrible in front of her and turning it into something else. It was a windy day, and the breeze kept blowing her hair into her face, and I wanted to hold those strands back so she could work without getting bugged by it. And I wished I could rest my hand on the back of hers as she drew, so I'd know what it felt like to lay those lines down on paper. I wished she could feel me there, not just hear me, but feel me next to her, watching her work, loving what she was making.

I wished she'd draw me too. But she'd have to see me to be able to do that, so it was never going to happen.

This time, in the library, Heidi was crying and blacking out all the windows in her drawing of a city built on top of a narrow hill. It looked like the whole tiny place was shutting its eyes, one at a time, and I never would've said anything like this to anyone, especially not Xavier with his feelings notebook, but watching her do that made me feel . . . well, they say you only die once. But on days like that, Heidi could kill me once or twice, easy. I sometimes gave her a hard time just to make it hurt less. So I watched her, folded over her tiny little world, turning it dark, and I felt the same inside.

CHAPTER SIX

Heidi

THAT EVENING, just as the last of the late fall sunlight drained from the sky, Heidi suited up in her basketball uniform, hoping to block a big shot, snag a key rebound, somehow redeem herself in the game. There was no chance of a wardrobe malfunction at least. Her shorts not only fit, they were made from polyester, a fabric that will, along with cockroaches and fruitcake, survive the apocalypse.

In the last three seconds of the game, her big chance presented itself. She stood below the net and caught a wild shot that rebounded off the rim. It *thwacked* her palms, and everyone in the gym roared, this huge sound that shook her organs and turned her fingertips to ice.

All she had to do was make a smart pass. She looked for someone open but couldn't find a hole, and time was running out. She tried to send the message from her brain to her arms to shoot. Scoring the game-winning point would be, in Jerome's words, epical.

Heidi stood there holding the ball.

Three! The crowd roared.

She could hear her parents yelling.

"Be the ball!" her dad said. "Be the ball!"

She wanted to. But she didn't know how. Most days, she felt like she could barely fill her big, clumsy body.

Two!

Jerome's voice filled her ear. *Don't miss. For once, for the love of . . . just don't miss.*

One!

She willed herself to press the ball toward the basket, bringing it closer to her face so she could give it everything she had. Then came the buzzer. She'd frozen, failed, wasted her chance. The crowd groaned; the air rushed from the room. Heidi looked up at the lights, bright stars surrounded by cages. They swam with watery rainbows.

Someone knocked the ball out of her hands. The murmuring crowd sounded liquid, distant. The basketball bounced away, *dub-dub, dub-dub*, like a heartbeat. It slowed. She saw colors and light. The heartbeat grew quieter and quieter. And then it stopped.

❧❧❧

The next morning, shortly after Jiminy woke her with his dog breath, she forced herself out of bed and into her clothes. She'd take a walk to the pond. As often happened, she had a deep urge to step right out of her body, leave it behind for a while as if it were a pair of dirty jeans. Since there was no chance of that happening, she wanted to settle for fresh air, a change of scenery, and time away from everyone who reminded her of what had happened at school, of everything that was wrong with her. Her parents had spent much of the previous night explaining to her how little it mattered what happened during the basketball game, a sure sign that it did matter. A lot. She also didn't want to be there when Rory showed them the video of her in the penguin suit. She was surprised he hadn't already.

She pulled on her jacket and, with Jiminy at her ankles, headed out the front door toward the street. The sun had barely cracked the horizon and it was near freezing out. She flipped her collar toward her ears, regretting she hadn't put on mittens or snow boots. Not even a hat. But she needed the air, and knew she'd never muster the guts to go outside again once she stepped back indoors, so she pressed on. Shaggy evergreens hunched their shoulders under thick coats of wet snow, and the sidewalks stretched before her, unshoveled, unwelcoming. Even the sky felt lower and moodier than usual.

The pond had always been a favorite place to forget. She thought of it as a gateway to peace. The water, usually still and green, rich with reflected images, had a way of calming her. It lay about twenty yards from a moderately busy road, ringed by a gravel path, hedged with rhododendrons, and it often froze during the darkest part of winter, shrinking beneath a silent lid of ice. A sagging blanket of snow covered everything around it like a sad, dirty quilt. Jiminy rolled in it like a lunatic.

"Stay close," she said.

A man wearing a maroon coat with AUDUBON SOCIETY silk-screened on its back held a clipboard and pen. He looked at her, nodded, and said, "There's a brown creeper."

Heidi looked down at her tan coat, wondering if he meant her. It would be a weird thing to say to a stranger, but maybe she was giving off the vibe. Or maybe he was some sort of mythological oracle guarding the gateway to peace, sent there to judge anyone foolish enough to go for a walk in such lousy weather.

She half expected Jerome to say something about the creeper comment. Ordinarily, he wouldn't let anything like that slide. But he was oddly silent.

Overhead, a bird sang, wrapping the pond in a sweet, silver thread of sound.

"See, see," the bird said.

Jiminy galloped down to the pond and romped on the ice.

"Jiminy!" She hoped he'd obey so she wouldn't have to walk all the way there to get him. He ignored her. She stepped onto the ice with one foot, then the other. Jiminy wasn't nuts. It felt terrific to be walking where she usually couldn't.

"Should you be out there?" the man in the coat said.

Heidi ignored him. What did he know? He'd called her a creeper. In all likelihood, the ice was fine. It had been freezing all week. Either way, she had to get her dog. She walked to the middle of the pond and whistled. There, the ice was no longer white but gray — the color of oysters and things drawn in pencil. She filled her lungs with cold air and exhaled, making her very own cloud.

The ice sighed beneath her feet.

"Jiminy! Come on, boy." He glanced at Heidi and ran in the opposite direction, up the bank, and off the pond altogether. That was a relief. She looked down at her shoes just as a sharp, low *crack* filled her ears. Then came a stuttering *creak* followed by an ear-ringing *snap*.

"See," the bird said.

Heidi froze.

Then the pond opened its mouth and swallowed her. She couldn't breathe. Her arms tingled and went numb. The best she could do was reach toward the sky, which unwound ribbons of light toward her through a sparkling cloud of tiny bubbles.

Where was Jerome? Why wasn't he saying anything?

The freezing water unlatched her brain and spun it around in her head. With her arms outstretched, she found herself dancing the tango, playing basketball. There was a sound, a *dub-dub*, of dancing feet and bouncing balls. The sound distorted and slowed. She saw colors and light and wondered why she'd never thought to draw an underwater city. Something like Atlantis. The look of the world through green-gold water was incredible. If she could've captured the bends of shadow and light, it would have been her most spectacular piece yet. Jerome would've liked it.

In the distance she heard him call her name. He sounded worried. How sweet. And then another voice, telling her what she wanted to hear. *Let go*. She did, releasing the cold, the light, the noise. All of it ceased, and for the first time she could remember, she felt completely and utterly at peace.

CHAPTER SEVEN

Jerome

I SHOULD'VE BEEN watching over Heidi when she went out onto the pond, but I wasn't because Howard had rung up my skull phone, which is what we call the implants in our heads that let us communicate with each other. He wanted to talk about dead cats again. That made one of us.

I listened to him just long enough to not make him mad. Then I pretended I was in a patch of bad reception and hung up. I turned around in time to see Heidi walk across the pond after Jiminy. And I guess the ice wasn't thick enough or she wasn't thin enough, because there was this big *snap!* and her hair sort of flipped up like it was attached to a string in the sky and then — *woop!* — she was gone and there was nothing but a big hole, and then time speeded up and it was only this guy in a puffy coat standing around the edge of the lake, holding a clipboard, looking at Heidi's dog like, *Are you gonna get her? I just ate and I don't want a cramp or anything.*

People suck when they think no one's watching.

Here's the thing. Someone's always watching.

Heidi! I called her name like it would make some sort of difference. I stared at that hole in the ice, hoping her hand would shoot out. Why wasn't the guy calling 911? I moved next to him and broke the rules and shouted the idea in his ear, which had so much hair inside, it looked like a shower drain.

Once he got over being scared out of his pants, he dropped his clipboard, stuck a hand in his pocket, and fished around for his cell phone. He first tried to dial with his glove on. He poked the buttons like some sort of ape before he finally ripped his glove off with his teeth and threw it on the snow.

There was a *ring-ring* and a 911 operator's voice said, "This is 9-1-1. What's your emergency?" and then he said, "I am reporting an emergency."

The slowness of it was killing me. I went closer to the hole and looked down. Her hair swished in the water. Her eyes were open. There were no bubbles rising from her mouth. Her arms reached up, like maybe she'd let go of a ball or a kite and she wanted it back. The only sound that cut through the cold air was a stupid bird that wouldn't shut up.

I wasn't going to be able to pull her out. When you're a soul, you can't lift big things, like people. If you really try or you're experiencing a major attack of feeling, you can knock something small off a table: a pencil, maybe, or a piece of paper. It takes everything you've got to move just that little bit of earthly stuff.

Keeping her safe was my last chance of staying out of Hell, so I couldn't let her go without a fight. I yelled her name and jumped in, and the water was beyond cold. The way my chest hurt reminded me of what it felt like to be alive, which almost made things worse.

It was hard to see underwater, and I fumbled around for what felt like forever. Then her fingers wrapped around mine. I thought I was maybe imagining it until I felt her glide through the water toward me. I pulled her close, reeling her in like a fish, and I wrapped one arm around her back. I'd had a lot of fantasies about the two of us that close, and I'd always tried to put them out of my mind. It seemed wrong. Figures that I'd get my wish like this.

With her head resting on my shoulder, I clawed back toward the light, using my free arm, kicking my legs like there was no tomorrow. I didn't know how I was doing it, but I *was* doing it. I was saving her. I was her guardian angel and I'd come through.

It was like a miracle. No, it *was* a miracle.

For a second I imagined the looks on the faces of the guys in rehab when I told them how I defied the laws of celestial physics and dragged a hundred-and-seventy-pound girl out of her watery grave. Howard would probably Chevy his pants. The rest of the guys would have to respect me for this. I might even ascend to Heaven, as long as no one spent too much time thinking about how it was my fault she'd fallen through the ice in the first place on account of I hadn't been watching her.

We busted through the surface of the water. Her head was still on my shoulder and I tried not to think about what would happen if I couldn't get her breathing again. In the distance, an ambulance wailed, but I didn't waste time waiting for it. I shoved Heidi up onto the ice, which was a lot easier than I thought it'd be, but I didn't question it because you don't Darcy Parker miracles when they happen.

I hauled my own self out of the water and dragged her off the ice and onto the snow a good ways away from the pond so there was no way she'd fall in again. Jiminy went nuts.

"I know, boy, I know," I said. "We gotta do the mouth-to-mouth thing." Jiminy barked at me like he understood.

Her face was still and her lips were blue and they were open enough so I could see the tips of her teeth. I felt panicky, but I'd seen on TV how they revive people. I could do it. I had to.

I unzipped her jacket and palmed her chest and pushed a couple of times. Then I moved around to the side of her and put one hand on her forehead and one hand under her chin. Her skin was cold and wet. Not how I imagined what it would be like to touch her.

Jiminy barked again. I leaned in, being careful with my forehead arrow, and made like I was going to take in a big gulp of air, not sure how well it would work on account of my not breathing anymore. Jiminy barked again and whisked around me like he was a little broom that needed to tidy the snow.

The siren got louder and I looked up. Hallelujah chorus time. The fire department could take over. Two guys in blue jumpsuits ran out and started putting on wet suits and breathing gear.

I waved them over. "Right here!"

Even after all this time, I still sometimes forget no one but Heidi knows I'm here.

Jiminy ran up to them and yapped his little head off. One of them looked our way, but he didn't come over. Instead, he was talking to the big guy with the clipboard. Ignore me, fine. But why were they ignoring Heidi? Couldn't they see she was right there?

"She went in there," Clipboard Guy said. He pointed at the ice. "I told her not to walk on the pond. What a shame."

I wanted to punch his neck for not actually helping, but it wouldn't do any good. I got myself together and turned back to my girl. I pressed my mouth to hers and gave it everything I could. Her lips were cold and had the sweet and dirty taste of pond water. I pushed on her chest again, but she didn't open her eyes or anything. *Please, please.* I leaned in, breathed into her again, giving it everything I had. Her lips moved under mine and I hopped away from her like she was a sparking power line about to rain down on the whole wet wreckage of me.

Her eyes opened and she turned her head my way. Then she coughed and pushed herself up on her elbows, blinking a couple of times real slow.

"Heidi," I said. "Thank goodness."

"Who are you? What happened?" She sat all the way up and touched a finger to her lips. Without thinking about it, I touched mine too, and I felt my skin get warm. "You fell into the pond, but it's okay because I pulled you out."

"Are you —" she said. "Wait. You sound exactly like the voice in my head. Like Jerome. What happened? Why can I see you? Why were you —" She touched her lips again, then her cheeks. "And oh my God, that arrow — does it hurt?"

I started to explain. Then I saw her eyes get huge, so I turned around to see what she was looking at. Holy Hell. Once I knew what she'd seen, I figured out what had happened. It felt like there'd been an avalanche in my skull.

"Is that —" she said. "Is that . . . me?"

She pointed at the ambulance guys, who'd made their way out of the pond and stood by the edge of it. Water streamed off their wet suits into the snow. Heidi's body hung between them. Her head tipped back and strips of hair dragged on the ground, and if my heart were still beating, it would've cracked open my chest and launched itself into the snow like a bleeding Molotov cocktail.

It took me a while to get the words out. "Yeah. That's — that's you."

My throat filled with concrete. I hadn't saved her. Not even close. I'd pulled her soul right out of her body and any second now she was going to *whoosh* away from me. She'd go to Heaven, I'd go to Hell, and that would be that. Sixteen years of her being with me, and it was over. Forever. For both of us.

I couldn't feel my hands or feet, and I couldn't find any of the words that I wanted to say to her, and when I could focus again, the ambulance was driving away, and Heidi was running after it, with Jiminy at her heels.

"Wait!" she yelled. "WAIT!"

They didn't.

I braced myself, and for the first time in I don't know how long, I prayed to the Creator. Not that I'd ever seen him or was even sure he really existed. But I prayed, and I meant it.

The Guardian Angel's Handbook: Soul Rehab Edition

Chapter 1, Subsection ii:
The Ten Commandments for the Dead

I. THOU SHALT NOT COMPLAIN ABOUT BEING DEAD.

II. THOU SHALT NOT ENGAGE IN DISCOURSE WITH THE LIVING.

III. THOU SHALT GIVE UP EARTHLY ATTACHMENTS.

CHAPTER EIGHT

Heidi

HEIDI STOPPED RUNNING once she realized she could never catch the speeding ambulance. She bent over and put her hands on her knees, expecting her lungs to be on fire. But they weren't. Strangely, she didn't even feel tired, just exposed and rootless, like a tooth that had been yanked from its socket.

Run home. She'd felt an overwhelming urge to go there, as if what had happened, what she'd seen, wouldn't be real if she were able to return to her family, to her cave, like a wounded animal. She started running again, and once again her lungs refused to burn. Her heart refused to hammer in her chest. She felt nothing at all as she glided along the sidewalk, no branches tugging at her hair, no snow crunching beneath her feet, no pounding of cement against her soles. It was like being in a dream, and except for the presence of Jiminy at her ankles, she would've thought she was having one.

She slowed to a jog just before she reached her house, staring at the figure on her porch. Jerome. Somehow, he'd known she'd come home. How he'd managed to beat her there was a mystery.

Leaning against a post with his arms crossed, Jerome looked like his voice sounded, but if she'd seen him at school or the mall or some other landmark of her life, she would've avoided him. He was big. Taller than she, but skinny, like his body had forgotten to expand outward as it shot upward. His hair was shaggy and black, and he'd tucked his faded jeans into a pair of combat boots held on with laces that were more knot than anything else. His green canvas jacket, which looked like he'd bought it at a military surplus shop, was maybe a size too big.

She stopped short, and Jiminy panted on the sidewalk behind her. In the distance, the neighborhood church bell tower started to ring.

"You're here already. How —" The sound of the church bells passed through her, each one feeling as round and solid as a bowling ball.

"I shooped," he said. He walked toward her, holding out his hands as if he were going to take hold of hers. "Thought you'd do the same. All souls can do it, at least all the ones I know. There's something I gotta explain —"

She stepped to the side, relieved the bells had stopped ringing on the ninth chime. "There isn't time. I need to see my family. Right now." Her voice caught. "This can't — this can't be happening." All of it felt strange and impossible, seeing Jerome and her own body, feeling the ringing of the bells and the appalling absence of her heartbeat.

Heidi pushed past him, raced up the stairs, and tried the doorknob. Her hand sliced through it as though it were a projection and not the simple, solid object she'd wrapped her fingers around nearly every day of her life without a second thought.

"I can't open the door," she said. "Why can't I turn the knob?" She turned to face him.

"Heidi."

He took a step closer. She looked at the arrow and put a hand on her chest. It was gruesome, sticking out of his forehead like that. How could he stand it? How was it possible even to survive something like that? He opened his mouth to speak, and she knew with absolute certainty he was going to talk about what they'd seen back at the pond. She didn't want to hear any of it.

"Stop. Don't say another word. I have to see my family. Maybe they can —"

Jerome reached out and started to put a hand on her forearm but appeared to think better of it. He shoved his hands into his pockets and looked at his boots.

"Heidi," he said so quietly she could barely hear it. "Any second now, you're gonna go to Heaven. You'll get to hang out with the angels. You'll love it."

She put her hands over her ears. "STOP! Don't say that. It's not true. I'm not —" But she couldn't find the word in her mouth. If she'd been crazy before for hearing him, what was she now that she was seeing him?

She fell to the snow and wrapped her arms around her head.

"Come on, Heidi. I know how you're feeling. Believe me. When I woke up in Gabe's office —" He interrupted himself, shaking his head. "Look, I'm sorry, but we've gotta get going. It's already past nine o'clock, which means I am late for group, and any second now, you're going to get pulled into Heaven, and once the powers that be write your name in the registry, I'm going to get sent someplace else. My only chance to survive is if I sneak you in through the back so no one notices. You'll be fine — I promise."

"Jerome." Heidi's voice was quiet, and she could only get out one word at a time. "Please."

A look passed across his face, and Heidi almost got up and went with him, he looked so desolate. Before she could speak, though, he shrugged and helped her stand. Then he turned and walked straight through the door as if there was nothing there at all.

With one hand extended, Heidi took a step toward the door. Jiminy barked and she turned to him. She couldn't leave him alone outside. He'd run into the street, get hit by a car. She froze for an awful moment, trapped between what she wanted to do and what she knew she had to do.

Jerome stuck his head through the door. "You coming?"

He caught sight of Jiminy. "Oh yeah," he said, stepping outside again. "I'll watch the mutt."

❧❧❧

It felt strange to pass through a door, like a million soft fingers stroking her cheeks and shoulders. Heidi shuddered, but didn't stop moving until she'd reached the family room, where her mother was reading a fitness magazine, her father was balancing his checkbook, and her brother, Rory, was playing his video game, as though this was any Saturday morning and not her last one.

"Mom, Dad!" she said. "I've had an accident!" She couldn't say the word *dead*. Even if it were true, maybe she could keep the reality of it at arm's length and spend the rest of her existence near her family, as Jerome had with her.

She tried saying their names again. "Mom? Dad?" Her voice wavered. If she let in the grief through any of the cracks, it would drown her all over again.

Heidi's mom adjusted her reading glasses and flipped a page in her magazine. "Rory, it's cold in here. Did you leave your window open again?"

"No," Rory said, clicking buttons on his controller. "I don't think so."

Her dad mumbled "carry the three" under his breath. He tucked a pen behind his ear and scratched his head. Why couldn't they hear her?

"MOM! DAD! I'VE HAD AN ACCIDENT. IT WAS BAD."

No reaction. She turned to her brother. The television screen carved a blue halo around his head, and the light shone through the tips of his hair. Even standing behind him, she could smell his cinnamon gum.

"Die, bastard, die!" he said. He was playing some sort of war game.

"Rory, your language," Mom said.

Heidi stepped in front of him and reached for his controller. Her hand went straight through. "Rory!"

"Aw, crud," he said. "My game crashed."

It was true. The image had frozen on the screen. An alien with a space helmet was caught in the moment of its death, its green exoskeleton split open, revealing a pomegranate splash of guts.

"That sucks! I was about to get a bonus life." He rebooted his game.

"Rory," her mom said. "Language!"

Heidi understood why they couldn't see her. But why couldn't they hear her? She cursed and reflexively covered her mouth, expecting her mom to scold her as she had Rory. She would've welcomed it, or any kind of reaction, but she got nothing. She lowered herself onto the couch next to her mom, who shivered and reached for a quilt.

The telephone rang.

"Answer it, Rory," Dad said.

"Just a minute." The video game blipped.

"Rory," Mom said.

The phone rang again.

"I can't pause my game right here! I have to get it to the next level before I can save my status."

The phone rang a third time. Once more, and the call would go to voice mail.

Heidi's mother stood. She placed her magazine down on the couch, marking her spot with a coaster from the coffee table. She pushed her glasses up the bridge of her nose and strode to the telephone.

On the fourth ring, she picked it up.

"Hello?" she said. "Hello?" Then she placed it back in the cradle, sighed, and said, "Let's see if they left a message."

"The phone isn't your boss," her father said. "You don't have to listen to the messages right away."

"I know, but it might be important." She dialed and put the receiver to her ear. "The caller ID says it's the hospital. Do we know anyone sick?"

Heidi moved next to her mother and whispered in her ear, taking care to pronounce each word clearly. "It's me, Mom. It's me. I had an accident at the pond."

Her mother's lips tightened, and the knuckles on the hand that held the phone turned white.

"Sweet!" Rory said. "Die! Die!" Digital explosions scuffed the air.

"Turn it down, Rory. I can't hear the message." Her mom stuck a finger in her ear. "Oh my God." She scratched down a telephone number on a notepad.

"The hospital," she said. "They want us to call right away. They said it's an emergency." She hung up. For a long moment, she seemed to move in slow motion. "Where's Heidi?"

Heidi had never seen her mother's face look that way.

"She's not in her room?" Her father set his pen on the coffee table.

"Heidi? Heidi?" Her mother ran down the hall, and Heidi followed on silent feet. "Heidi, are you in here?" She spun around once in the center of the room.

"Yes," Heidi said. "YES!" Her mother heard nothing. The Vincent Lionheart vampire figurine she'd bought for

Megan stood on the shelf, next to an unobtrusive Moleskine notebook full of cityscapes. Heidi had picked up Vincent on a shopping trip with her mom the weekend before. If she could knock him on the floor, it might send a message of sorts. But her hands swiped through him with nothing more than a tingle.

"She's not here, Warren." Heidi's mom ran back into the family room.

Heidi took one last look at her notebook, wishing she could put it someplace safe, hating the idea of people flipping through it and thinking she was pathetic for drawing so many of them. There was nothing she could do about it, so she turned to follow her mom back into the family room, where she was already dialing the hospital. It took her mom two tries to press the right numbers, but she finally lifted the receiver to her ear. It rang once, twice, three times.

"Come on, come on, answer," she said.

Someone finally picked up. Heidi's mother explained why she was calling. A voice buzzed in response. Her mother's knees buckled as she reached for the wooden chair behind her, putting her arm straight through Heidi's belly. For the first time since her accident, Heidi felt warmth.

"Warren," her mother whispered, dropping backward into the chair.

He took a step toward her, his face taut and gray. He didn't say a word.

"It's Heidi," she said. She held the phone to her heart. "They found her. In the pond."

"No." He blanched and covered his mouth with his hand.

Rory's game blipped; another alien exploded in a cloud of crimson mist.

"Turn it off, Rory," Mom said, her voice barely more than a whisper.

"I'm trying!" The television screen went blank. Rory dropped the controller and stood, wiping his palms on his jeans. "How did she fall in? You're not supposed to walk on the pond."

"We have to be with her," her mother said. "We have to be with her right now."

Heidi tried to grab the sleeve of her mom's sweater, but her hand slipped through and her mother moved entirely out of reach. "I'm right here! I AM RIGHT HERE!"

She yelled until her throat ached, but no one looked her way. She pleaded with them as they grabbed their coats and shoes, but they walked through her as if she didn't exist. Rory opened the door and Jiminy bounded in, dripping muddy water. He bounced up to Heidi and ran circles around her ankles, but nobody cared about that or the mess.

The door slammed. She burst through it and nearly tripped over Jerome, who sat on the porch, holding his head in his hands.

"Jerome!" she cried. "They couldn't hear me! Should I get in the car and follow them?"

She didn't want to go where they were going — the morgue, most likely. The thought of seeing her dead body again filled her with terror and revulsion. But she couldn't bear the thought of never seeing her family again, and if she didn't go with them and was taken away to Heaven like Jerome said . . .

"What should I do? Jerome, tell me!"

Car doors slammed and the engine started up. She reached for Jerome's shoulder and he turned his face toward hers. She gasped. The arrow had started bleeding a bit, and his pupils were so dilated she couldn't tell what color his eyes were. The skin below them had ripened into soft plums. Something terrible had happened.

"Come with me," he said. "Just . . . please."

"But I didn't get to say good-bye to them." She gestured toward the car, which was backing out of the driveway.

"Heidi."

Inside, Jiminy barked like crazy, reminding Heidi she'd never see him again either. She felt as if she could fall apart right there, disintegrate on the welcome mat of her home. In front of her, her family was disappearing in a cloud of bitter exhaust, on their way to make arrangements for her body. Beside her was Jerome, who held her hand and was begging her to break into Heaven with him. In one direction was her body, in the other was her soul, and she felt trapped between the two.

She took one more look at Jerome and had an epiphany. He was as real as she was. He wasn't something she'd imagined, which meant she hadn't been as crazy as she thought, or even crazy at all. Besides Jiminy, he was the only one who could see her, talk to her. Maybe he could finally show her who he really was and why he'd been inside her head her whole life.

"Heidi," he said one more time. "Please."

"Okay," she said. And she meant it.

He stood and took hold of both of her hands. The color had started to return to his face. He looked into her eyes and said, "Let's hope this works."

She opened her mouth to say, "Let's hope what works?" but before she got a single word out, the world melted into light and streaks of color, and the only thing that remained solid was the connection between their pairs of hands. Heidi thought she might very well throw up.

The Guardian Angel's Handbook: Soul Rehab Edition

Chapter 1, Subsection ii:
The Ten Commandments for the Dead

I. THOU SHALT NOT COMPLAIN ABOUT BEING DEAD.

II. THOU SHALT NOT ENGAGE IN DISCOURSE WITH THE LIVING.

III. THOU SHALT GIVE UP EARTHLY ATTACHMENTS.

IV. THOU SHALT HONOR THINE HEAVENLY ADVISORS.

CHAPTER NINE

Jerome

GABE CALLED my skull phone when Heidi was inside saying good-bye to her family. He used his loud voice, which had a way of splitting my head in two.

"WHY WERE YOU NOT IN GROUP THIS MORNING?"

"Uh."

"YOU WILL REPORT TO MY CHAMBERS IMMEDIATELY."

"I, uh, can't right now on account of I —"

"THERE IS NO OTHER DEFINITION OF *IMMEDIATELY*. THE WORD MEANS NOW!"

So, yeah. Good thing Heidi agreed to come with. I didn't want to be the guy who stood between a girl and her last good-byes with her family and stuff, but I really needed to see if there was anything I could do to fix the situation, or at the least, slip her in the back door of Heaven while I was on my way to get my apple handed to me in a paper sack. Once she was all settled, I could maybe talk Gabe and Xavier into giving me a do-over. I'd do a better job if I got a second chance. That was a promise.

After a pretty smooth shoop, considering it was Heidi's first time, we landed at the service entrance, which isn't as fancy as the main gate. But I'm not allowed in the front, and anyway, trumpets and hand bells would only make my headache go all the way down my neck.

"Here we are," I said.

She was all, "Here? But we're at the mall. In the back entrance. Behind the employee parking lot."

"Chevy," I said.

"A Chevy? Are we going for a ride?"

"You don't see it? The glowing doors? Right under the stone angel thing? Covered with a sign that says HAVE HOPE, ALL YE WHO ENTER HERE? With the doormat that says PLEASE WIPE YOUR SOULS?"

"I see parked cars. I see a girl in an Orange Julius uniform trying to light a cigarette. I see a regular door with a sign that says NO ENTRANCE FOR UNAUTHORIZED PERSONS. There's graffiti on it that looks like a bald guy with stars for eyes."

"Chevy," I said.

"Jerome, don't take this the wrong way, but did that arrow give you, uh, brain damage? Because I've heard that people with head injuries sometimes repeat words at inappropriate times, and I just wanted you to know I'm not going to judge —"

"Shush. Gotta think."

Something was pretty flasked up if she couldn't see Heaven's service entrance, which is behind the mall because it has a really convenient layout and plenty of parking if anyone needs to wheel in something big, like an enlightened circus elephant. If Heidi couldn't even see the door, there was no way I was going to get her in it, and Gabe was waiting. I substitute-cursed myself out for losing the guardian angel handbook, while I rubbernecked a bit to see if any of the other guys from group were hanging around. That would've stunk, especially if one of them was Howard.

Luckily, we were alone. Even so, I wanted to be quick about stuff. I didn't want Heidi to get the idea that anything was messed up about the situation. Or more messed up. It's bad enough finding out you're dead without knowing there's some problem with where to put your soul.

I talked fast so I could get to Gabe before my head got its wish and exploded.

"Okay, here's what we're gonna do. I'm gonna go in and talk to my guy, and you're gonna walk around inside. Check out some stores. Sit on a bench and do some people watching, but be careful when you do it. Benches and chairs are just like doors, and you can fall through if you aren't paying attention. Wait, no. What you want to do is this: deep sniffing at the Mrs. Fields — seriously. It's awesome. You won't mind not being able to eat human food once you fill yourself up with high-grade cookie vapors. But you gotta do me a favor. Don't talk to anyone, especially not anyone who's dead. And if this guy named Howard comes up to you wearing an ugly-apple plaid shirt

81

and asks you if you're into planets and/or cats, do NOT talk to him."

"Why not?"

"He's a psycho, that's why."

"How long are you going to be?" She bit the corner of her lower lip.

"Probably not too long," I said, trying to keep it casual. "You got somewhere else to go?"

"Jerome," she said, "I don't want to be alone." Her eyes started to get shiny, so I looked at a really dented-up car and thought about how easy it would be to pound it out with a mallet.

"I have to do this thing and it won't take hardly any time, so go sniff some cookies, okay?" I had to be tough, even though part of me wanted to go straight to Mrs. Fields with her.

She wiped her eyes. I made a fist and chucked her under the chin to show some appreciation. Then she went "Ow!" because I think she maybe bit her tongue.

For a second I wanted to be one of those guys from France or wherever so I could've kissed her on her cheek instead of chin-chucking her, because it seemed more Rico Suave than "See ya later." But only for a second.

She grabbed my sleeve.

"Jerome," she said, and I knew I had about two seconds to get out of there before I changed my mind. I peeled her off me and punched my code into the security pad and went through the service entrance, past the janitorial and diaper supply closet, and into my lobby. I tried not to think about her chin or her cheek or any part of her, even though I would've loved to have brought her along, on account of she would've understood what I'm really about better than I could've explained even if I used all the words I knew.

Your rehab lobby is your own personal space, meant to help you imagine Heaven and do what you need to do to get in. My lobby is twice the size of my old bedroom. It has a lot of vending machines lining the walls, along with vintage album covers and guitars from Kurt Cobain and Jimi Hendrix, and Jim Morrison's actual leather pants, which I got mostly because by the time he died he was too fat to keep wearing them. I don't know how this is supposed to help me get into Heaven, though. It's just stuff I love. Anyway, all of those guys made it in. If you do something with your whole heart, you are forgiven a whole lot of stuff that normal people go to Hell for. If I had known this, I would have definitely kept up with my plan to become the Frogger champion of the world.

Howard says his lobby and service entrance don't look like mine, but I stopped listening when he was going on about a microwave, twenty cases of pizza rolls, computer parts, and lots of little stuffed animals with their heads switched.

A holographic picture of Gabe's head and upper body lowered from the ceiling.

"JEROME!"

My head rang like a gong.

"Dude. I am right here. You don't need to use my skull phone."

"THIS CONVERSATION IS BEING RECORDED TO ENSURE THE INTEGRITY OF OUR INTER-ACTION."

You know it's worse when they start being all official.

"Okay, fine. I'm listening." I put my hands in my pockets in case I got the shakes. In the background, the stuff Gabe calls music was playing. When he was alive, he was all into old-school rock, and he had his earthly record collection covered by the heavenly choir, Nun of the Above, which that jerk-off Howard does sound engineering for. I'd get a monster shock if I said what I thought of their version of "Runnin' with the Devil." Howard has no respect for guitar tone, and when Eddie Van Halen finds out what he's done to that song, there's going to be hell to pay. Literally, I hope.

"YOU WERE MARKED AS ABSENT THIS MORNING. WHAT WAS SO IMPORTANT THAT YOU DID NOT PARTICIPATE IN GROUP THERAPY?" Gabe shifted his toothpick to the other corner of his mouth.

I took one hand out of my jacket pocket and smacked myself in the forehead, in the universal "Oh, I am such a dumbapple" gesture.

But I *am* a dumbapple to hit my forehead, on account of the arrow. It took a couple seconds to absorb the pain before I could talk again. On the bright side, it wasn't hard to make a sad face for real. Gabe's shoulders shook up and down a little bit and he might have been laughing at me, but it could have been my vision, which goes haywire when someone touches the arrow.

"Dude," I said, when I could finally talk. "I'm sorry. I forgot."

"YOU HAVE THIS APPOINTMENT EVERY DAY AT THE SAME TIME."

"Dude," I said. "I'm seventeen. Cut me some slack."

"Please don't call me *dude*. It's disrespectful," Gabe said in his normal voice. He crossed his arms across his sweater vest. "Also, you have been seventeen for sixteen years. It's getting old, son. It's not like you can stay in rehab forever. At some point, they're going to make me send you down. I'm afraid that point might be now."

Then he went back to the voice that would be recorded. "YOU HAVE REACHED YOUR QUOTA OF ABSENCES FOR THE TERM. IF YOU MISS ANY MORE MEETINGS, YOUR ENROLLMENT IN OUR PROGRAM WILL BE TERMINATED. PLEASE PRESS ONE TO INDICATE YOU UNDERSTAND."

I touched my chin. That's known as "pressing one" to these people. I had to breathe out through my nose real hard so I didn't get crazy mad.

"Jerome," Gabe said.

"What?" If he didn't bring Heidi up, I wasn't going to.

"Is there anything else you want to tell me? Anything at all? About the soul you're guarding? If you don't want to make a disclosure here, you can always refer to your handbook for guidance."

Grown-ups can be stupid, even the professional ones assigned to deal with kids like me. No, there was nothing else I *wanted* to tell him. *Yeah, Gabe, I want to tell you I killed my human so that you can send me down to one of the levels for the rest of eternity.*

Idiot!

"Gabe? There is something else."

He put his hands together, all prayerlike, and he tilted his head a little bit to the side, like he was posing for his stained-glass portrait.

I made my most sincere face and said, "It's important."

He smiled and his eyes got bright, like he was a kid who'd seen Santa.

"I really, really . . . like your vest."

For a second I think he believed me, and then I saw the two halves of his mustache dive down like a pair of burrowing prairie dogs. I would never admit this without feeling a red-hot pitchfork in my sitting bits, but I actually felt kind of bad. I sometimes forget that the guy is proud of his vests, which he wears on weekends. If you spent your human life wearing a religious dress and sandals instead of actual clothes made for a dude, maybe having a vest would be sweet.

"Can I go now?" I said. "I have to look after Heidi. You know, protect her soul and all that."

He opened his mouth like he was going to say something. The toothpick hung there. That was some sticky saliva. He pulled a watch out of his pocket and looked at it. Then he put it away, made prayer hands, nodded once, and said, "YOU MAY GO IN PEACE."

I swear he does the loud voice to rattle my skull. He knows it hurts me worse than it does the other guys. No way was I going to return the prayer nod after that. He could mark it in my permanent record if he wanted.

Gabe disappeared in his cloud of incense, which reeked. If he were a car, his engine would need a serious tune-up.

Much as I wanted to, I couldn't shove my ringing head in a bucket of cold holy water. I couldn't sneak Heidi in the back way on account of she couldn't see it, so I had to figure out what else I could do with her. For that, I needed that handbook. The next group session was in less than a day. If I hadn't figured something out by then, I was looking — at best — at spending my eternity on Level V, Sloth, where they hand wash dirty underwear for the entire population of Hell all day, every day. The soot stains are epical. That alone was serious motivation.

THE GUARDIAN ANGEL'S HANDBOOK:
SOUL REHAB EDITION

Chapter 1, Subsection ii:
The Ten Commandments for the Dead

I. THOU SHALT NOT COMPLAIN ABOUT BEING DEAD.

II. THOU SHALT NOT ENGAGE IN DISCOURSE WITH THE LIVING.

III. THOU SHALT GIVE UP EARTHLY ATTACHMENTS.

IV. THOU SHALT HONOR THINE HEAVENLY ADVISORS.

V. THOU SHALT NOT COVET THE FOOD OR THE DRINK OF THE LIVING.

CHAPTER TEN

Heidi

IT WAS A long walk around the mall to the main entrance, through an icy parking lot littered with cigarette butts and lined with struggling trees, but Heidi didn't mind. In truth, she felt most comfortable on the edges of things. She put a tentative hand on her hair, which went Medusa when it got wet. There was no telling the damage it could cause anyone who looked at it.

She made her way to the glass doors at the front entrance. Behind her, cars cruised the lot, looking for parking. The air smelled of food-court grease, tissue paper, and new shoes, three scents that always lifted her mood. Maybe Jerome was right. This was a good idea.

She stepped on the automatic door sensor and waited. Nothing happened. She stomped. Still nothing. She jumped. Then she remembered. These things would never work for her again. She'd have to walk through the glass.

She held her hands out in front of her and took a tentative step in case the glass affected her differently than the wooden door at home. Her hands slid right through. She felt molecules swirling around her wrists. She pulled them back. With her body stripped from her soul, nothing separated her from anything else. She was one with the universe, just like they talk about in those woo-woo shows on television at two A.M. She had no words to capture it. Bizarre. Mind-melting. Freaky. Was this what it felt like to belong in the world? She held her hands there, just enjoying the dance.

The glass doors *whuffed* open, and she felt sudden heat. Three boys had walked right through her, one of them wearing a puffy vest and baseball cap she'd recognize anywhere. Sully. If she'd followed him out of the assembly instead of doing the *Talentpalooza!!* tango, would she be here? Everything might have been different had she made that one choice, listened to Jerome. She wouldn't have frozen at the basketball game, might not have needed the walk, might not have fallen through the ice. She might still be alive.

The doors closed. She stole a peek at the back of Sully's jeans as he walked away and then, in her mind's eye, saw his freckle-spattered face, as though the artist who'd made him had finished the job with a good shaking of the brush. He'd walked right through her without noticing, which meant she could walk beside him without his knowledge. She could smell his shampoo, listen to the swishing music his vest made as his arms brushed the fabric. She ran through the door to catch up, wincing in anticipation of pain she might feel passing through the glass. But it didn't hurt. She was part of the glass. It was part of her.

Then he turned and looked over his shoulder, directly through her, and laughed at something, and any courage she might have possessed evaporated. Death hadn't changed everything. He was still himself. She was still Heidi. And even though she was invisible, the thought that she wouldn't be welcome, wouldn't be what he'd want, made it impossible to keep going. And what was the point, anyway? There wasn't much of her left, not anything you could see or hold or feel.

She stopped and steadied herself. Sully and his friends flowed into the crowd. She watched them disappear, letting the voices of strangers wash over her, feeling them walk through her, seeing if she once again felt at one with the universe.

She didn't. She felt like nothing at all.

❧❧❧

But at least Mrs. Fields smelled as good as Jerome promised. If she couldn't be one with the universe, merging with warm chocolate chip cookies was a good consolation prize. She leaned over the counter and felt the vapors twirl through her. Then she moved closer so she was standing in the counter, fanning the sweet, buttery warmth upward, feeling it fill her arms, her chest, her head. Eating chocolate chip cookies was good. But becoming one with them? That was something else, something infinitely better. Even after the clerk whisked away the tray and loaded the cookies into the display case, she felt warm and silky sweet. She had to close her eyes to concentrate on it. How could Heaven even come close?

The experience left her giddy. She had to sit on a bench, taking care not to become one with its molecules and slip through to the tile floor. A group of senior citizens doing mallercise creaked by, giving her time to muster the courage to look for Sully and his friends. Eventually she found them at the food court. They sat at a metal table, facing a tray full of future heart attacks. Sully was working on a paper bowl of garlic fries, stuffing them in his mouth two and three at a time, wiping shiny fingertips on his pants every so often, the sort of thing that Heidi would call disgusting if Rory were doing it, something she wouldn't dream of doing herself.

Somehow, though, it was fine when Sully did. She wondered for a moment why she cut him all that slack, and none for herself, but she had no answer. Instead, she sat in the empty chair at his table and watched him eat, stunning herself by wishing she could be a fry, held between his fingertips, brought slowly to his mouth, as though all she needed to imagine contact with another body was to lose her own altogether.

He picked up his soda, and Heidi tried to hyperventilate out of habit. Ice cubes clicked against one another in his wax-coated cup. Beads of condensation twinkled and dripped over his fingers. He wrapped his lips around the straw and sucked until he'd drained the drink. Then he stood, wiping the salt and grease off his palms and onto his thighs. He went to the soda machine and helped himself to a refill. It was embarrassing how much she enjoyed watching him without his knowledge. Had Jerome felt the same way about her?

On Sully's way back to the table, he slapped his hand against his hip pocket and pulled out a buzzing phone. He worked his thumb around the screen as he walked.

"Either of you guys know someone named Heidi?" he asked his friends.

She didn't dare move. Could he see her? Why was he asking about her? Did he ... Could he possibly? ... Maybe he liked her?

"Nope," said the one in the blue flannel shirt. Heidi was fairly sure his name was Owen. He went to a school across town. She'd seen him at track meets. He was fast, even if he had an embarrassing tendency to make victory fingers as he crossed the finish line.

"Really tall girl? Reddish hair?" said the other boy, who was a couple of years younger. "Her brother's in my class. Why?"

"Tammy texted me. She fell through the ice at the pond this morning."

"Tammy fell through the ice?" the other boy said.

"No, asshat. Heidi did." Sully used his thumb and middle finger to flick his friend's forehead.

"Bummer," Owen said. "Was she hot?"

"I don't know," Sully said. "Can't remember her."

"Not hot," said the boy in Rory's class. Roger. His name was Roger. He had a blob of sour cream from his burrito on his lip. "Huge. Like a cross-dressing lumberjack."

"Yeah, I figured I'd have remembered who she was if she was hot," Sully said. He took the lid off his cup and crunched a few ice cubes between his molars. "Wait. Was she the one in your talent show video?"

Heidi was drowning all over again. She reached for the edges of the table for support, but panicked and her hands flashed through. She felt weak and sick, as if someone had punched a hole in her soul. Even the food court lights seemed dimmer than they had been just a few moments before.

Sully cursed. Soda had splashed all over his lap, darkening his crotch. Ice clattered on the floor. He stood, wrapped in the laughter of his friends.

Then came the hand on her shoulder, warm and solid.

"Don't tell anyone I did that," Jerome said. "It's against the rules."

"The rules?"

"I can't knock shi — OW! — off tables."

"You did that?"

Sully mopped his pants with a napkin.

"Guy's a jerk," Jerome said. "He's Howard's soul, but Howard's in Victoria's Secret again. You'd think he'd have figured out the secret by now. There are no nipples on the womannequins."

"How long were you standing there?" Heidi wiped her dripping nose.

"Long enough," he said.

"Jerome?" Her voice was pebble-small and hard in her throat.

"What?" He grabbed her hand and pulled her to standing. She was glad to see he looked much better than before.

His arrow had stopped bleeding, and his face was a normal color again.

"I want to get out of here. I need some air."

"You got it," Jerome said.

They left Sully and his friends behind. Heidi only half noticed the bulky figure in a plaid shirt who materialized in the cafeteria just as they were leaving.

THE GUARDIAN ANGEL'S HANDBOOK: SOUL REHAB EDITION

Chapter 1, Subsection ii:
The Ten Commandments for the Dead

I. THOU SHALT NOT COMPLAIN ABOUT BEING DEAD.

II. THOU SHALT NOT ENGAGE IN DISCOURSE WITH THE LIVING.

III. THOU SHALT GIVE UP EARTHLY ATTACHMENTS.

IV. THOU SHALT HONOR THINE HEAVENLY ADVISORS.

V. THOU SHALT NOT COVET THE FOOD OR THE DRINK OF THE LIVING.

VI. THOU SHALT NOT LIE.

CHAPTER ELEVEN

Jerome

WE WENT OUTSIDE the mall and it was kind of darkish because the sun had gone down and most of the clouds had blown away and the sky was nothing but a cold mess of stars.

She was standing close enough to me that I could still smell the cookies on her. "Jerome," she said. "How high have you gone?"

At first I thought she was asking me about drugs. I started to explain how there aren't any in Heaven, but that wasn't what she was talking about. She meant the flying kind. Pretty much everyone dead tries it out after they get over the shock of it all. Everyone but me. I never went much above the roof of a semi because I have this fear of heights that would give a lesser guy worse shrinkage than the cold.

But she didn't have that problem, and her feet were halfway to the second floor of the mall by the time I noticed, so I sucked it up and hurried to catch her, because at this point the only thing worse than killing her would be losing what was left.

"What gives?" I said. My voice sounded like someone was throwing rocks at my neck. "There's this thing I have to find. We don't have time to be messing around up here."

"What thing?" she said. "I thought I could maybe see the entrance to Heaven if I went to the sky." She squinted.

"It's not there," I said. I tried not to look down. "It's, uh, complicated."

We were seriously far up. Cars looked like bugs, and every so often, the world flashed white when we went through one of the few cloud shreds still hanging around.

After a minute I said, "You know how the service entrance to Heaven was at the back of the mall?"

"I guess so. I never saw it." Her voice sounded kind of crabby.

"I guess so, I never saw it," I said back at her.

Then I saw the look on her face and remembered that this business wasn't all her fault. Or even mostly. I was supposed to be looking out for her.

"Look," I said. "Heaven's sort of a trick. The front entrance is different for everyone."

I reached my hand toward hers, and I guess she got the message because she reached the rest of the way and grabbed my fingers, and then I didn't feel so floaty up there, and I hoped she also knew I was saying sorry.

"I never actually saw it myself," I said. "I just heard about it."

"It seems kind of harsh to do it like that."

"I don't think it's meant to be that way. What this angel guy, Xavier, said was that you couldn't get there if you didn't know where you were going. The back door was pretty much for us guys who had work to do on our souls. It was the service entrance, you know. The front was for people who'd figured it all out."

"Like, people who were good all the time?"

She turned so she was facing me, and somehow our free hands ended up kind of holding each other, and we spun in a slow circle with the stars above and the world below. We were surrounded by blackness all shot up with starlight and it felt huge and cold and lonely except where our fingers touched. I hadn't touched a person like this for sixteen years. I hadn't touched a girl like this ever, unless you count that one time Darcy agreed to do the snowball with me at Skate King. I felt like I almost couldn't breathe for a minute, and I had to close my eyes until the feeling went away.

"I used to think that and it really got in my grille," I said. "But Xavier said something like it was more about finding your purpose." I had pretty much decided my purpose was to ignore Xavier, so I maybe wasn't getting all the details right, but I gave it my best shot with her. "I think it was going all out on something. It didn't really matter how good you got or how good you acted, as long as that something was what you gave the world. Basically, making your own heaven on earth while you were alive. That's the thing. Living the best life you can."

She was quiet for a minute, right down to her fingertips. "Oh."

"You figure it out?" I said. "Because we could try to find your entrance if you did."

"No," she said. "God, no. The opposite. I can't even see the back door. I have no shot of getting in. No shot."

I couldn't look straight in her eyes without losing it.

"Nobody wants you in there more than me," I said. "Nobody." That was maybe the truest thing I ever said to her, or anyone.

She didn't say anything for a really long time.

"I never thought of drawing a city from above. I wish I had." She looked down through our feet. "And it's really, really quiet."

Also true. The sound of wind burned a little bit in my ears, but everything else I was used to — cars honking and people yelling and dogs barking — had stopped.

"I can see my house," she said. She let go of my hands and pointed, and I pretended to look, but it would have made me mess my pants, so I just watched her face, appreciating the way her forehead squinched when she was trying to find landmarks below us. "I can see Megan's house. And school."

"Yeah," I said, feeling all the warmth leave my fingers. "They are down there and we are up here. That is a fact."

"It's my whole life," she says. "It seems so small."

"Well, duh," I said. "It's far away. It's a lot bigger up close."

"That's not what I meant," she said. She looked up and to the left, like maybe something was written over my shoulder that would help her explain stuff, but when I turned to look, nothing was there. "I mean, everything

I did or cared about is the size of, I don't know, a piece of rice. It's like all those drawings I made."

"No, this is a top view," I said.

"That's not what I'm trying to say." She covered her face with her hands and was still, and she started drifting away from me in this slow way.

"My life," she said. "It was a small thing in the grand scheme. But it was everything to me. And I never did anything with it. I just sort of floated along, waiting to figure things out, and now it's over and I'm never going to have even that little chance again, that chance to know what I was meant to do and who I was meant to be. I did what people wanted me to do, what people told me to do — parents, teachers, friends, *you* — and now there's nothing left of it, nothing left of me."

I didn't know what to say back to her. Sometimes, when people say things that are sad and true and unfixable, there isn't anything you can say.

But then I got a killer idea and I zoomed back toward her until we were almost touching again.

"There is something left. Want to go somewhere? Have an adventure? Do all the things you ever wanted?" If I went far enough and fast enough, maybe Xavier and Gabe wouldn't know where to find us. And maybe they wouldn't care. What did two lost souls matter, out of all the rest?

She punched my arm and we started spinning in a circle.

"Don't be ridiculous," she said. "I'm only sixteen. My parents would —"

"They'd what?" I changed the way my body was in space so we'd stop spinning, and I looked her right in the eye. If this were a movie, this would be the part where the guy would kiss the girl. Heidi'd never been kissed before. And I knew she wanted to be. It was the one thing I could give her. And it wasn't Heaven by any stretch. But it would be something, if I weren't so chickenchevy.

"You're right," she said. And then any chance of kissing passed. I could tell from her face that she was thinking again about what it meant to be dead, to not have a future. She wasn't thinking about kissing. And definitely not kissing me.

We started to sink back down to earth. I held her hands all the way.

"I know where I want to go," she said. We were right under a streetlight, and her face was all kinds of shiny. "I want to see the Eiffel Tower. I don't care of it's pouring, even. I'll draw its reflection in a puddle and then we can go to Buckingham Palace and I'll draw that and —"

"Slight problem."

"Don't you like Paris? We could see the museums and sniff croissants and sit by the river —" She touched my field jacket.

I held up my hand to stop her right there. Not the touching part. That, I did not mind. The Paris part. Somewhere not all that far from us, a train whistle blew.

"We can go anywhere I know how to get to. Someplace I've been before so I can imagine it. Like camping or Six Flags or something."

I closed my eyes for a second and wished she'd choose

Six Flags because the popcorn there makes for great sniffing, and when I opened them, Howard was standing right behind her. He reached for her.

"Don't even think about it," I said.

Before he could lay one of his grubby fingers on her, I grabbed her wrist and we shooped like nobody's business in the direction of the passing train. I probably should've warned her, because she looked like someone who'd just stepped off the Kingda Ka coaster, which has a really sick four-hundred-and-eighteen-foot drop.

"We're on a train," she said, when the world stopped its sliding. "We're on a train."

I looked around to make sure Howard hadn't followed us.

"Let's just find somewhere to sit, okay?" I didn't want to tell her that Howard had just tried to make a grab for her. Hopefully, he hadn't heard the train whistle and gotten the same idea I did.

We found an empty table in the dining car and sat across from each other. The train was moving at a good clip, all shimmying and rumbling, and the sound and movement started to take the edge off.

"You said, 'Don't even think about it.' What am I not supposed to think about?"

"Watch," I said. I slipped my hands through the salt and pepper shakers really fast. "Magic!"

That would've worked a lot better on the four-year-old Heidi. She put a hand on my wrist so I couldn't do any more tricks.

"Where are we going? What are we doing?" Her eyes had the saddest tilt to them, and it seemed like as good a time as any to explain about the soul rehab program and Gabe and Xavier. For the longest time after I finished, she was quiet, sitting there by the window while the world streaked right by her head.

"Am I going to Hell, then? Is that it?"

For the first time all day, I cracked up. But I stopped when I saw the look on her face. "You? What'd you ever do bad? Creator knows I've seen everything. No, you're not going to Hell. I did think you'd already be in Heaven by now. I must've screwed things up bad at the pond."

Heidi leaned back against the bench just as we went through a bunch of trees that made the world look darker than ever. The only light that came through every once in a while shined from the porch lights people had left on at farmhouses. Otherwise, we were in the dark and I had no clue where we were even going.

"This is really happening, isn't it?" she said. "I keep thinking I am going to wake up and have it all be a dream, that tomorrow, I'll have another chance."

Her voice went that bendy way it goes before you cry, and she stopped talking and bit her lower lip until it turned whitish. I hoped that'd keep her from springing an eye leak, but I came around to her side of the table anyway, in case she wanted to do it on my shoulder. I could always lift her head off of me in case she started leaking snot on the canvas.

The tracks sloped uphill and the train lurched. She

turned toward the window so our shoulders didn't even touch. There was a tunnel ahead, a hole cut into a mountain.

"What about you?" she said. "How long did it take you to get over being dead, and knowing you'd never get to do any of the stuff you wanted to do?"

"No point in talking about that."

"Come on. What else are we going to talk about?"

"Truth?"

She nodded. The train whistle blew again, and the lights flickered as we hit the tunnel.

"Never thought about my future because I knew I didn't have one."

Heidi stared at me like I'd just sprouted horns.

"I've never met anyone who didn't think about the future before." Her face was a big question mark. Darcy Parker would've been proud. "It was pretty much a rule in my house. You saw how it was. Good grades. Impressive activities. Check and check. It was all so we could be successful. All I ever really wanted to do was draw, but you know what my parents thought of that. I don't even think they noticed when I stopped showing them my stuff. But even then, I still thought about the future as this thing, this thing with possibilities, this thing that would actually happen at some point."

She got real quiet.

I poked her in the arm a little.

"Well, it wasn't like I wasn't thinking about anything. Just not the future. Best I could do was have a good time as long as the ride lasted."

She put my hand back on the table. "Did you?"

"Actually, yeah. I just didn't realize it at the time. But what would plans for my future have done to make my life any better? What was the point? I saw what Pop's day was like and didn't want any part of it. He got up before sunrise. Went to work at the base. Busted his butt fixing planes. Came home. Drank beer, watched *America's Deadliest Animal Attacks* or whatever on TV, fell asleep in his La-Z-Boy. On weekends, he'd fix stuff that got broke around the house or work on his model train set, which we used to do together until that one time I spilled Coke on a switch tower and he yelled at me until his voice kicked out. I kept my distance after that, and so did he. It was like I broke the switch tower and he broke what was left of us. Every so often he'd ask me about homework or getting a job, but we both knew we were just going through the motions, and that there was nothing much ahead for me, less even than he had."

She sat there watching me and we finally blasted out of the tunnel. My nose started to sting a little bit, but I just rubbed it and kept on going. I was glad she didn't ask me any more about Howard or rehab or Pop. I didn't have any answers about why she couldn't Commune with the living, or why she hadn't flown up yet. I wished I knew where to look for the handbook.

I felt fully exhausted all of a sudden. "A life like my pop's was gonna be as good as I could get — and probably not even that much on account of I could never live up to his way of doing things. Guy couldn't even stand being around me."

"You don't really believe all that, do you? Your dad loved you."

"Nope," I said. "Trust me, there wasn't a lot to love. I usually made a mess of things."

"All parents love their kids. It's a rule."

"Maybe in your world. But in mine, no way. I was watching him once when you were taking a nap. He was at work, talking with his buddies, who were all going on about the dumb stuff their kids had done. His supervisor was all, 'But your boy, he kind of won on that score, right? No offense or anything.'

"My dad got this look on his face, the one he used to get when I'd flask up really bad, where it looked like he was two parts shocked, three parts disappointed, and one part like he wanted to punch someone. And he said, 'Yeah, guess so. Shoulda probably put "took him long enough" on his grave, right?' I shooped out of there real fast after that. Haven't watched him since."

Heidi's mouth hung open a little bit, and I tried not to stare at her lips. There was something about the way the train lights hit that top part of her lip, the part where it dipped under her nose. It was the perfect shape. I'd never noticed it before. I touched that part of my own mouth, just to see if mine matched, but I couldn't tell.

Even though I don't drink earthly stuff anymore, all that talking made me wish I had something from my lobby vending machine to wash the taste of the words away, like a Sermon on the Mountain Dew, only I couldn't take Heidi with and there was no way I could leave her alone anywhere, not with Howard on the prowl.

We leaned against each other for a while, just listening to the wheels against the track. The sound was a lot bigger than what I imagined it would be when I was a kid and still allowed near Pop's model trains. It wasn't something that was just in your ears. It went all the way through you.

"So, rehab," she said. "Don't take this the wrong way, but why haven't you gotten out? Does rehab go on forever?"

I should've expected that she'd ask that. I'd wondered it fifty or a thousand times myself, but there wasn't a good answer, so I was all, "Duh, because you would've missed me too much."

I sort of punched her again on the arm, and that's when I realized that was the opposite of true. I would've missed her. Completely. Her face did that thing where it turned red all the way out to her ears. "What about girls in rehab?"

I cracked up again. "You've seen me, right? I have an arrow sticking out of my forehead. I've seen the kind of guy girls like. Ones like the stupid vampire doll you got Megan. I am not that kind of guy. I am the guy who hands the socket wrench to the guy who fixes the Volvo *that* guy drives."

She got a puzzled look on her face and then she was all, "Uh, that's not what I meant."

Chevy. Of course it wasn't. I messed with the cracked button on the cuff of my jacket. That button would always be broken, no matter what.

"Nope," I said. "No girls in rehab. Not in our section anyway."

"So they probably wouldn't take me, even if I had nowhere else to go," she said. She was quiet for a while and opened her mouth a couple of times without saying anything. Then, right before I made fun of her for looking like a fish face, she dropped the bomb, a quiet one, but the words exploded all through me.

"Why didn't you tell me any of this stuff before, Jerome?"

"This stuff?"

"You know, about rehab. About the afterlife. About dying and what it was like. You just took up space in my head —"

"You never said you minded."

"I thought you weren't *real*," she said. "I thought I was crazy."

I didn't know what to say to that, and the look on her face gave me a prickly feeling. It crossed my mind I could sing "Freebird" or something to remind her of some of the good parts of me being with her, but before I got a chance, her eyes went *woop!* and got all wide, and her body started to flicker again worse than it had before. She called my name and I reached for her hand. It felt all full of static like a balloon you've rubbed on your head, and I held on tighter, hoping that I wasn't hurting her.

"You're okay," I said. I looked in her eyes, but they didn't look all that okay, and I hoped that was the kind of lie that wouldn't count against me when the end came. "Just hang on. We're going to shoop to Megan's house. Maybe you can Commune with her, like a best friend thing."

I didn't actually think that was gonna work, but I didn't know what else to do. Something was messed up, big-time, and I didn't know how to fix it and could only hope I wasn't gonna make it worse. The second she turned solid and warm again under my hands, I closed my eyes and took us there, hoping she'd survive the trip.

THE GUARDIAN ANGEL'S HANDBOOK: SOUL REHAB EDITION

Appendix F: The Problem of Dislocated and/or Lost Souls

Although Heaven is highly organized, it is also fantastically busy. Every twelve seconds, a human dies and must be evaluated for placement in Heaven itself, in a rehabilitation program, or in one of Hell's nine rings. And this doesn't account for the activity in our wholly owned subsidiaries, Pet Heaven and General Animal Heaven, where creature souls by the billions flow in.

On occasion, a soul isn't processed quickly enough, or belongs to a toddler or small child who's unable to wait in line. On *very rare* occasions, souls split free from their vessels while the vessel still lives. This can happen when a soul is, for whatever reason, not adequately connected to its body. Any number of things can cause this: drug abuse, ennui, even an accident in which the body is revived after the soul completes its journey through the tunnel of light.

If you should happen to find a dislocated soul, it is your duty to return it to your counselor, and quickly. Without protection from an earthly body or an officially recognized heavenly dimension, a soul will dissipate into the universe and be reabsorbed, never again to manifest consciousness. Soul dissipation generally occurs within twenty-four hours of corporeal separation, depending on the resilience and capacity for desire of the soul.

Your counselor has all the knowledge necessary to (a) restore a soul to its body or (b) direct it to its proper eternal destination. Your counselor is also monitoring you at all times and will be aware if harm befalls your ward. Your counselor is not allowed to intervene, however, as the ultimate disposition of your soul depends on the benevolent exercise of your free will.[5]

---

5 In other words, you're allowed to make your own mistakes, and if you do, you're going to go to Hell. Could we speak any more plainly?

The Guardian Angel's Handbook: Soul Rehab Edition

Chapter 1, Subsection ii:
The Ten Commandments for the Dead

I. THOU SHALT NOT COMPLAIN ABOUT BEING DEAD.

II. THOU SHALT NOT ENGAGE IN DISCOURSE WITH THE LIVING.

III. THOU SHALT GIVE UP EARTHLY ATTACHMENTS.

IV. THOU SHALT HONOR THINE HEAVENLY ADVISORS.

V. THOU SHALT NOT COVET THE FOOD OR THE DRINK OF THE LIVING.

VI. THOU SHALT NOT LIE.

VII. **THOU SHALT NOT UNDERMINE THE DIGNITY OF THE LIVING.**

CHAPTER TWELVE

Heidi

THE NEXT THING Heidi knew, they were standing in front of Megan's house. She pressed her hands against her face, hoping to push the fog out of her head.

"Aren't you going to go in?" Jerome sounded antsy. She lowered her hands, trying to make eye contact.

"What just happened? I felt like my whole body was starting to, I don't know, vanish."

"Really?" Jerome said. He turned her toward the front door, nudging her through it. "You looked totally fine to me. Let's go talk to Megan already."

Heidi felt uneasy entering Megan's house without knocking. Mrs. Lin had always told her to make herself comfortable, but she might as well have been saying "Go roller-skate with a giraffe on the patio." Heidi had wished for the power to make herself invisible more than once in her presence, especially when Mrs. Lin had her home leg-waxing kit going.

"It's just sugar and lemon juice cooked on the stove!" Mrs. Lin would say, slathering her legs in goo. "If you don't mind a little leg hair, you can eat the stuff!"

Heidi's great fear had been that someday Mrs. Lin would wax her legs and make her eat the peelings. The thought made her uncomfortable on every level, and maybe even on levels she wasn't aware she had. Heidi didn't touch her own legs all that often if she could help it. Instead, she preferred to treat her body as if it were a distant relative, one she'd acknowledge politely on holidays.

With a jolt, Heidi remembered something Mrs. Lin said about the leg waxing: "Someday, Heidi," she grunted, ripping a strip of hairy wax from her shin, "someday, you will join in the fun of this life. I have psychic gifts and I see your soul, and it is hungry enough to eat the sugar and lemon juice, even with the hair."

Heidi couldn't imagine ever being that hungry. Even now.

"You comin'?" Jerome said. He jerked his thumb toward Megan's room.

"How'd you know — wait — you watched me here too?"

"Rehab guardian angel. My job. But don't worry. You didn't do anything too embarrassing. Usually."

As if. Megan's house was an epicenter of personal embarrassment, ranging from middle school kissing practice to things Heidi didn't even want to review in her own memory. Her face blazed and she put her hand over her mouth.

Jerome leaned against Megan's door. "Yeah, about that. When you do actually kiss a boy, go easy on the

ChapStick. We don't want to feel like we've been eating ham. Not that ham isn't really good —"

Something awakened inside her, buzzing her head and heating her skin. She recognized the feeling: anger, the first she'd felt of it in ages. Here she thought she'd been crazy, but instead, Jerome was watching her — judging her — even when she was doing things that were supposed to be private. The closeness she felt to him on the train evaporated.

"Shut up, Jerome. Just shut up and leave me alone with Megan."

She stood there, momentarily stunned that she'd actually said something like that. She never told people to shut up. She hated conflict, avoiding it even more than she avoided Mrs. Lin's wackadamia-nut grooming rituals. Still, a small part of her felt free. Maybe it was something to do with being outside of her body at last.

She closed her eyes and passed through Megan's door, ignoring Jerome as he followed her into the room. Megan had fallen asleep with the light on, and her jeans and sweater lay in piles on the floor. That was unlike her. Megan was an extreme folder. She'd even bought a scored blue plastic sheet on an infomercial so she could get her T-shirts the same size for stacking, which she used religiously until she discovered a better method of folding in a Japanese video online. She'd converted all her fellow employees at the Gap to it, until she quit that job so she might dedicate herself more fully to honing her psychic abilities, something her mom was certain would get her into college. Heidi thought it was crazy but didn't feel entitled to be particularly judgmental on that score.

"Megan?" Heidi whispered into her ear, hoping to rouse her gently.

Megan stirred and rolled onto her back. She flung one arm over her head. Her eyes were puffy, her skin raw. She'd been crying, which was oddly satisfying. Still, Heidi wanted her to wake up and she didn't, and the frustration of it made her start tearing up again in front of Jerome. She wiped her eyes hard, as though she could push the tears back inside.

"Megan!" she said, louder this time. Nothing happened.

Jerome stepped forward, licked his finger, and stuck it in Megan's ear. Then he bent and whispered something. Megan's short lashes fluttered. She opened her eyes and sat up. Her blanket, which had been pulled up to her shoulders, slipped down.

Great. She'd gone to bed topless. One more opportunity for a Jerome privacy invasion. "Megan! Cover up!" Heidi yelled, but Megan didn't even blink.

"Heidi, relax," Jerome said, turning to face her. "You know she wouldn't care."

"She might not, but I do." She stepped between Jerome and Megan, trying to block his view.

Megan stretched, yawned, and reached for her glasses as Jerome positioned himself against her desk.

"It's nothing I haven't seen before," he said, crossing his arms. "Come on, Heidi."

Heidi glared. "Is that something you're proud of?"

She took a step in his direction, and Jerome shied backward until he was sitting on the desk. He swallowed hard.

"You guys were funny. I once even made a game out of the things you always used to do." He reached into his pocket, pulled out a notebook, and flipped to a hand-drawn bingo card, mostly filled out, cataloging various embarrassments. "Look, this one was almost a slantwise win."

Heidi's mouth fell open. He'd made a game of their friendship. A game! And if he'd done that with Megan when the two of them were together, what had he done with her when she was alone? A slap to the face would've felt better.

It took her a while to find her words. "How would you feel if someone spied on you?" She clenched and opened her fists, trying to do something with the energy that was pooling in her hands. "What if that was a person you thought liked you? A person you —" Her tongue stumbled. She couldn't say any more.

Jerome started to talk, but appeared to think better of it.

Megan slipped her bra on, picked up her T-shirt, and snapped out the creases before she pulled it over her head.

Jerome cleared his throat. "If I'd said anything, you'd've been embarrassed." He sniffed and rubbed his nose. "It was better this way."

Heidi sat cross-legged on the floor, her chin in her hands. "I'm embarrassed now. Mortified."

He looked up toward the ceiling, as if help might come from above, and his voice was quiet and strained. "Look,

I never showed anyone the game. I never told anyone what you did. That means it's as good as not happening. And you have to admit it's kind of funny. I even give myself bonus points when you guys do the whole pregnancy thing."

"Only Megan does that."

Megan had a whole stages-of-life routine, in which she'd go from being an infant to being an old woman in the span of two minutes. The part where she was pregnant was Heidi's secret favorite — Megan would put on a huge striped shirt, stuff a pillow under it, and yell "MY WATER BROKE."

Heidi crossed her arms and gave Jerome a hard look. "The things you do when no one is watching are the true test of your character. They do matter. A lot."

There was a long silence, broken by the sound of Megan zipping her jeans.

"I know," he said, his voice no more than a whisper.

Heidi had a sudden urge to take his notebook from him, to take it and rip it up. She marched to the desk and grabbed at it, but he held it over her head. She moved in close and strained upward until she realized their bodies were almost touching. She stepped back. It was one thing to be next to him when he was listening to her, to what she chose to share, and trying to make her feel better. It was another thing when her life had already been opened like a can of tuna.

She lowered herself once more to the floor and looked at her feet.

"Heidi, don't get mad at me for this. Come on. I was just keeping track of you, and I had to do something to keep quiet. I hate not hearing myself talk. I go crazy. Scooch over."

He took a step toward Heidi, as if he planned to sit next to her, but stopped when she looked up suddenly, her eyes squinted in anger. He flopped down on Megan's bed instead.

Megan, fully dressed, sat in her chair, opened her desk drawer, and pulled out a small bottle of reddish-black nail polish. Vamp. The stuff they'd been saving for some unspecified important thing — and it had already been opened. Heidi was aghast that Megan had used it without her. As Megan painted, a tear slid down her cheek. Heidi had to press her hand against her mouth to keep from crying out.

Megan whistled air through her lips to dry each nail, and Heidi made herself look at Jerome. "Can't you help me? I want to talk to her. To say good-bye, to tell her I . . . I loved her before it's too late."

He stretched out on the bed with his hands beneath his head. "I've done everything I can think of. Just let me say whatever you want to say."

"And have her hear your voice? No, thanks. She'd think she was losing it. I wouldn't wish that on anyone."

"I'll make it high," he said, sitting up. "Like this."

"Jerome, come on. That's idiotic. Aren't there instructions or anything? How'd they activate your voice when you got to rehab?"

Jerome pinched the bridge of his nose. "I don't know," he said. "It just always worked for me. Let me do your talking for you. It's the least I can do." He cracked his knuckles and looked at her expectantly.

"Not in a million years." She flicked his toes. "God, get your shoes off her blanket."

"Come on. I'll tell her whatever you want." He swung his feet over the edge of the bed. "Anything. Tell me what I should say."

She looked at the ceiling. There were so many things. So many sentences that started, "Remember that time . . ."

But none of them seemed right, especially since they almost always ended with Heidi being a reluctant participant at best. Heidi maybe hadn't been wrong to resist Megan's wackier plans, given how *Talentpalooza!!* turned out. But it wasn't as if she died of embarrassment. She'd drowned. And Megan was right about the thing she said in the cafeteria. Now the penguin incident really did seem like no big deal, and instead of memories of a lifetime of boldness, Heidi was left with something that felt decidedly cramped. She was like the rose she'd once sketched in a middle school art class, a flower that shriveled instead of breaking free from the protective cage of leaves around its bud. No wonder Megan had gone ahead and used the nail polish. She'd been humoring Heidi all along. Their friendship was based on pity.

The weakness struck again, crashing like a wave over her, dimming the lights, prickling her soul with white-hot needles of pain. She slipped all the way to the floor. Jerome said something she couldn't quite hear. He hopped off the bed, wrapped his fingers around hers. She held on.

"Let's get out of here," she whispered.

As the world darkened around her, Jerome's face lit up.

"I remember where it is," he said. "But you have to promise to keep your eyes shut."

Heidi neither knew nor cared what he was talking about. She nodded and closed her eyes. As he grabbed her other hand, the world slid away all around her.

THE GUARDIAN ANGEL'S HANDBOOK: SOUL REHAB EDITION

Chapter 1, Subsection ii:
The Ten Commandments for the Dead

I. THOU SHALT NOT COMPLAIN ABOUT BEING DEAD.

II. THOU SHALT NOT ENGAGE IN DISCOURSE WITH THE LIVING.

III. THOU SHALT GIVE UP EARTHLY ATTACHMENTS.

IV. THOU SHALT HONOR THINE HEAVENLY ADVISORS.

V. THOU SHALT NOT COVET THE FOOD OR THE DRINK OF THE LIVING.

VI. THOU SHALT NOT LIE.

VII. THOU SHALT NOT UNDERMINE THE DIGNITY OF THE LIVING.

VIII. THOU SHALT NOT UTTER OATHS.

CHAPTER THIRTEEN

Jerome

WHEN HEIDI WAS crying about not being able to talk to Megan, and going all blurry around her edges, I remembered where I'd stashed the handbook. At my dad's house in the little drawer of mystery under the oven. I used to hide stuff there before I died, like spare cash, report cards, that sort of thing. It was a good hiding place even though it was a little dusty and greasy, because no one ever opened it. Opening it would've meant we put pans away, and we only ever washed things on an as-needed basis.

But even if Dad had opened the drawer, he wouldn't have found the book because it's a celestial object. If you've ever walked from one room to the other and forgotten what you were doing, you most likely passed something an angel hid. Celestial objects give off vibes meant to keep people from noticing them, and sometimes the vibes are strong enough to erase your last couple thoughts. Howard thinks it's hilarious to hide some of his Chevy in schools. Jerk.

When we got to Dad's house, I slapped my hands over Heidi's eyes before she could see the place. I wished I could bring her anywhere but there, but the good news was, her edges had crisped up again. Maybe the air at my dad's house was good for giving people a dose of reality.

"I'm already closing my eyes," she said. "You don't need to do that. And you're squashing my nose."

I stood behind her with my arms sort of around her so I could reach both her eyes, and she felt warm and good, and she still smelled a little bit like cookies, so on the one hand, I thought about staying where I was. But on the other hand, I wasn't going to be able to get into the drawer if I had my palms stuck on her face.

"Fine," I said. "Keep 'em closed."

I walked into the kitchen, which wasn't far from where she was standing, and every so often, I looked back at her. Dad wasn't home, but he'd left a lamp on, and the light from it shined through her hair and blazed up the side of her face so that she sort of looked like one of those pictures they take when you're graduating high school. If she had put her chin on her fist and stayed there for a year, boom! Senior portrait.

"What are you doing?" she said.

Her eyes were still closed.

"I'm staring at you, you dumbapple," I said. Tip: If you tell people what you're actually doing in a certain kind of voice, they think you're lying. "Good work keeping your eyes shut. If there was an actual job doing that, you would be employee of the month."

"What's that smell? It is not good, Jerome. Not good."

I ignored her and bent down and stuck my hand through the drawer and rummaged around in there and pretty soon I felt the handbook. I shoved it in my pocket. Then came the sound of my pop's key in the lock. Heidi opened her eyes. The door creaked and Pop walked in looking about a thousand years old and like maybe he'd stopped at a bar on his way home from work.

"Who's that?" she said, taking a step backward. "Where are we?"

"Nobody," I said. "We're nowhere."

I touched her elbow real light and we shooped back to her house so fast it made my head spin. It was worse for Heidi, judging by the way she hung on to me.

"Jerome, you have to tell me first before we do that." She shoved me away and took a couple of wobbly steps, like she was dizzy or something.

The scene at her house was totally different. People kept coming up to the door, bringing casseroles to one of her mom's work friends, who was stationed in the entry. We hung out in the bedroom to check out the manual without getting bugged.

I'd always liked her room better anyway.

It was like the garage of her life, a place where you keep everything that used to be important on account of it might come in handy someday. She still had a shelf full of smelly old kids' books and a teddy bear that looked like it got chewed on by a dinosaur. She had her shrine to that vampire guy: the poster with him bending down over his girlfriend's neck, and Megan's doll-in-a-box thing she put on the shelf next to it, only someone had taken him out of the box, which was gonna hack Heidi off once she noticed.

But she also had her desk and a computer and a bunch of humongous books that she used when she was doing her homework and sometimes, when I used to watch her, I could imagine what she'd look like all grown up. It was a real mind-flask. I mean, someday, she'd be older than me. She'd have a job and an apartment and a husband and kids, or, knowing her, a bunch of cats wearing sweaters Megan had knitted.

Maybe I would've still been in the picture, the one angel who never made it out of rehab, and I'd be there with her, telling her what to say to the people who gave her Chevy at work and at bars and stuff, because when she was old enough, we were for sure going to hang out at the ones that had sports on TV and darts and wet T-shirt contests every Saturday night. Well, maybe not the darts because those are just little arrows and I've had enough of those.

But she never was going to get old enough, was she?

There was only one chair, and Heidi sat on it. I was on the bed all by myself, which was fine because I was not thinking about the sort of thing I used to think about doing when I was in bed with a girl, namely, getting a little handsy with her milk cartons. Not that that ever actually happened.

She was still mad at me because of the bingo thing.

"It's just really embarrassing that you did that," she said. "I feel like Megan had no privacy at all. Like I had no privacy."

"Look," I said. "I'm sorry. What would you have done if you were me?"

"I can't even imagine being you," she said, in a way that made me feel like something you wouldn't want to step in. "And that's not the point. The point is, you weren't respectful of *me*."

She crossed her arms and wouldn't look at my face. Gabe's instruction manual felt crummy in my pocket, especially given my other assets, so I pulled it out and cracked it open.

"What is that?" she said, pointing at my hands.

"Book. Instructions."

"Instructions for what? Helping me talk?"

"More than that. All of death, I guess. Never really read it, so be a little more *shh* so I can figure something out."

The one time I looked at the handbook, I would've died of boredom except for the fact of my already being dead. It has, like, seventeen chapters, some with footnotes at the end, which is the worst. They put the longest words there and they make them so small you have to push your face into the paper. Who needs that? And there's this chart with arrows and things. Just looking at it makes my head hurt.

Also? There are no pictures. You'd think with the kind of technology Heaven has that can send messages directly into our skulls, that'd be the least they could do. Or maybe they could figure out a way where we don't have to read, like maybe with the air TV thing.

"Heidi, I don't know what half of this Chevy means."

"Chevy," she said. "Is that swearing thing going to happen to me? Let me see the book."

I wouldn't let her, just in case she found out something bad. I wanted to find out why she hadn't been summoned to the gates and all that stuff before she did, so I could fix it without getting her any madder at me than she already was. I also wanted to figure out how she could talk so she could get her last words out like she wanted. I flipped through the manual to see if I could find something that would explain everything. When I got to the part about swearing censors, I decided to do a test because that was the easiest thing.

"Say a bad word. Swear."

She shook her head and crossed her arms over her milk cartons.

"I don't think so, Jerome. Can I please see the book?" She held out her hand. "Does that have instructions for Communing?"

"I'll show you if you swear."

"Jerome, swearing's embarrassing!" Her ears were so red they went see-through at the tops. "And I don't want to get a shock."

"It's not like I said I wanted to touch your girl parts or anything. Just swear."

"Okay, fine. But I'm not going to say the worst word, just in case."

She closed her eyes for a second and I could tell she was thinking. There was no change in her cartons, but that didn't surprise me because everyone knows those bits aren't involved in making thoughts.

"You're an —" She paused, like she was afraid it was gonna hurt. "You're an asshole."

My body jerked all on its own when she said it. That word causes a pretty harsh head buzz. Nothing happened to her, though. It was weird and unfair.

"I can't believe that didn't hurt you."

"Maybe I didn't get a shock because it's true. You are a world-class a-hole at least half the time."

I took out my Megan Bingo notebook and pretended to make a mark, just to bug her. Bull's-eye. Her eyes went dark and squinty.

"Jerome," she said through her hand. Using the worst word of all for emphasis, she told me to show her the handbook.

After I got over my involuntary spazzing, I gave her some friendly advice.

"Don't make a habit of saying that word. Once they get your chip in, bang! And, also? You look real stupid covering your mouth all the time. If you're gonna talk, talk. Stop hiding behind your hand!"

I didn't say it out loud or anything, but it made me mega-nervous that swearing didn't fry her head. Because the Ten Commandments for the Dead? The ones that are in the manual? THOU SHALT NOT UTTER OATHS is the eighth one. They take it totally serious. It confused me when I was new in rehab, because I was getting zapped all the time, even without saying oaths. Then Xavier explained to me that the rule referred to not saying swearwords, any of them, and not only the word *oaths*.

If they don't want you to swear, they should say it plain. Like this. DON'T SWEAR. I had the book open to the page with the commandments.

"Let's look together." She sat by me, crossing her arms.

"Look at that," I said. I planted my finger on the page. "It's in crazy moon language. Good luck figuring it out."

Heidi read it out loud. "THOU SHALT NOT ENGAGE IN DISCOURSE WITH THE LIVING."

I looked over at her to see if she picked up on what was funny about that. She looked back with confused eyes.

"Discourse," I said to Heidi. "Man, that's messed up. I can't believe they care if we have sex with people who are still alive. It's the dead ones you're not supposed to touch. I had an uncle once who worked at a funeral home and he went to jail for —"

"God, Jerome," she said, once more not getting shocked for saying an oath. "You're lucky you died before your SATs. Discourse is talking. *Intercourse* is sex." She turned all red.

Huh. I did not know that. All this time, I thought we weren't supposed to be having *sex* with living people. But it turns out that I could've been doing that all along, and it was the *talking* that's not allowed. Chevy! Sex and no talking sounded like Heaven, am I right?

"Look who's all smart and stuff," I said. I was only kidding, but she reached over and twanged my arrow, and it took a minute before I could make words again.

"I can't believe this," she said.

"What? That there are no pictures? I know —"

"No," she said. "The First Commandment says you're not supposed to talk with the living if you're dead —"

"And?"

"You talked with me *every day*. Almost the whole day

131

long. And I've been trying to talk with the living. You should have warned me!" She got off the bed and took the book with her. "If the doorbell rings one more time . . . stupid casseroles. Didn't I at least deserve lasagna?" She had a point.

"You know that saying, that every time a bell rings, an angel gets his wings?"

"Yeah?" she said.

"Total bull."

"You're completely annoying. You know that, right?"

She maybe had a point. The worse I felt, the less I could control what came out of my mouth. But it's unfair to blame someone for this. You don't get mad at people for being tall or having brown eyes. So why blame them for chronic, incurable mouth diarrhea?

She poked her head through the wall, sneaking peeks at the people milling around, mostly her mom's friends on account of her family wasn't there. This was not improving her mood. I could see it on her face when she popped back in the room, so I tried to cheer her up.

"I'm pretty sure these commandments are more like guidelines," I said. "You know, stuff to work with."

"Jerome!" She slammed the book down on her desk. Even though it's spectral, it made the papers on her desk flutter. You can do that sort of thing when you have a lot of emotion zipping around in your essence, like I did when I dumped the soda on Sully's crotch and knocked the salt and pepper shakers over.

"Commandments aren't guidelines. They're firm rules!" She sat, leaning against her desk.

"Really?" I sat next to her on the floor and tried to

give her some puppy eyes. It doesn't work all that good with a forehead arrow.

She made a plate with her hands and rested her face in it the way people do in pie-eating contests. Only, without the pie there, it was a much sadder thing to watch.

"Which level of Hell are they going to send me to?" she said. "According to your book, I've broken the rules. Almost all of them."

She lifted her head and I saw a hard, bright look in her eyes. She reached for the book again and started flipping from the front to the back, where they describe the levels of Hell. "I mean, I wasn't being ungrateful or cruel or wasteful. I didn't steal anything and I wasn't hypocritical. And I'm certainly not guilty of deceit, am I?"

"I don't know," I said. I'd been meaning to ask Xavier what *deceit* meant for a while, only he was always so mad when he was accusing me of it.

"I want to talk to your teachers," she said. "Now." She crossed her arms again.

"Xavier's pretty busy." I knew that'd be a dead end. "So this deceit thing means —"

"It means lying. I know I haven't done that," she said. She climbed onto her bed, still holding the book in her hand. "Which makes one of us."

"Like you said, I talked with you all the time when you were alive," I said. "If you were going to go to Hell for that, I'd already be there."

"Really?" She sat up and leaned against a pillow. "Because I don't want to go to Hell. I don't even want you to go there."

"A hundred percent sure," I said, even though I wasn't, which was pretty nice of me, considering I now knew this to count as deceit, which would send me to Level III, where I'd have to scan newspapers to make microfiche in the library of infinite bad news and school board minutes.

"Well, that's good to hear," she said in a voice so small I could have set it on the head of a nail. She started getting all leaky-eyed again. I looked around her room for a Kleenex. Maybe I could move one and she'd use it instead of my sleeve or her finger. "But just in case I am, I want to be able to say good-bye to people, you know? It sounds stupid, but I just want, you know, closure."

The snot and tears started bubbling out again. She was the juiciest dead person I'd ever seen. Maybe it's because she'd died underwater. I thought about this TV show where a kid fell through the ice and drowned, and when they revived him he coughed up green water like he was a human fountain.

And that's when it hit me why she might be having some trouble talking with the living and shooping and seeing the service entrance of Heaven, but I didn't want to admit it to myself because I would be in way worse trouble with Gabe and Xavier.

Chevy.

Because if there was one thing worse than having your human die in an accident, it was what was going on with Heidi. It was totally possible that there was not even a level of Hell for people who did what I had maybe done, though the maggot level was probably about right for me. This whole thing happened on account of me. I'd pulled her soul out of her body. When I was trying to revive her, I was killing her. Maybe if I hadn't touched her, they'd've been able to bring her back. Maybe she wouldn't be dead.

If I'd been a halfway decent person, I would've told her then and there. But I didn't have the words to say it, and the scared part of me wanted to lead her as far from the truth as I could.

I took the book from her and the doorbell rang again. Heidi stopped her sniffling.

"Corn dogs." I said. "Do you like them?" I tried to make my voice sound normal.

"They're okay. Why?"

"Because I know this place . . ." Maybe if I told her while we were sniffing corn dogs . . .

"Jerome!" She tried to take the book back, but I wouldn't let her. It didn't matter. She saw one of the commandments anyway. "No! I coveted."

"No, you didn't. I'm pretty sure."

"The cookies, Jerome."

"You didn't covet them. You sniffed them. It's totally different." My voice sounded like I was going through puberty in reverse. I punched myself in the neck to make it stop, and when I could talk again, I said, "What's *coveting* even mean?"

She went over to her desk and tried to pick up this fat red book with gold letters on it. Her hand went right through.

"Darn it," she said. "This is a dictionary. You're lucky I can't pick it up or I'd throw it at your head."

We had a book like that at our house, and Dad used it to prop up the table in the kitchen. It had one short leg because of this thing that happened when I was, like, six, and we were always looking for stuff to make it not wobble. Rocks, cups, baseball gloves . . . we tried a lot of stuff. The book turned out best because of how flat it was, which was the most use it ever was to me.

"Okay," I said. "So?"

"You use it to look up the meaning of words."

That explains why Mrs. Domino used to talk about them all the time. I always stopped listening when I heard the *dic* part.

"*Coveting* means 'wanting.'"

"No problem," I said. "I covet all the time. It's no big deal. Nothing happens."

"Are you sure?" she said. "Because I think —"

"Exactly. Stop with all that thinking. Look at this. It's cool. Commandment Nine: THOU SHALT NOT INHABIT THE BODIES OF THE LIVING."

I stopped. I didn't know that was possible.

"Who'd want to do that?" she said.

I could think of two reasons, or three, if you count a girl's boobs separately instead of together. If I'd read this far in the manual before, I for sure would have tried to inhabit a girl's body and try it out, head zaps and all. But I didn't mention that to Heidi, because she might have thought I meant *her* body, and I wasn't necessarily ready to commit, especially with Tammy Frohlich and Heidi's mom, mayor of MILFtown, USA, in the picture.

Instead, I said, "If you're inside someone's body, you can use it, Heidi. Sheesh."

"Use it?" she said.

"Be alive in it. Walk around. Talk to people. Say your good-byes and things." I was starting to understand why Gabe switched on the loudspeakers when he was talking to me. People can be so dense.

"I don't know," she said. "Wouldn't the other person mind? Wouldn't I want to get permission first?"

Permission! I would've started laughing right then and there except I didn't want her to cry at me again. I was a real applehat for not figuring out earlier why she hadn't gone straight to Heaven and why she could swear. She totally met all the angel requirements. All except the one where you actually have to die like in a normal, human way.

"Better to shoot for forgiveness," I said. "Besides, how would you ask?"

"I don't know. I haven't the slightest idea how you'd even occupy a body. I mean —"

I cut her off. "Why don't you start small? Like with an animal." I pointed to the fishbowl on top of the bookcase.

"There's no way I'm going inside Fred," she said. "I can't breathe underwater, and besides, even if I could say anything, it would probably sound bubbly."

She had a point. Still, she was making stuff hard. I looked around her room. There was the stupid vampire doll she got for Megan. I would give almost anything to see that thing talk, and for the money she spent on it, it should. In several languages.

"Try the doll," I said. "It's not alive or anything, so it's not technically against a commandment, but maybe it will work anyway."

"What? Oh . . . He's not a doll. He's a collectible figurine. They're totally different," she said, like anyone would actually believe that. "Hey! I can't believe someone took him out of the box." She walked over to where the doll stood on a shelf, wearing his little black coat and old-man shoes. "I don't think I'm going to fit, and I don't want to do anything that's going to diminish his resale value even more. That would upset Megan."

"Heidi, don't be a dope. You ever heard the expression 'can't take it with you'? It's real. You shoulda seen the air gun I left behind. It was a .177-caliber Beeman rifle. My cousin got it and he's using it to shoot squirrels. It's practically a crime."

"The poor squirrels," Heidi said. "Your cousin sounds like a real sicko."

"Who gives a Chevy about squirrels? I'm talking about that beautiful machine in Mike's hands. He doesn't wash them after he goes number two."

Heidi reached out one finger all nervous-like toward the doll.

"That's the stuff," I said. "Now imagine you're —"

I guess she has a good imagination, because *whoomp!* I couldn't see her soul anymore. The doll wiggled a little bit on the ledge. It blinked. I almost Chevy'd my pants because it was so creepy. And then it — I mean, Heidi — talked in a little squeaky voice like the kind you get when you suck the helium out of balloons.

"Omigod! I'm inside Vincent Lionheart!"

I wished I had a video camera because it was that funny hearing a girl's voice coming out of a tiny vampire's mouth, but it wasn't all that realistic, because his lips didn't move right, so on second thought, it probably wouldn't make the best video. People would think it was a fake.

Heidi tried to cover his mouth with her hand and it made her fall off the ledge and somersault through the air like someone jumping off a skyscraper in a movie. She screamed as she fell, making this chipmunky sound. The doll flipped under the bed and Heidi swooped out.

"Jerome! Vincent Lionheart's off his ledge! We have to put him back."

"Yeah," I said. "Good luck with that." I flumped up her pillow. Might as well be comfortable.

That was maybe not a good move. Heidi had eyes full of murder. Or at the least, punching. I sort of hoped she'd let loose. Instead, she just yanked the handbook away and started flipping until she found something that made her stop. I didn't think her face could get any whiter than right after she came out of the pond, but I was wrong. She faded to the color of new snow and looked at me for a long and rotten moment. She didn't blink, and if her hands hadn't been shaking, I would've thought someone had pressed the PAUSE button on her.

She finally spoke in a low and terrible voice. "Did you know about this?"

"About what?" From experience I knew the best answer to this question was usually "no."

"About what happens to souls if they don't go to heaven in twenty-four hours."

"Uhhh," I said.

"Jerome!" she said. "My soul will DISSIPATE in twenty-four hours if I don't get into Heaven!"

Dissipate. I hadn't heard that word before.

"Do you even know what that means?" She was shouting at me. Her hand was not in front of her mouth. I backed up a little bit so I was between the pillow and the headboard.

"No?" I said.

She started crying again. Huge tears.

"It means," she said, stopping every once in a while, "it means I'm going to disappear. We have been goofing around and sniffing cookies and not getting any messages through to the people I love, and I have —" She stopped to look at the clock on her bedside table. "I have only about fourteen hours left until I am gone forever. FOREVER."

She crumpled herself on the floor like an old Kleenex and cried. "I hate you, Jerome. I *hate* you."

I can't remember exactly what I said back. But I think it was this: "Uh."

Just like I hoped she would, Heidi launched herself off the carpet and came at me with both fists flying. Girl packed a wallop. I leaned back and let her do her thing. I deserved it. In a way, it was a relief, so much so that I even laughed during it. What's more, I'd always be able to say I got busy with a girl in bed. I don't remember exactly what she said when she was done with me. But she took the handbook and left me there, and she didn't look back.

THE GUARDIAN ANGEL'S HANDBOOK: SOUL REHAB EDITION

Chapter 1, Subsection ii:
The Ten Commandments for the Dead

I. THOU SHALT NOT COMPLAIN ABOUT BEING DEAD.

II. THOU SHALT NOT ENGAGE IN DISCOURSE WITH THE LIVING.

III. THOU SHALT GIVE UP EARTHLY ATTACHMENTS.

IV. THOU SHALT HONOR THINE HEAVENLY ADVISORS.

V. THOU SHALT NOT COVET THE FOOD OR THE DRINK OF THE LIVING.

VI. THOU SHALT NOT LIE.

VII. THOU SHALT NOT UNDERMINE THE DIGNITY OF THE LIVING.

VIII. THOU SHALT NOT UTTER OATHS.

IX. **THOU SHALT NOT INHABIT THE BODIES OF THE LIVING.**

CHAPTER FOURTEEN

Heidi

Thirteen hours and fifty-six minutes left.

SOMETHING HAD BROKEN inside of her. For her whole life, she'd carried this terrible secret, knowing it made her different from everyone else. For the past couple of years, she'd even thought it meant she was crazy. But no. The voice was real, and he was using her to keep himself entertained instead of doing his job and keeping her safe. He'd watched her when she thought she was alone. He'd even made a game out of her friendship with Megan. He was the thing that made her hide herself away from the world, the voice she listened to when she should have been listening to her own.

It was as if she'd collected all this shame and sorrow in her heart, layered it with sand, and filtered it with tears until all that was left were the stony remains of things she'd hoped to do and be. Then the whole mess of it had shattered inside her, cutting her most tender parts on its jagged edges.

Jerome had broken the rules. He'd let her think she was nuts. And then he'd let her die and set her soul to wander and, through his own stupidity, condemned her to disappear in just a few hours. His presence had already erased her life. Soon, it would obliterate her soul.

She wasn't the sort to go around hitting people, but she poured her rage into her fists and pounded them at Jerome's belly and chest, as though doing so would be her salvation. Her hands thumped against him, one after the other, filling her ears like the heartbeat she no longer had. It felt good. Necessary. She didn't even feel like she was still dissolving, although she knew her fate had been sealed. But maybe anger was the thing that could hold off the inevitable. In any case, the rhythm of it, *thump-bam*, *thump-bam*, made her feel alive again, almost.

She wanted to provoke a reaction from him. An apology. Tears. Anything. But instead, he laughed through part of it, a jittery giggle that inflamed her further. How could he be enjoying this? What was wrong with him? Where was the part of him that was supposed to care about her?

Her hands throbbed, but she kept on hitting and would've continued indefinitely but for another sound, a short, sharp bark that pierced the darkness in her like a star.

Jiminy.

He was outside again. Either the casserole brigade had been careless with the front door, or Rory had left his window open. Jiminy loved climbing on Rory's bed and using it as a launching pad to freedom. He could never get back in, though, and he'd stand in the juniper bushes below, barking himself hoarse.

He needed someone to let him back inside. He needed Heidi. The thought of this lifted her out of her haze. She stopped hitting Jerome. Her hands felt hot and strangely empty, and Jerome lay on the bed, putting ragged breaths between each word.

"You . . . done . . . yet?"

She didn't bother answering. It wasn't as though he cared about her, or had ever cared. It had only felt that way, and maybe that was the thing that hurt most of all.

She slid off the bed and rubbed her knuckles on her thighs, hoping to soothe the ache in her fingers. Vincent Lionheart was under the bed, gathering dust. It pained her to see her gift to Megan there, but she couldn't do anything about it, and Jiminy needed her to lead him back to where he belonged.

Before she passed through the wall to the garden, she gave Jerome a warning.

"You'd better not be here when I get back, or I am going to tell everything you've done."

She didn't know whom she'd tell. She also didn't know how she'd do it. So far, she had zip when it came to finding her voice, or any way into Heaven. But Jerome was going to pay for what he'd done, maybe with the people who gave him headaches. Or that guy . . . Howard. If Jerome didn't want her to talk with him, then that was probably exactly what she should do. She took the handbook and shoved it into her back pocket, intending to study it as soon as she'd taken care of Jiminy.

She slipped through the wall of the house and felt the brief tickle of plaster, the shrill whistle of insulation, and the crackling vibration of the cold siding throughout her soul. Outside, the air smelled lightly of pizza rolls. Had someone actually brought that for dinner? That was worse than a casserole.

She looked around for Jiminy, acutely aware of the dwindling time her soul had left. In the distance, a car rumbled. She recognized it as the diesel engine of Mrs. Thorpe's ancient Mercedes. The car was a monster with huge, round headlights and a chrome grille that grimaced as it prowled the streets.

Jiminy burst from the shadows and stood on the sidewalk under a streetlamp, his tiny paws studded with clumps of snow. He barked at her, wagging his tail.

"Jiminy!"

He heard her call, bless him. He was the only one besides Jerome who knew what had happened to her, who knew she was still here. He bounded toward her, diving up and over the freezing slush piles that glowed lavender under the light of a shrinking moon. With Jiminy, at least, nothing had changed. He stopped and cocked his head.

That's when she noticed the squirrel. Out much later than normal, probably starving, frantically looking for home. In so many ways she could relate, even as she hoped Jiminy wouldn't see it as it dashed for a tree, its eyes mirrors in the evening light.

But of course Jiminy saw. He gave chase, sliding once in a deep patch of snow. He bounced right back up and kept running. Mrs. Thorpe came closer, her car's engine rumbling ever louder. The squirrel blurred into the middle of the street. Jiminy followed, barking.

The car rounded the bend. Heidi ran after them, shouting, "Stop, Jiminy, stop!"

He didn't.

Neither did the car, which carved a loose S in the icy street as Mrs. Thorpe braked. The squirrel made it across in time and dashed up the tree to scold Jiminy, who stood in the road with his back to the car. The headlights framed his silhouette in the snow. For a terrible moment, that image held still in her mind, a sketch from a book of nightmares.

Jiminy was wagging his tail when the car struck him. His body flew through the air, over the sidewalk, and past a snow-covered rhododendron.

Heidi ran to him.

"Jiminy! Jiminy!" She slid and stumbled, her vision crooked with tears.

Behind her a car door popped open and a voice said, "Oh my God. Oh my God." The car's engine grumbled and its headlights blasted two slashes of light into the darkness.

When Heidi finally found Jiminy, he lay on his side beneath a bush, taking quick breaths. His collar was gone, torn off somehow by the impact. He looked up at her, his eyes dimming with each passing second, as though he'd been waiting to see her one last time before he let go. Was that the look she'd had in her eyes when she was dying?

The light disappeared and her soul grew heavy, as if someone had filled it with sand. Jiminy exhaled. She reached out to stroke his fur, and as she said his name, he stepped out of his body, as if to come to her call one last time.

He shook himself the way he did when he was just out of the bath and touched his damp nose to her face. It felt the way it always had, warm and sweet, and she smiled until she understood what it meant.

Then he barked and galloped off after the squirrel, completely unaware that he had died. Either that, or it made no difference to him.

She couldn't let this happen to him. He couldn't die. Not like this.

"Jiminy!" She called for his soul to come back, but he kept running after the squirrel.

If she didn't do something soon, it would be too late. His body was so still in the snow. An idea seized her and she hoped it would work, commandments be damned. If she could keep his body alive and lure him back inside, she might be able to undo this horrible accident.

She pressed her hand to his heart and willed herself inside his still-warm corpse. A soul-tearing sucking sound filled her ears. Something tugged brutally on her essence — far more powerful than whatever had pulled her inside Vincent Lionheart. She braced herself, fearing that she'd made a terrible mistake. That instead of keeping his body safe, she'd hastened the destruction of her own soul.

She was caught in a hot vortex of light that lifted her, spinning and twisting what was left, filling her eyes with blinding streaks of brightness. Then came that strange almost-sound that remains after musicians have stopped playing, the vibrating memory of melody, and it coated her with a swirling, liquid peace.

For one long moment, she felt better than she ever had, and she wondered whether that was how it felt to have your soul melt into the universe, to disappear. Maybe it wouldn't be such a terrible end.

Then her arm blazed. She looked at it and tried to move it, but couldn't. Agony. More shocking, her arm was no longer an arm but a bloody paw covered in black and tan fur, growing more swollen by the second. It felt fat and foreign and on fire, and wherever Jerome's handbook had gone, she could no longer reach it and was therefore cut off from anything that might help her figure out what to do next.

The world around her had turned into a strange place, hot and painful and alive with smells: diesel fuel, wood smoke, the anxious breath of small animals, the needles of a Douglas fir tree, low clouds full of pending snow. She inhaled them and felt their shapes touch her mind and was instantly dizzy with the oddness of it all.

Footsteps crunched in the snow. A shadow blocked the light. Her tail — her tail! — wagged feebly when she looked up and saw Mrs. Thorpe, as though the love Jiminy always felt for everyone had stayed in his body and was responding, even without the presence of his soul.

"Oh, you poor thing!" Mrs. Thorpe said. "I couldn't stop in time! But you shouldn't have been playing in the street. No, sir."

She took off her coat, spread it flat on the ground, and placed Heidi on top of it. The pain, so deep she could drown in it, took her breath away. Her breath. She was breathing again. She'd never realized air was such a heavy thing or that a still-beating heart could feel so broken. Mrs. Thorpe wrapped the coat around Heidi and lifted her against her chest.

"I can't take you home," she said. "Not on a day like this. Oh, what a day it's been. Oh, my. I suppose I should take you to the vet so he can look you over."

She set Heidi on the backseat of her car, and Heidi wondered whether she should try to fasten her seat belt. She'd have to ask for help with it. That's when she remembered. She'd made Vincent Lionheart speak. She could probably do the same with Jiminy — use his body to say what she wanted to her family, to Megan. A little part of her thought about just staying inside Jiminy's body as long as she could, and maybe even living the rest of her life as a dog. She whimpered.

"Oh, you poor thing," Mrs. Thorpe said. "We'll be at the vet soon."

It couldn't be soon enough for Heidi. The army of pain marched through her paw, up her arm, toward the cage of her ribs, and into the soft nest of internal organs that quivered there.

149

A strange voice, distant and cold, whispered in her ear. It wasn't Jerome playing around, though the voice was male and vaguely familiar. She couldn't see who was speaking.

Let go, he said. *Come to me. You want to join me.*

For the time being, she ignored him. He might be a hallucination. A real one, for a change. In any case, she couldn't leave Jiminy's body, not just yet. She focused instead on the pain, which grew more insistent every second. She'd always loved riding in cars, looking out the window, watching the world blur by. It made her feel detached from everything. Floating, padded, protected. But her injuries stripped away this buffer, and for the first time she could remember, she noticed every angle, every bump, every burst of the streetlamps they passed. It hurt, but she wanted it to. She wanted to feel every minute of what it was like to be alive again for as long as it lasted. Feeling it was better than fading away.

The car slowed and turned into a parking lot. Mrs. Thorpe caught the edge of a curb with her tire and Heidi felt its shape slide through her, a solid block of suffering. She whimpered again. The car stopped.

Mrs. Thorpe sucked in her breath. "Such a bad night to be driving."

She killed the engine and looked back at Heidi.

"We're here," she said. "And you're still alive — that's good news."

Mrs. Thorpe pulled her keys from the ignition. She opened her door, grunting as she eased her bulk out of the car and plodded through the crusted heaps of snow, looking cold without a coat. Her shoulders rode up to her ears as she wrapped her arms around her body. Heidi absorbed every movement and sound, and most especially the small gestures Mrs. Thorpe made. Each one was a poem dense with meaning. No wonder Jiminy had always seemed to know how she felt.

The back door opened.

"Oh, dear," Mrs. Thorpe said. "I don't think that blood will ever come out."

Heidi examined her paw. There was blood on it, to be sure, but nothing that wouldn't wash out in a warm bath. It took her a second to realize Mrs. Thorpe was talking about her coat.

"Sorry," she said, before she thought better of it.

Mrs. Thorpe stepped back. She looked over each shoulder.

"Who's there?"

Heidi's voice had sounded grotesque, like peanut butter smeared over gravel. She itched to cover her mouth with her paw, but didn't, knowing how much it would hurt to move it.

"Hmm," Mrs. Thorpe said. She slid her arms beneath the coat and lifted Heidi. "Was probably just in my head."

Heidi pressed her jaws together to prevent any more slips. It felt strange, having a mouth full of small, pointed teeth. It made her miss her old teeth, her old mouth, her old body, something she'd not thought possible. She'd spent the better part of her life wishing she'd been someone else, anyone but the awkward, oversize girl who heard a voice in her head and couldn't stop drawing cities. Now she'd give anything to be back inside that body, able to move fingers, able to pick up a pen and hold it in her hand.

Mrs. Thorpe stepped up to the sidewalk outside the emergency vet. Underneath its neon sign, her face flashed red and blue.

"There, there," she said. "We're almost inside." She shouldered the door open and announced, "I've found a dog! It was hit by a car! Please, oh my goodness — can anyone help me?"

Who knew Mrs. Thorpe was so good at deceiving people. What level of Hell would you be sent to for hitting a dog with your car and pretending you didn't?

Come with me. The voice again.

Out of the corner of her eye, a light flashed in the distance. Probably just the reflection of headlights on the windows. If this voice was another guardian angel, like Jerome, she'd be able to see him. The thought made her wish she had someone there with her, someone who loved her, someone who'd make her feel better, or at least say something funny. Jerome. She was missing him. Or maybe missing what she'd thought he'd been for her. She closed her eyes and let herself think about him, even though part of her still burned with anger about what he'd done.

He'd no doubt have a crack about Mrs. Thorpe's huge ass. He'd definitely think it was weird and cool that Heidi was inside Jiminy's body. She wondered whether she'd see him again, and if she did, whether she'd forgive him. Something had begun to nag her about what had happened at the pond, something she didn't let herself think about until now because it was too tender a notion: She didn't struggle. She didn't try to get out of the water. What might have happened if she'd tried?

Something shifted in her and she knew she would forgive Jerome if she ever saw him again. This wasn't entirely his fault. He wasn't perfect, but neither was she. And while he'd damaged her life, he'd also enriched it in more ways than she could count.

The pain worsened. Without thinking, she said his name, and it came out sounding like the saddest howl she'd ever heard. And then she was floating in someone else's arms through a hall so brightly illuminated she had to squint. Shoes squeaked on a linoleum floor. People mentioned X-rays and anesthesia and operating rooms, but their voices felt remote — quieter even than the whisper. Her limbs came to rest on a cold steel table and she opened her eyes reflexively, noting the sensation of having three eyelids, an upper, a lower, and one she'd never noticed on Jiminy that slid over her eye when the others had sealed.

The light overhead was the brightest one yet. She screwed her eyes shut; even the afterglow felt blinding. Drawers opened and closed. Fingers flicked against a hard plastic syringe. A hand parted the fur on her back. Then came the jab from the needle, a sickening warmth, the swift flight of pain, and darkness.

THE GUARDIAN ANGEL'S HANDBOOK: SOUL REHAB EDITION

Chapter 1, Subsection ii:
The Ten Commandments for the Dead

I. THOU SHALT NOT COMPLAIN ABOUT BEING DEAD.

II. THOU SHALT NOT ENGAGE IN DISCOURSE WITH THE LIVING.

III. THOU SHALT GIVE UP EARTHLY ATTACHMENTS.

IV. THOU SHALT HONOR THINE HEAVENLY ADVISORS.

V. THOU SHALT NOT COVET THE FOOD OR THE DRINK OF THE LIVING.

VI. THOU SHALT NOT LIE.

VII. THOU SHALT NOT UNDERMINE THE DIGNITY OF THE LIVING.

VIII. THOU SHALT NOT UTTER OATHS.

IX. THOU SHALT NOT INHABIT THE BODIES OF THE LIVING.

X. **THOU SHALT NOT INTERFERE WITH THE NATURAL ORDER OF THINGS.**

CHAPTER FIFTEEN

Jerome

Six hours left.

I WANTED OUT of her room before she came back, but I couldn't find my body's gas pedal or whatever it is inside of you that lets you get up and do something when your motivation's left the building. I stayed there long enough that the house got totally quiet, even the part of me that might have been moaning. People stopped bringing casseroles. Cars stopped cruising by, and it had started snowing again, little flakes at first, then a whole lot of them. Through the window, it looked like the sky had worse dandruff than my uncle Mort.

But it was soothing to watch. The snow, not Mort's dandruff. That was sick and you know some of it got on his food when he was eating, which is why I wasn't sorry when he went to jail for the Florida swampland deals.

It was like I'd been born into a family with a curse. We had these trouble magnets inside of us, pulling us toward the wrong things all the time. Mort and his scams. My other uncle and his thing with those corpses. Then there was me and Mike and anything that could get blown up, or shot at with arrows, or run over by his car, or covered with glue and most of the feathers in his pillows. And of course, that poor, stupid cat that trusted us and shouldn't have.

Cursed. Every last one of us.

My dad always said I had a choice in the matter, but that wasn't something I ever felt. When you wanna do something so bad and all you hear is that devil on your shoulder, and your body is an engine going as fast as it can to get you to that spot where your idea is waiting, where does the choice come in? Even knowing what happened and how I felt when the cat's eyes lost their shine and its body stopped twitching, could I say for a hundred percent certain that I wouldn't do the same thing again today if Mike was egging me on? Was my soul any better now than it was then?

By the time I made it outside, it was the middle of the night and there was no sign of Heidi or Jiminy. Not even Jiminy's footprints. The snow had filled in everything and it would've looked all perfect, like one of those paintings at the mall, except for the part about a missing soul and a missing dog and me having no clue where to look for either.

I tried to shoop to wherever she was at, but it didn't work. I couldn't figure out why. She might have broken my shoop when she was using me as her own personal punching bag. Or maybe she got pulled into Heaven. I hoped that was the case, but good stuff like that is not the Jerome Way of Things Happening. More likely, she'd already fallen apart. She didn't even get the full twenty-four hours, and as hard as it was to imagine her gone — just gone, like that — I had to face the fact. I owed it to her to be that much of a man.

And I hoped that the end for me was worse than it was for her. I was so out of last chances that it was just a matter of figuring out which level of Hell to send me to. I'd broken so many commandments, they might have to split me up and send hunks of me to every level.

I had to lie down again and I moved my arms and legs through the cool white fluff the way kids do when they're making a snow angel. I didn't even leave a wing pattern. Whoever thought I had the makings of a guardian angel was a world-class dumbflask. There was no way to make me an angel. I couldn't even make the kind kindergartners make in snow. Of course I never stood a chance in rehab. I couldn't help myself. Why would I be able to help anyone else? I had to laugh and cry at the same time, all sloppy and wet and shaky.

Jiminy ran up and licked my face. He smelled like kibble, and you know what? That stuff tastes better than anyone gives it credit for. It took me a few minutes to figure out what the problem was in this scenario, besides his dog breath. If Jiminy could lick me, it meant only one thing.

He was dead.

Chevy.

The thought of it wrecked me because I knew how much Heidi loved that dog, and I also knew how everything that had happened since the day at the pond — since before, really — was at least partly my fault. It wasn't as bad as what happened with the cat, but it seemed like death went where I did and maybe it would be better for everyone concerned if I was locked up someplace I'd never leave.

I lay there for as long as it took the lopsided moon to slide a couple hand widths across the sky, and by then, I wasn't laughing anymore. My body shivered, but not from the cold. Jiminy lay next to me, and I got why Heidi liked him so much. He was all right for someone who spent a lot of time licking his balls. I was sorry he'd gotten killed, even if it wasn't totally my fault. Gabe and Xavier could just add this to the list. It's not like I could be any more damned than I already was.

Then I caught a sniff of something in the air: pizza rolls.

Howard.

Heidi and Howard. Together. If she hadn't fallen to pieces yet, he'd probably taken her. Either that, or she'd gone with him all on her own, just to get back at me. Maybe she wasn't worse off, though. Maybe he didn't want to hurt her. Maybe he knew how to keep her soul from disappearing. Maybe he knew something more than I did about getting her into Heaven. Maybe it was time for me to give up on Heidi, to give up on myself, time to let someone else take over.

Something skittered in the bushes, and Jiminy ran after it, leaving me completely alone. He'd find his own way to the creature gate of Heaven. I couldn't show him anyway. Only Howard and his crew knew where it was. They once went cow tipping there and the authorities had to put extra security in place because cows enjoying their eternal reward do not deserve to be tipped, apparently.

For about the millionth time since my death, I wished I could ask my dad for advice. Xavier and Gabe try, but it's not the same. Nothing's the same as your dad, and even if he thinks you're worth less than the sack the groceries come in, you never stop wanting to have the kind of relationship where he smacks you manly-like on the back and tells you what he'd do if he was in your shoes.

The smart part of my head knew this was never going to happen, and I didn't have time to waste on wishes or watching my old man sleep. Heidi's and my clocks were ticking down together. But even knowing that wasn't enough to keep me away from stopping by, just to spend a little time near him. I tried to get up the guts to talk with him, to say sorry, but I couldn't make a single sound come out.

Pop's place smelled like bacon. It was the only thing he knew how to cook besides something from a box or a can. A pan of grease on the stove had hardened and turned tan and there were little flecks of burnt meat in it. It was pretty satisfying huffing the fat for a while. I don't know why people sniff glue or gas when there's bacon. Erase your brain or have an orgasm of your entire face? Come on!

159

He was asleep in his La-Z-Boy with the blanket my grandma crocheted for him pulled up under his chin. He'd started sleeping there after my mom left. When I was little, I thought it was because he was guarding the place in case she decided to come back and he wanted to give her the what-for. But then I read the note he always put on the kitchen table, alongside a can of Schlitz. *WELCOME HOME*. I was probably like six or eight at the time and I'd come to the kitchen for a drink of water because my throat used to turn into sandpaper at night.

This was before me and Pop had stopped talking to each other. And even though stopping talking had felt like a good way to stop fighting, it turned out to be a bad thing, because each word we didn't say was like a brick we stacked into a wall, and pretty soon that wall felt so big, we had no way of getting over it.

Anyway, however old I was, I was still little enough that I couldn't read without sounding stuff out. Pop heard me and busted out of his chair like a bear that had sat on a beehive. He yelled a bunch of stuff and he came at me all fast with his arms spinning at the air like sideways propellers, and he kicked at me, but I was more awake than he was, and definitely less drunk, and so his foot went into the kitchen table and there was this crack and the power of his kicking had busted one of the legs right off.

Only it wasn't a clean break. There were a lot of splinters and he said some bad words and I stood there and watched him try to get the table propped up again. He had one hand holding the Schlitz and one hand holding the table, and he was trying to get the leg in there using his knees, which wasn't working too good. I wasn't sure if I should offer to help or if that would make him worse, so I stood there in my underwear and T-shirt, feeling the cold air on my legs and noticing the patterns the streetlights made on the floor when they slid through the blinds.

"I want a drink of water," I said. Pop didn't answer me for a while. Alls I could hear was the kitchen clock ticking and the occasional car zooming by. Their headlights had a way of making shadows from the blinds slide all the way across the room like claws. I wondered if he'd fallen asleep there holding up the table and the Schlitz. Nope. He was awake, but his eyes were puffy and his chin was wobbling, like maybe the table was heavy.

So I was all, "Here," and I scooted in there and got the table leg out from between his knees and I worked it as best as I could so the splinters lined up.

Pop took his hands off the table and the beer all slow, like he was a magician doing something complicated with a rabbit and a hat.

"As long as we don't put any food on it, it should work good as ever," he said.

He rubbed his palm over his face and then over the skin on the back of his neck, which was always one of the most interesting things on him because it was red and crinkled and full of dents like the ones on those red rubber balls at school. I reached out my hand and put it on it real soft. It felt warm. My hand might have tickled because he started laughing, the quiet kind, where no sound comes out but your whole body shakes. I didn't want to look at him in case he was laughing at me standing there in my underwear, but me and Mike had used my pajamas to make a scarecrow and I only had the one pair. My legs were goose bumpy and I was real glad when Pop stopped laughing. I took my hand off his neck and he said with a kind of rough-edged voice, "What say we get you that drink of water and you go back to bed?"

He was still squatting and his eyes were lower than mine, which made me feel pretty grown up.

"Sure," I said.

"We'll fix that table leg tomorrow," he said. "I got all the tools for the job."

I drank every drop of the water in one gulp the way I'd seen Pop do it, but I don't think he noticed, because he didn't say, "That's the stuff," the way he did when he finished his drink. He was probably still thinking about the table.

We did try to fix it the next day, but Pop maybe didn't have all the tools that he thought. We had to sand the leg down where there were splinters, and even though we got it reattached all right, the table was wobbly. I had the idea of sanding down the other legs to match, but Pop said no because it would make the table too short and he wasn't going to sit at a midget table for the rest of his life. I decided not to say anything else after that, because he used to sometimes get really mad when things didn't go right, and part of me wondered if he was going to get it in his head to kick one of the other legs off. If there was one thing worse than one busted table leg, it was two.

Afterward, the table always had a lean to it. We tried sticking a bunch of stuff under it, but someone was always accidentally kicking it out and the table would — *woop!* — go slantwise, which is no way to eat, especially when you're working on something slippery, like a bowl of SpaghettiOs.

The dictionary did the trick, once we figured that out. Other than that, we were used to it. You can get used to a lot of stuff by living with it.

I could never quite figure out why Pop kept sleeping in the La-Z-Boy, though. After he stopped putting out the can of Schlitz and the note, he still parked himself there every night. Habit, probably. Or maybe it made it easier for him to get up in the morning, seeing as how he was already at something of an angle.

Now I stood over Pop again and watched him sleep. I was close enough that I could smell his aftershave, which always reminded me of limes. The light from the street bled through his whiskers, turning them from reddish to gold, and he snored a little bit, making a quiet noise that sounded like he was gently sanding wood.

"What you dreaming about, old man?" I said, not expecting my voice to work.

But it did and he woke up and grabbed on to the armrests of the chair. His face had a scared look, like my words went straight into his dreams.

"Jerome?" he said.

He looked from side to side quick-like. And then I could see the memory sink into his face. It was probably the light, but for a minute it looked like remembering took the color out of things, because his face turned from a sort of pork-chop pink to gray. He knew it couldn't be me, but that's only because he doesn't know what happens after you're dead. He blinked his eyes a couple of times real slow, closed his eyes, and fell asleep again, and his blanket slipped down to his stomach.

I looked at the clock. At most, Heidi had three hours left. Three hours is a lot of time if you want to kill it, and it is not enough time if it's all you have. I didn't want to kill time anymore. I didn't want to kill anything. I'd had enough of that for one lifetime.

It made sense to me now why Heidi wanted to say good-bye to her people. I wanted to do the same, for Pop, and for Mike. That seemed like as good a way as any of filling my last hours before going to Hell.

It was against the rules, but I focused all my emotion on getting Pop's blanket up under his chin. The guy might not have been the dad I wanted, but he didn't deserve to freeze in his sleep. Nobody does. I figured that was as good as I could do by way of good-bye. I took one last look at him and memorized him in his favorite chair. Then I shooped to Mike's.

CHAPTER SIXTEEN

Heidi

Three hours left.

HEIDI'S EYES OPENED and the room spun into slow focus. At first, she wasn't entirely sure where she was, or even who she was. There was the voice again. The voice, and a blinding light.

Come to me, it said. *Don't make me come and get you.*

She fought the urge to obey and float out of Jiminy's body. That had always been her default setting: listen to the other voice in her head, forgetting what her own was telling her. But an image of her family formed solidly in her mind. If there was any way she could get back to them and restore Jiminy's soul, she would do it. That it was a violation of one of the commandments in Jerome's handbook didn't matter. She was already outside the system, a lost soul. It wasn't as if things could get any worse.

The anesthesia cloud began to dissipate and she realized the white light that surrounded her came from the overhead fixture in the operating room. Squinting blocked the worst of it, and she could still make out the blurry shapes of the vet and his assistant as they tidied up the room, pushing sweet antiseptic wind over her face every time they passed.

The vet spoke: "You know, I'm sort of surprised we were able to get this little guy stitched up on the inside."

"So it wasn't just me?" the assistant said. "I thought he was a goner, for sure. Someone up there must want him to live."

"That's one way of looking at it," the vet said. "Okay, so we're going to have to shave that down before we do the plaster."

They were talking about Heidi's leg, or Jiminy's leg — whoever it belonged to was no longer clear. The limb was numb from anesthesia, but she could still feel the buzz of the clippers and the pressure of the cast as they wrapped the wet plaster. It ached like a bad tooth. Worse, though, was the plastic cone the assistant strapped around Heidi's neck. It blocked everything but the circle of room in front of her face, and it amplified the smell of dog breath. Within a few minutes, she'd coated the inside of the cone with a depressing, damp film of stink. A whine escaped her mouth and she sank lower on the metal table. Then a hand grabbed the fur between her shoulder blades.

"No collar or microchip," the assistant said. "Shame."

"I hate that," the vet said. "There's gonna be a hell of a bill for this. The Good Samaritan lady only left twenty dollars. Here's hoping we can find this guy's owners before we have to put him down."

"That's more than most leave. Dog's lucky he got found. If we don't find the owners, someone'll want to adopt him. He's adorable."

The vet grunted. "Can you believe it's only six A.M.?"

Six. Heidi had three hours before she disappeared for good. Three hours to get Jiminy's body back to her house, find his soul, and make the swap. The knowledge should've filled her with a sense of urgency, but the lingering anesthesia was so strong. She wanted to rouse herself, but it felt hopeless. How would she find Jiminy's soul if she couldn't even stand? Even her eyelids were more than she could keep open. She wished Jerome were nearby. He'd keep her awake.

Find me, Jerome. Find me and save me. She whispered it in her head like a prayer.

The assistant moved Heidi into one of the many small cages stacked against the wall. Most of them held animals: rabbits, cats, snoring dogs. Inside it reeked of 409. Heidi couldn't believe she was feeling nostalgic for her mother's organic cleaning products. The assistant stroked her on the nose, closed the door, and fastened the catch with a metallic snap.

"All set," she said. Heidi read the woman's plastic name tag. CORINNE.

She sniffed and noted that Corinne had eaten a hot dog with mustard and relish for dinner, along with a side of Cool Ranch Doritos; her breath also seemed to carry on it a whiff of Diet Coke. She inhaled again. Was that Head &

Shoulders shampoo? Her dad used that. And had Corinne been crying? She smelled the tiniest bit sad. Heidi suppressed a sympathetic whimper.

"Oh, little guy, did you sneeze?" Corinne said. "I hope you're not allergic to cats or it's going to be a long day."

Corinne flicked off the light, and the room became a dark box. Her shoes squeaked as she departed. Heidi fought the anesthesia for a few more seconds, but it was like wrestling a cloud. She knew there was a chance she'd never wake up if she fell asleep. And that was her last thought before her eyelids drifted shut.

CHAPTER SEVENTEEN

Jerome

Two hours left.

I DIDN'T LEAVE a last will and testament that said Mike could have my stuff, so it used to get my goonies in a twist every time I saw my vintage Heather Locklear calendar on his wall, and for a long time I couldn't come here after I got my chip installed because I'd swear myself a skull-melting headache. Now, though, I can handle it pretty good, which is why I was okay going to Mike's for good-byes.

Also, I thought looking at Heather would help me relax, and Mike has her on July these days, which is pretty much awesome. Heather's a collector's item, which is more than I can say for Mike. He still lives with my aunt and uncle, which was definitely not our plan for total world domination.

Don't get me wrong. I haven't lost my edge in rehab, but the guy could use a haircut. It was pretty sweet having long hair in the back and short in front when we were kids, but you need to have the hair in front to make the hair in back make any sense. It's *business* in front, not *bald* in front.

Sometimes I wonder what would've happened if the arrow had gone in Mike's head instead of mine. Maybe I would've been the fat thirtysomething with wizard hair, still sawing logs on the lumpy twin bed in my old room.

Doubtful, though, because I was always the brains in the operation, and Mike was the balls. He got all the girls. Well, both of them, but that was two more than I ever had. It seemed like alls he had to do was snap at a girl and say, "Ever rode so fast on a skateboard your whole world blurred?" and the females would line up.

Crystal was the first and they went out forever. Like four months. He used to give me the play-by-play of their dates. Mike and Crystal broke up before I died. He'd started dating this girl named Cori, who was way out of his league and he knew it. But she thought he had nice eyes and she was always looking into them and talking with him about doing better in school and how they could work with animals together or something totally uncool like that.

He had sex with her four times. Twice in one afternoon when her parents were at work. And then she baked him chocolate chip cookies afterward. It still cuts me a little bit when I think about it. I was mad at him because he didn't deserve sex and cookies any more than I did.

Mike and Cori were actually supposed to be at a movie the day he shot me, only I told him it was her or me, and he agreed to blow her off. And then the thing happened and he felt guilty because I was dead and he'd stood her up, and she dumped him, and after that he went through a real bad time with the drugs, and as far as I know they never talked to each other again, but Cori has a kid with a bent thumb exactly like his and I think if he'd known about it, he might have called her instead of dropping out of high school, rotting away in his Metallica shirt, and only working enough hours at the Walmart to buy gas for his Chevy.

He really drives one and it also is a piece of Chevy. If I were him, I'd paint it so the door matched the rest of the body. You can tell the door's pink and the body is maroon even when it's dark out.

I decided to hang out with Mike until it was time for group, make it kind of a long good-bye. If I was having my last night ever outside of Hell, I wanted to spend it with him. The truth was, I was scared out of my head and I wanted to be with the guy who'd been my best friend. Maybe it's because we were blood relatives, but I'd never met anybody I liked so much in the afterlife, which, when you think about it, is kind of a big deal. I know I was only in the rehab part and not full-frontal paradise, but if the people you hang out with every day on Earth are better than the ones you're stuck with for forever, it makes you think real hard about your idea of Heaven.

I was gonna miss Mike when I was gone for good.

There was so much to remember about us, mostly stupid, which is sort of the best kind of stuff. The dirt bombs we chucked at cars. The tree we fell out of when we were trying to build a fort. The beer we stole from my dad that one year on the Fourth of July when we were trying to burp the Pledge of Allegiance.

When you miss someone, they leave a person-shaped hole behind in the world that nothing can ever fill. If you don't keep thinking about them, the edges of the hole shrink and fade. You can't let go or the last of them disappears.

And it wasn't just Mike I'd miss. It was Heidi. I'd miss her too. I already did, and I could almost hear her telling me to find her and save her, even though it was too late and she wouldn't want me even if I did find her. The hole she left was so big I could dive inside. Its edges were sharp enough to shred me.

It was that feeling, that torn-up sort of missing, that made me finally call Howard. He was my enemy. But if there was any chance . . . Maybe he'd found her and kept her safe. Even if he didn't have her, maybe he'd just feel sorry for me and use his giant brain to help me look for her. I'd give him anything he wanted. Anything. I couldn't stand Hell, knowing I hadn't done everything possible.

My time with Mike was up. I left him a message as best as I could, just in case. I had this feeling it's what Heidi would've wanted me to do. I went MacGyver with a Scrabble set, some shaving cream, and his old, messed-up Rubik's Cube with the stickers peeled off. Told him what I thought he needed to know to have a happy life. It took it out of me to manipulate all that matter, but I couldn't stick around till he woke up. Chances are, he'd think it was someone flasking with him anyway.

But maybe, just maybe, he'd believe.

Howard didn't pick up until the seventeenth ring.

Jerkbox. I know he has caller ID. He was all bragging about it this one time when we were polishing Gabe's chariot wheels, which was supposed to be a punishment for us whizzing on them, which I only did because Howard told me if you made the yellow water on solid gold, your hair would stand up straight. That's something I'd only ever been able to do with toothpaste.

When he finally did answer, he used a girly voice that tricked me for a minute, so I hung up because instinct sort of took over. Me, girls, and phones have never mixed.

Then my skull phone rang and I kind of freaked out. I was standing outside of Mike's house and I jumped behind the garbage cans that he never puts back in the garage. I might've knocked one over, which is a super-hard thing when you're trying but amazingly easy when every nugget of your soul is splitting in two on account of panic.

I was lathered up because (1) I didn't have caller ID because Howard wouldn't share, and (b) was it Howard calling or Gabe? Also, (c) I will never get used to the ringing in my head. NOT COMFORTABLE AT ALL.

I manned up as best as I could even though the stuff in the garbage — foot fungus cream and a crusty bottle of Rogaine — made me almost want to cry for the lameness of Mike.

"Hello," I said, using my voice of not caring.

"Hey, asshole," Howard said in his normal voice. One other thing? He reprogrammed the swearing sensor so he can say whatever he wants. He likes to lord that over the rest of us, and the reason so many of the other guys follow him around all the time is because he promises he'll show them how to upgrade too. I'm not falling for that.

"Howard," I said. "What's up?"

"What's up, my fairy princess? What's up? Jesus, man. You called *me*." I could hear him breathing.

I almost told him it had been a wrong number, but then I would have been back where I started and it wouldn't have fooled him anyway.

"I need your help."

He didn't talk for a long time, but I could hear him crunching and swallowing. I could imagine nasty pizza roll crumbs and sauce all over his face, which is still reddish from the carbon monoxide he killed himself with in his parents' garage.

"Howard," I said. "Come on. I need a favor."

He belched. Then he started laughing.

"You need my help? This better be good, Handcock." Howard always used my last name in conversations because he thought it was funny to put a *d* in the middle where one doesn't belong. Pretty rich coming from a guy whose last name is Lipschitz, a name I can't even say without feeling the thunder of the Lord in my sinuses.

I wanted to hang up, but if I did, I had no idea how I was going to fix things with Heidi, if I even could. Group would start in about an hour, and by then, her time would be up for sure.

"I'm serious, man," I said.

"I'm listening."

I told him what had happened at the pond and everything after. The sun was coming up all around me and I got this pinching feeling in what used to be my heart. It's not that I'm a sucker for pink skies or anything, it's that part of me knew it was my last sunrise. They don't have them in the nine rings of Hell. No sunrises. No sunsets. They also don't have clocks that would help you measure the time passing. Hell is all about stuff not changing. It's part of the punishment. If people won't change, let them not change forever and see how they like it.

Howard only interrupted me once, when he heard about Megan Bingo.

"You were holding out on us, Handcock," he said. "Guys would have liked to see that."

I could sometimes be a real idiot. I flicked my arrow so that I'd stop getting distracted by the color of the sky and get my head in the game.

"C'mon, man," I said. My head felt like I'd dunked it in gas and shoved lit matches into my ear holes. "Sorry about that. You know you're supposed to be watching your own soul. I didn't want to give you the temptation."

"I got a cam on mine," he said. "I only shoop in when the kid's about to get in major trouble."

A cam. Howard would have been rich if he'd stayed alive. That had to burn. Before we died, computer geniuses were the dorks who dreamed of inventing robot girlfriends because the real thing wouldn't go near them for a million bucks. Over the next few years, those guys became zillionaires with hot chicks in their basements. Live ones. Who didn't charge.

175

"So Heidi's soul is wandering around by itself," Howard said. "I knew she'd popped loose when I saw her in the mall. Thought you maybe did it on purpose, you dirty dog. Followed you guys to her place, but then she disappeared. I sent her a few messages, but she didn't answer."

"Messages?"

"I hacked her soul once when you weren't paying attention."

"What do you mean? Do you have her?" I wanted to reach through my skull phone and grab his throat and squeeze like there was no tomorrow, because there wasn't. "C'mon, Howard. Give her back."

"I don't have her, asshole. But I'm gonna get her right now."

"Where is she?"

"Her dog's dead and the body is missing," he said. "And you still have no idea where to look for her soul?" He laughed at me again, and I got so mad it felt like he'd broken a rack of pool balls in my skull.

"That's why I'm asking you for help." My voice sounded stupid, like someone about to cry.

"More like begging."

"Yeah, fine." The words took a long time to work their way out of my mouth. "I'm begging you."

The sun was all the way up and the sky was a lighter shade of blue than my favorite jeans, which I wish every day I'd been smart enough to die in. People were doing their thing, driving their cars slowly through the slushy streets. A noisy brown bird, the same kind that had been at the pond the day Heidi died — the day I killed her —

sat on a bare branch yelling at me. It sounded like he was saying, "See? See?" Sort of like he expected me to be stupid, like my old man and everyone else did.

"I always knew you'd beg me for something," Howard said. "But I figured you'd want me to reprogram your sensor so you could swear again. I had no idea it was going to be this good."

It took everything I had not to tell him off.

"There's only one place she could be, you dumbshit."

Only one place? But where?

"And this is exactly what I've been waiting for, so thanks," he said. "It's going to answer a question I've been wondering about ever since I got here. A little experiment with a lost soul, in the name of scientific and philosophical exploration. Best thing you could've given me. Enjoy your trip to Hell, buddy."

I felt emptiness in my head and knew Howard had hung up. The bird was still telling me I was an idiot. I stood and kicked some of the garbage I'd been sitting in. I was mad enough that an old StarKist can rolled across the sidewalk and landed in the gutter.

I gathered up my feelings enough so I could chuck a rock at the bird, and I got a memory of the time Xavier and I were taking a walk around the pond. Rehab has a nature section in it because delinquents are supposed to be soothed by green stuff. There's a heart-shaped lake in the middle, with a path that goes all the way around — kind of like a better version of Heidi's pond, now that I think of it.

Xavier picked up a rock, and I first thought he was going to clonk me with it so I sort of turtled my head into my shoulders, but he didn't hurt me. He threw the rock into the water and said, "What do you see?"

I squinted for a minute, thinking maybe I was going to see the Loch Ness Monster, which would be awesome and totally the sort of thing that should be in Heaven. Or maybe he'd managed to hit a trout on the head and stun it, and it was going to come floating up, and an eagle would come screaming out of the sky and grab it in its claw, which would have been weird because that was totally going to be the art on the cover of Mike's and my first album: *This Is Free Lunch.*

"What do you see, Jerome?" he asked.

I took a long time to answer. Truth? I didn't see anything. The rock sank. The end.

"Water?" I said.

"And what is the water doing?"

How was I supposed to know? It was being wet. Water doesn't do much unless you're thirsty or you have balloons that you want to fill and drop from the roof.

"I dunno," I said. I kicked some pebbles, but they stopped short of going into the pond. "It's not complaining that you threw a rock at it?"

Xavier shook his head and put his hand real light on my shoulder.

"Look at the ripples," he said. "The rock caused all those ripples. They start out as a small ring, but given enough time, they'll reach out and travel all the way to the edge of the lake. Do you see yourself in that?"

"Which one is supposed to be me?" I asked. "Am I the rock or the ripple?"

Xavier laughed at me. Tears came out of his eyes and he squeezed my shoulder like it was a roll of soft toilet paper.

"What's so funny?" I yanked my shoulder away from his hand. I hate it when people laugh when you're not trying to be funny. That's against the rules of jokes.

"Sometimes," he said, "you help me see things more clearly. We are all the rock. We are all the ripple."

At the time I thought, well, glad one of us is seeing things clearly, because I am totally confused, and then I realized another thing that would have been awesome to hit: a mermaid, especially if I knocked her clamshells off.

But now I think I understand what he was getting at. I was the rock. I made the ripples. Even when the water in the pond was frozen, I created ripples. I'm also a ripple because what people do affects me.

It sort of figures that the day I learned that the things I do count for something was the last I'd have a chance to make a difference. With the handbook gone, I had a choice. I could confess to Xavier and Gabe and write my ticket to Hell. Or I could try Howard one more time. There was a chance he was bluffing. Or maybe he'd take pity on my soul.

It was my last hope for saving Heidi. My last chance for saving myself.

Knowing Howard, it didn't count for much at all.

THE GUARDIAN ANGEL'S HANDBOOK: SOUL REHAB EDITION

Appendix G: The Ten Commandments for the Living

I. THOU SHALT HAVE COURAGE.

CHAPTER EIGHTEEN

Heidi

Fifty minutes left.

HEIDI'S EYES FLEW open. What time was it? How long had she slept? Was she too late? She swung the cone around and found the clock. Almost eight A.M. Her heart lurched. She'd slept two hours, and her head still felt wrapped in a blanket of fog.

"Jerome?" she said. No one answered.

She couldn't see Jiminy's paws, but she could feel them pressed against the mesh of the cage, just as she could feel every inch of him merged with her soul: his paws, his legs, his fur, his little tail. She had never been so close to him or missed him so much. He was always happy, even when he was chasing squirrels and cars without catching them. He never thought about looking stupid, as far as she could tell. He didn't mind being his size. He was just happy to be alive in the bright, smelly world.

Maybe that was the key to a good life — the acceptance of things as they are. She wished she'd known this earlier, when there was still time.

She didn't have much left, maybe an hour or so, if the handbook was right. As strange as it was, she was glad to be inside Jiminy's body. It was partly the familiarity of it, and the hope that she'd be able to restore him to it, sparing her family a second death in as many days. But there was something more. It felt almost as if it was offering her some protection against the universe's desire to reclaim her soul.

That said, it wasn't easy staying inside. It took all her energy just to hang on. How on earth did Jiminy manage? A terrible thought struck. What if the same rules applied to animal souls? What if Jiminy only had twenty-four hours before he disappeared forever too? She had no more time to waste and couldn't spend her last moments in a cage, not when she might still make a difference for Jiminy and her family.

It would hurt, balancing on her broken front leg while she used her other paw to slide the cage open. It would be worse landing on the floor below. But she wasn't going to wait for anyone to rescue her. She'd escape. Find Jiminy. Bring him back home, back into his body, back to her family. If possible, she'd see to it that Megan got her Vincent Lionheart. After that, if there was anything left of her, she'd find Jerome and make him introduce her to his soul rehab counselors. They sounded like teachers, and teachers were almost always helpful.

With her good paw, she reached for the latch. It clicked open. The door swung wide and she made herself jump. When she hit the hard ground below, the pain was so terrible she almost flew out of his body on impact. But she hung on, trying her best to work her way back into Jiminy. She felt clumsy and dull, like a limb that had fallen asleep, and she could feel herself seep out through his fur. She lay on the floor, fading with each passing second. The voice whispered, *Just let go. Come to me.*

The last scraps of the old Heidi were tempted. It would be easier to do what someone else wanted her to do. But it wasn't what she wanted, and it wasn't the right thing either. She gathered her courage for one last try, squeezing her essence into a sphere, tucking it deep in the hollows of Jiminy's heart. She closed her eyes against the searchlight of pain that hunted her, and she held on until she felt ready to extend slim feelers from her soul through the fibers of Jiminy's body. Creeping, gliding, reaching, she urged herself onward, stopping to rest as her soul encountered the worst of the wounds. She pushed past them as you might walk barefoot on broken glass. It hurt like nothing she could've imagined, suffering she never could've endured before.

During her human life, any sort of ache was a flashing red light. When she saw it, she'd stop, too afraid to venture forward. She wanted the sure thing. The green light. She didn't know then that she could press on through the pain. She let the red swallow her and she started moving again, knowing in the deepest part of her that the pain wouldn't consume her. It would merely change her.

And she could live with that. She had to.

At last she was firmly inside Jiminy. She rested a moment. The linoleum tiles were cool, and they smelled of disinfectant and wax. She lifted her head to see the expanse of gleaming floor beyond the plastic cone. The light bounced off it like sunbeams off a lake, and it was almost beautiful. If Corinne would steer clear a few more minutes, Heidi might actually make it out the door.

She stood and tested her weight on her injured leg. The cast was a help. The end wrapped around her paw like a boot, taking pressure off the broken bone. The lampshade around her neck would have to go, though. She thought about using the table as leverage. It was a tall, stainless steel one with a top that stuck out a good six inches, leaving a useful gap between its legs and the wall. If she could walk through the gap backward, she could force the cone off.

Getting under the tabletop was the easy part. With her leg in a cast and her chest full of cracked ribs, walking backward was close to impossible. She took a few halting steps. The effort left her shaking and breathless. But she almost didn't mind. It was good being in a body again.

The table leg and wall caught the cone. Heidi tucked her chin and felt the plastic slide against her throat. She gagged twice, and the sound alerted all the other dogs that something interesting was happening below. A brown Chihuahua started saying, "Hey! Hey! Hey!" and it took her a moment to realize she'd translated dog to English. Then the rest joined in, all of them yelling "hey!" until the inevitable happened.

Corinne returned.

The door swung open and sent a breeze up Heidi's back, ruffling her fur. Her legs shook. It was going to hit her. She braced herself and held her breath.

"What's going on in here?" Corinne said. "You guys have been yapping all morning."

The door just missed her. Jiminy's body fit neatly in the triangle of space between the door and table, a space that was now reassuringly dark.

"What the —"

Corinne had noticed the empty cage. Heidi heard quick footsteps, then the creak of the cage door and the jiggle of the handle as Corinne inspected the latch. More footsteps. Heidi imagined Corinne scanning the room, her ponytail swinging from side to side. She prayed she wouldn't look behind the door.

Then Corinne's retreating voice as she darted from the room. "The new dog. He's missing!"

That's when Heidi realized her plan had certain limits. She'd made it out of the cage, but how was she going to get out of the animal hospital? It wasn't as if she was going to find a secret, magical doggie door leading outside. She'd have to pass the reception desk and walk through the lobby to escape through a door she could not open.

The red light flashed again in her mind, but she ignored it. She might not get out of the hospital, but she could get out of the room. One step at a time. That's how she'd do it. She went at the cone again, willing herself not to gag. With a lurch, she freed herself. The cone slipped off and rolled across the floor. She hoped the noise wouldn't draw Corinne back.

With the cone off, the cool air was a revelation on her face. She tipped up her nose. So many scents. It was hard to focus. She took one deep sniff and caught the odor of the outdoors: cold air, car exhaust, old corn dogs from the 7-Eleven down the street. The smell made her think of Jerome, and her borrowed heart beat faster.

She poked her head out the door into the hallway. Corinne was to her left, peering under the couch in the lobby. To her right, the vet chatted away on the telephone, giving advice on the proper treatment of some sort of intestinal parasite. Heidi looked left again. Corinne was pushing herself upright.

Should she make a run for it? Let loose a cat or two and stage a diversion? Crawl to Corinne, whimper adorably, and hope she let Heidi outside for a potty break?

There was no great choice. But before Heidi could make even a bad one, an angel materialized in front of her, wrapped in a shroud of diamond-white light.

"That's unexpected," she said.

"For you, maybe," the angel replied.

THE GUARDIAN ANGEL'S HANDBOOK: SOUL REHAB EDITION

Appendix G: The Ten Commandments for the Living

I. THOU SHALT HAVE COURAGE.

II. **THOU SHALT BE LOYAL.**

CHAPTER NINETEEN

.

Jerome

Thirty minutes left.

MY PLAN WAS to shoop to Howard's lobby. Maybe he'd even be there working on some new invention to make someone else's afterlife hell. Or maybe he'd be microwaving pizza rolls and decapitating stuffed animals. Whatever he was doing, maybe he'd talk to me and take pity and agree to help.

I landed outside his door and automatically looked up at the security camera. Before I knew it was there, I put honey and thumbtacks on his doorknob and got caught on tape and had to do some serious penance. I felt like giving him the one-finger salute in the camera for old times' sake. But I didn't. Because that would have been counterproductive, to use one of Gabe and Xavier's favorite vocabulary words.

Instead, I pressed the doorbell and listened to Howard's custom ringer. He'd programmed it with the Death Star theme from *Star Wars*. Like he'd even fit inside a storm trooper suit. The Emperor's fat-guy robe, maybe. I counted all the way to sixty Mississippi. He didn't answer. Either he wasn't there or he was ignoring me on purpose.

I turned the knob. Locked. If this had been a cop show, Heidi would've been in the room, gagged and tied to a chair, and when she heard the doorknob rattle, she would've gotten a look of hope in her eyes, just before they went to a commercial for extreme-flavor chips. I let that be my inspiration. The Heidi part. I like regular chips better.

Back in my human life, Mike and I used to practice breaking into places. Open windows were easy. Smashing a window was an option, but I'd once torn the bottom of my pants climbing through one, and my dad wouldn't buy me new jeans until I told him how I'd ripped them, and it meant I had to go to school showing everyone my London and France until the school nurse took pity and gave me a pair she said her son had outgrown, but she forgot to take the price tag off. Also? My dad made me pay to fix the basement window myself even though he couldn't prove I did it.

Eventually, I got pretty good at breaking the sort of lock you can pop with a credit card. You slide it in the gap, massage it back and forth a bit, coax the knob, and then *snock!* There she goes. I first started breaking in to get into my house when I'd forgotten my key, but pretty soon, I was working my way toward cooler exploits. My dream was to be able to use those little locksmith pins that you stick in the actual lock, working them one by one, until the teeth of the lock line up and smile their way to opening. A night at the arcade after hours. Sweetness.

I never had enough money to buy the actual set, but it wouldn't have mattered if I'd died with them in my pocket because Howard didn't have that kind of lock anyway. Or windows. He'd rigged up this fancy gizmo with a metal flap that slipped over the door so no one could go sliding a credit card in the gap. Instead of having a spot for a key or an awesome set of tools, the door locked with one of those calculator pads. You had to type in a code.

I might never have been good at math, but I knew the odds of my guessing the right numbers: somewhere between Vegas craps and zero. And chances are, Howard had booby-trapped it so anyone monkeying around outside, namely me, would get a bucket of cold holy water dumped on his head.

I leaned against the door and slid all the way down until I sat in a heap on the ground. There was no way I'd get through this in the, what, thirty minutes I had left. I wished I could have gone ashes to ashes, dust to dust instead of Heidi. Disappearing forever — that would be better than what I was facing. Stupid Howard. Stupid calculator lock.

Then an idea hit me like a cartoon frying pan. Calculators. I hadn't had a lot of reason to touch them in my life, but whenever I did, there was one thing I made sure to type. 58008. If you do that and turn it upside down, it says one of the most beautiful words in the English language. There are other words you can spell with a calculator, like *hello* and stuff, but those were for people who were lame.

I stood and punched 58008 onto the keypad, half expecting that bucket of cold water or an explosion of pitchforks. Instead, there was a buzz and a click. The knob turned. I pushed the door open and I was in.

"Heidi?" I called out. The place was dark and smelly. I wanted to gag. We had unlimited access to incense, and even though that smells like something I can't say, it wouldn't have hurt his lobby one bit. I felt around for a light switch until I remembered that Howard had hooked everything up to a Clapper like the kind they used to sell on late-night TV. He had half the guys convinced that he'd invented it. As if. I clapped the lights on.

He'd made some changes since I'd last been in the place. The stuffed animals were in a trash can with their guts spilling over the edge. On his wall was an old-school chalkboard like the kind they don't have in schools anymore, and he'd covered it with all sorts of math I didn't understand. There was a pile of books on the floor, books by Kierkegaard and Nietzsche and Camus, names I didn't even want to pronounce. But I found something good on his desk. His soul guardian's handbook.

I opened it hoping I'd find something about Heidi's situation but gave up in two seconds because the thing was so covered with Howard's own writing, it was almost impossible to read. He'd shoved some extra pages in the back and they fell out and spiraled to the floor.

I almost lost my lunch when I saw what he'd written on one of them.

if death isn't the end, what is?
when a soul disintegrates, does anything
happen to the pieces?
do they retain any memories?
or is that the final nothingness?
if there is no final end, then life means nothing.

I NEED TO WATCH A SOUL DISAPPEAR.

Heidi. That's why he wanted her. He had some idea that his existence would have meaning the second she was completely erased. I wanted to go fetal on the floor. I wanted to have never been born so I didn't have to feel what I was feeling, that life was one long struggle you could never win. But none of that was an option. Just as I turned to leave — I couldn't look at any more of this stuff — something hard smashed into my jaw from below. One of Howard's keyboards, swung by one of his minions. The one named Troy. If I'd been shorter or Troy had been taller, the keyboard would've connected with my arrow and it would have been game over right there.

As it was, it just meant a split lip. I touched it and tasted blood. That was going to leave a mark. Probably even one you could read, the keys had gone so deep. It was a real shame I didn't have enough time to take care of Troy. I would've liked to turn him into a set of luggage.

"You're not supposed to be in here," he said. "I'm telling Howard."

"Where is he?" I could feel my lip swelling. Pretty

soon, I'd start to talk funny. There wasn't going to be any dignity in this.

"He's out."

"Thank you, mathter of the obviouth." And there was the lisp.

An alarm dinged and the two of us swung our heads around. It was Howard's computer letting us know group was starting. That also meant Heidi's thirty minutes were up. My soul went numb.

"You're not leaving," Troy said. "We can do this the easy way, or we can do this the hard way."

I guess I'm not the only one who likes a cop show.

"Thut up," I said. I looked around, hoping to find something I could use. My lip stung. I touched it and noticed the sound my jacket made. My field jacket. The one I got from my dad. The one every guy in rehab wanted, especially Howard and therefore even more especially, his minions.

I slipped it off. I hadn't taken it off since I'd been in heaven, partly because you can only change clothes in a lobby, and partly because it was the one thing I had that still connected me to my dad. It had been his when he was in the Army, and it smelled like him and still had the shape of his arms in the sleeves. It was the last piece of hope I had that we'd be the family I wanted.

"This is all yours if you let me go to group and don't tell anyone I've been in here."

Troy's eyes lit up like a slot machine.

"I won't tell a soul," he said. I left before I had to watch him put it on.

CHAPTER TWENTY

Heidi

Fifteen minutes left.

SHE WAS STILL a little loopy from the anesthesia, which is why she thought at first the angel who'd materialized in front of her might be Vincent Lionheart come to life. The aura around him was that beautiful. Then he took a step closer and she realized he wasn't Vincent. Not even close. And if he was an angel, she felt a tiny bit less sad about not getting into Heaven. The angel was homely, shaped like Mr. Potato Head, and dressed in an oversize plaid shirt that hung over a belly the size of an Easter ham. A blot of pizza sauce hung below the corner of his lower lip. His expression, simultaneously creepy and eager, made her shudder.

But his voice was friendly enough, so she decided to give him a chance. Everyone deserved that.

"I have found you at last," he said. He pressed his hands together, as if in prayer, and bowed.

"Me? Why were you looking for me?"

"I have come for your soul," the angel said, gesturing at her with one palm. His aura pulsed when he said *soul*.

So this was it. Someone was taking her to Heaven. She expected to feel happier about it. The truth was, she'd hoped that someone would be Jerome. He'd been there for every other step in her life and it felt wrong to take the last one without him.

"My soul?" She tried to keep her voice down so Corinne wouldn't hear. She was also stalling for time. She wasn't ready to go just yet. There had to be a way she could put Jiminy back together.

"Your soul!" the angel said. He flung his fingers wide on either side of his ribs. Jazz hands. Megan did it all the time to make Heidi laugh. But she couldn't let herself laugh at someone who by all or at least some appearances was a messenger of God.

"Where's Jerome?" she asked. "Did he send you?"

"Jerome is about to be sentenced to eternal damnation," the angel said. His voice echoed magnificently. "Think of him no more."

It was hard not to think of Jerome. Her head had been painfully empty since she'd left him. And as angry as she'd been, she still wanted to know he was okay. She wanted to hear his voice again, if only one more time. She hoped he'd forgiven her for hitting him. And she hoped he knew she'd forgiven him for everything else.

"Eternal damnation?" she said, hating the way the words sounded coming out of Jiminy's mouth. "Like, forever?"

"Oh, who cares?" the angel said. "Jerome's a world-class ass."

This time, his voice didn't have the fancy echo. In fact, he sounded like he maybe had a sinus infection. He cleared his throat, and the echo returned. "And now thou shalt come with me."

Heidi couldn't believe it. He said "ass" and he didn't get a shock. Maybe he was a higher-ranking angel than Jerome. If that was true, she'd have to obey him even though she wasn't ready to leave. She felt her options go from zero to less than. She stalled for time.

"Where are we going? I don't think the vet's going to let us walk out of here."

"Thou shalt leave that detail to me," the angel intoned. He reached inside his flannel shirt and removed what looked like a television remote control. He pressed a couple of buttons, mumbling, "function, function, glow level seven," and was instantly bathed in light that made the ones in the operating room look defective.

"Am I supposed to go into that?" Her heart thudded. Oh, God. This was it.

"Only if you want to crash into me," the angel said. "Duh." He shook his head and scratched again. "Humans."

"I'm actually a dog right now."

"Only the unimportant part," the angel said. "In fact, we might as well ditch the pooch carcass here."

"No! I can't. I—" Footsteps. Corinne was coming back.

"If you don't, it will make things so much more difficult," the angel said.

"What things?"

She moved in for a sniff. Something was off about him,
something she wanted to understand. Beneath the outer
layer of pizza rolls, he didn't have a scent. Nothing. Most
people, she'd noticed, especially since she'd become a dog,
smelled like something, something soul-heartening. Bread.
Grass. Sweat. Shampoo. When she was close to him on the
train, she noticed Jerome's comforting musk. But this angel
smelled . . . empty. The fur between her shoulders rose.

She was probably being silly. Yes. That was it. It had
been a long, terrible night and she was still woozy from
the surgery.

"I don't have time to explain," the angel said. "And
more to the point, you don't have time for me to explain."

The only way he could've known her soul was about to
dissipate was if he really was an angel. She'd have to go
with him. But maybe he'd give her just a few moments more.

"I need to keep my dog alive," she said. "Until I can
get his soul back in his body."

The angel slumped his shoulders and let his head fall
toward his chest. He sighed heavily.

"I have never been able to understand earthly attachments," he said. "When I was a human, I had none. I was
happy."

"Is that how you became an angel? No attachments?"

"An angel? Ha —" The angel paused to scratch his
nose. "Yes," he said. "I am an angel, and a lack of attach-
ment is how I achieved my exalted state."

"Please help me." Her voice sounded so pathetic. "Please."

"Help you?" the angel said. "We have to get you to my — my esteemed colleagues."

"If I'm going to spend eternity in Heaven, there has to be time for me to do this one last thing on Earth. I need to do this. I need to save Jiminy and say good-bye to the people I love."

"Gahhh," the angel said. He stuffed his hands in his pockets. "Fine. Follow me."

He fiddled with the remote control again and the world around her went hazy.

"I don't want to do it," she said. "I don't —"

"What, you don't trust me?"

She didn't. But she didn't want to seem rude or offend the one soul who might help her now. She opened her mouth to speak, and the bell on the door of the veterinary office dinged. A thirtysomething guy with a head half full of long hair walked in. What was it called when a balding guy had a mullet? The melting pony?

"Cori!" he said.

Corinne walked out and stopped abruptly. "Mike?"

She wanted to watch what was going to happen. She had that fluttery feeling you get when you're watching a movie and you know there's going to be kissing.

The angel's white light spread until it swallowed her. She felt something tug her fur. She staggered outside. The angel whisked away the light as a magician retracts a silk handkerchief, leaving her shivering on the sidewalk in a softening bank of slush. Her leg ached. A maroon Chevrolet was parked crookedly nearby, its lighter-colored door hanging open.

"Come on, then," the angel said, glancing back over his round shoulder. "Let's get all that stuff over with. We're late enough as it is."

CHAPTER TWENTY-ONE

Jerome

Five minutes left.

I FELT NAKED without my jacket and drunkish from getting whacked on the head, so I stumbled a bit as I walked into group. People were at activity centers, which is how we start sessions. A couple of guys were playing Yahtzee. I hate how the dice rattle in cups. It makes my arrow hurt. I would rather play poker, but that involves bluffing, which Xavier and Gabe view as a form of lying and so we're not allowed.

I tripped on the leg of the Yahtzee table and knocked my arrow on the corner of it when I went down. It hurt so bad I thought I'd never get up. I grabbed my head and listened to the moaning sound coming out of my mouth. It was like a herd of cows was in my throat. Then I saw a pair of tasseled loafers in front of me. Xavier.

"Jerome," he said. "It's hard to talk with you when you're in the fetal position." His knees popped as he squatted next to me. "What's wrong? I know there's no food poisoning in Heaven, and we upgraded your sensor to keep you out of Applebee's, so don't pretend you're having another Riblets incident."

"Xavier," I said.

My voice sounded like someone had stepped on it, but at least the lisp was gone. I stared at the carpet real hard, wishing the strands would rearrange themselves into letters telling me what to do. He put his hand on my back, right where the wings sprout out on greeting-card angels. I turned my head and squinted. Xavier obviously didn't know what I'd done or he wouldn't be doing the comforting thing.

"So what's the verdict on the carpet?" he said. "See anything interesting there?"

"Smells," I said. "Like feet."

Xavier offered me a hand up.

"Don't need any help," I said.

"Regardless of whether you think you need help," Xavier said, "I am offering it. That is what I am here for."

He stood and did his little clap-clap thing to let people know group was starting. The echoes were not a sound I needed just then. Everybody put down their half-finished lanyards and Yahtzee dice and headed to the folding chairs. They socked each other's shoulders and settled down in their seats like it was any old group session where we'd report on our humans and then sing uplifting hymns and wait and see if anyone had accumulated enough points to fly up.

I'd never felt more alone in my whole life or any of the years that came after Mike shot me. It's bad enough to know you're going to Hell with the weight of someone's lost soul on your shoulders. It's something else to know you're going by yourself and to see everyone just doing their thing like nothing unusual was happening.

Once everyone was seated, Xavier glided to his chair, cleared his throat, and said, "Does anybody have anything he'd like to share?" He looked right at me.

A new kid named Irving piped up because he hadn't learned yet that sharing in group is likely to lead to uncontrollable confessions.

"Um, Xavier?" he said in his squeaky little unchanged voice. "I don't think Howard is here?"

"Why, thank you, Irving, for helping watch over my flock." Xavier squinted and scanned the room. "Has anyone seen Howard? Is he not feeling well?"

I wasn't going to open my snack hole at first. I didn't know where he was, but I knew what he was doing, watching Heidi's soul disappear from the world forever, and loving every second of it. Xavier put one long finger on his temple and massaged. He put his other pointer finger in front of his mouth and shushed us.

I'm calling him, he mouthed, like we couldn't tell.

He let Howard's skull phone ring and ring, and his face got more confused-looking by the second. I don't know if skull phones are like those things that suck the water out of air, but the waiting was having that effect on my mouth. My tongue felt like a lump of cotton. A lump of nasty cotton living in the armpit of a bum who has an apartment at the dump and not even the good kind of dump with busted car parts. The kind with fish heads, banana peels, and old transvestite wigs.

Xavier lowered his finger. "Does anyone know where Howard is? We've had reports of Canadian succubae sightings. Or he could have been detained by a wayward hellhound. If anyone has information he isn't revealing, this will count as a blot on his soul. I don't believe I need to say that for some of you striding the edge of expulsion, those may very well be the points that send you through the double doors."

He pointed and made his fingertip audio equipment do a thunder sound.

Troy, who'd come into group right after me, crossed his arms over his chest. My jacket was way too big for him.

"Jerome!" Xavier used his loud voice.

I had to shake my head to snap out of it. *Look cool. Look cool.*

"What?"

"Your face," he said. "It looks troubled. Is there something you want to tell me?"

He made church-and-steeple hands and looked at me with his lips touching the steeple part, like he was daring me to let a lie creep out of my mouth in a holy place.

I have lied in all sorts of places, both when I was a human and since I became a rehab soul. I've gotten to where I don't think of words as truth or lies anymore. They're things I put out there to do what I need. They're like a socket wrench or a hammer or my favorite tool, the Sawzall, which does exactly what it sounds like it does unless you take it to the bumper of your dad's Pinto, because then it becomes a Sawznothing.

I opened my mouth with the idea of lying, but then I looked in Xavier's eyes. I started thinking about ripples and I couldn't stop, and I knew that no matter what, I didn't want my last ripples to be false ones.

I closed my eyes to make them stop stinging, and I used my skull phone to call him so the other guys wouldn't hear. It was hard sending a message with my brain because normally I use my mouth. But I guess my brain has some usefulness to it, because he nodded right at me and whispered, "Hallelujah." Then he did clapping hands again and announced that during the rest of group today, it would be A/V time featuring a showing of *Steel Magnolias*.

I almost hurled until I remembered that I wouldn't be watching it. I'd be confessing my sins with Xavier and Gabe. The movie screen swooshed down and there was a lot of clanking as the guys rearranged their chairs. And then I was out of the group room and in Gabe's chambers, and he and Xavier were in front of me. Waiting. That's when the clock struck nine.

The Guardian Angel's Handbook:
Soul Rehab Edition

Appendix G: The Ten Commandments for the Living

I. THOU SHALT HAVE COURAGE.

II. THOU SHALT BE LOYAL.

III. THOU SHALT TELL THE TRUTH.

CHAPTER TWENTY-TWO

Heidi

Zero minutes left.

FOR THE FIRST time since she'd gone into Jiminy's body, Heidi noticed the world was no longer in color, or at least in as many colors as she'd known in her human life. The sun was a white wound in a gray sky. The rest of the world was a landscape of textured black and white, stitched in a thousand shimmering shades between. It was the world as she'd always tried to draw it, only better.

Her nose deepened the picture, picking separate strands of fragrance out of the air: here, car exhaust; there, squirrel. Braiding everything together was the richness of a burning cedar tree — infused with the warmth and wind and rain and moonbeams it had absorbed over the course of many human lifetimes — now slowly turning to ash in someone's fireplace.

And then there were the noises. The high chatter of birds. The low moan of passing cars. The chuckle of melting snow in the storm drains, like a secret joke between the sidewalk and the street, punctuated with the intermittent punch of barking dogs announcing, "I'm here! I'm here!"

She'd observed a bit of it earlier, as Mrs. Thorpe drove her to the animal hospital. But it was dark then. And she was hurt. Now that she was patched up and hungry to remember everything for as long as it lasted, it felt sublimely strange to perceive the richness of ordinary human experience through the senses of her dog. No wonder Jiminy always held his ears up. No wonder he poked at the air every so often with his nose. He was paying attention. She wished she'd done the same. She wished — she wished . . .

"Why do you keep touching my back?" she asked the angel.

They were walking toward Heidi's house to see if Jiminy had gone there — it wasn't far, maybe a mile. The going was rough on the icy sidewalks. Most of the snow had been cleared, but any lingering anesthesia that might have blunted her pain had vanished, and the salt stung her footpads.

She knew enough to understand why the angel wasn't offering to carry her. He couldn't. Even if he didn't mind breaking one of the Ten Commandments for the Dead, he probably didn't care enough about her to lift her. Besides, she didn't want to look like a flying dog. That would attract the kind of attention she didn't need. Still. His fingers kept wrapping around her spine as though it were a purse handle.

"I'm, uh, I'm petting you," he said. "Ruffling your fur. I thought dogs liked that." He took his hands away, pressed them into his pockets, and whistled an ugly melody through his teeth.

It didn't feel like he was petting her. This was way too rough. She growled. Something about being inside Jiminy had stripped away her old reserve. She felt like a peeled orange, alternating bursts of sweetness and bitterness, and she resolved to walk faster. The sooner she made it home, the better. She disliked being with this angel. It wasn't just the creepy song he was whistling. It was his palpable absence of goodwill. He made her feel worse than any-one who'd made fun of her at school — and they'd only just met.

"Do you think you can do what you need to do in, say, five minutes?" he asked. "We're kinda running late."

They stood on the steps outside her front door. Melt-ing icicles hung like earrings on the eaves, shedding sparkling drops onto the softening soil below. The warm breath of the house had melted the snow, revealing a skirt of earth. Soon, crocuses would reach their fingertips through the surface, followed by their purple and golden heads.

"Yo," the angel said. "I asked you a question."

She turned her face toward him.

"Five minutes?" She whispered so no one inside would overhear. "Can't I have more time?"

The church bells started ringing and the angel rolled

his eyes. "It's nine o'clock," he said. "You've made me late already."

Nine o'clock. She was supposed to have dissolved by then. And yet she hadn't. She still felt as solid as she had an hour before. Something about being inside Jiminy must be keeping her safe. As hard as it was to hang on, doing so was making a difference. She hoped the protection would last long enough for her to find his soul and put it back where it belonged.

"Look," she said. "This might take a while. I'm going to have to find Jiminy and figure out how to get him back inside his body. I'd also like to say good-bye to my family and Megan. I'm sure you understand."

"Foolish human," the angel said in his reverberating voice. It gave her the shakes. "Your dog's spirit has most likely made its way to animal heaven. We'll need special permission to go there."

He might have mentioned that before. But no matter. She'd talk to her parents first, say good-bye. One thing at a time, one step at a time. "I'm gonna scratch on the door. That's how Jiminy asks to come in."

The angel rolled his eyes again, and she felt herself blush beneath her fur. She hated how stupid he made her feel for wanting to do these last few things. At least no one could see it through the fur.

"Are your ears turning red?" the angel said. "That's totally weird."

Fighting an urge to tuck her tail between her legs, she sat on the welcome mat and scratched the door with her cast. Then came footsteps on the tile, the nervous rattle of the chain coming loose, the slow turning of the knob. She stood and wagged her tail when she saw Rory.

"Jiminy! What happened to you?"

Rory had a coat on, as if he was just getting ready to leave the house. He lifted her and she felt every one of her internal injuries ignite.

"Mom! Dad!" Rory carried her into the family room at a run. She thought she might throw up, it hurt so much. "Jiminy's back and he's all busted up! Look! He's wearing a cast!"

Her parents emerged, also dressed in their winter coats. They looked terrible, as if they hadn't slept. A sweet pressure built up behind her eyes, but she had no tear ducts to release the pain. Instead, she barked and wagged her tail, looking about for Jiminy's spirit. She saw no sign of him.

The angel stood behind her, studying their family portrait. She growled, hating the hungry look in his eyes.

"Jiminy!" Her mother squatted and held out her hands. Heidi thumped her way across the floor and into her mother's arms. She breathed in her mother's scent and wanted to kiss her and embrace her.

"What happened to you, Jiminy? You disappeared on us. We were so worried." She leaned her forehead against Heidi's. "I'm glad you're home."

Heidi whimpered.

"Ticktock," the angel said. "I haven't got all day. You haven't got all day."

She shot a look at her parents, alarmed. But they hadn't heard him. The clock on the wall inched toward five minutes past. A pen and paper. That's what she'd need. It would be quicker to use Jiminy's body to talk, but her voice coming out of his mouth was monstrous. That was the last thing she'd want to do to her parents while they were still dealing with her death.

She slipped out of her mother's embrace and tottered through the hall to the family room. As usual, her dad had left his work on the coffee table. She picked up his pen in her mouth, wishing it were one of her beloved Pigma Microns.

"Jiminy, drop it," her dad said.

She resisted the urge to obey. The pen weighed a thousand pounds and its barrel tasted of salt and minerals. She arranged the pen so it was tip down, nosed her father's work out of the way, and looked for something to write on. Her mother's fitness magazine. It would do. It would have to. In fact, it might even make things easier.

"Jiminy!" Her dad's voice was sharper now. "Drop it!"

Heidi hurried and circled the letter *H* in HEALTH.

The angel leaned over her shoulder. The scent of imitation pepperoni and cheap tomato sauce assaulted her. "Why don't you step out of the dog already?" he said. "Get this over with?"

She growled.

"Dad, look!" Rory said. "Jiminy circled the letter *H*!"

"Don't be silly, Rory," her mother said. "Get the pen before he makes a mess."

"He's circled the *E*!"

Heidi paused. She wanted to drop the pen. It was making her drool.

211

"Warren, look at this," Heidi's mother said. She stood next to Jiminy. "What do you make of it? The dog's circled two letters."

"*HE*? What's that supposed to mean?" Rory said.

Heidi scanned the page for her next letter. There. An *I*, right in the headline "INVISIBLE TOXINS IN YOUR FRIDGE."

"He circled an *I*!" Her parents grabbed each other's hands. Exhausted and in pain, Heidi pressed on. She hadn't thought about what she'd write beyond her name. She found a *D* in the "UNSEXIEST DISEASES EVER" headline, and circled the *I* next to it, to conserve her energy.

"Heidi!" her mother said. "Jiminy spelled Heidi's name! What are the odds?"

"It's a message, Mom," Rory said. "A secret message from beyond! Maybe it's Houdini with dyslexia."

"Don't be ridiculous, Rory," her father said. "You sound like that fruitcake Patty Lin." But he peered at the magazine, his mouth slightly open.

"It could be a message," her mother said. "Rory's right. On *Oprah* once they had this —"

"Shh," her father said. He held up his hand. "Jiminy's circling another letter."

Heidi hovered over the magazine. It was hard to concentrate with everyone gathered around. She wanted to cry again but settled for a muffled whimper.

Heidi says good-bye. That's what she'd write. It was stupid, what people with absolutely no imagination might say. But it was the shortest thing she could think that also worked. Maybe once she delivered the message, she'd be able to use her voice without freaking them out entirely. Maybe then she could say "I love you" as well.

She found an *S* in a headline that read "INCONTINENCE AFTER CHILDBIRTH: 5 CURES." She was almost glad she'd never be having babies. Then she spotted an *A* in "STOMACH SHRINKING IN TWO WEEKS."

"YOUR CHEATING HUSBAND" had the *Y*, the *S*, a *G*, and an *O*. She was getting close.

"Heidi says go!" her mother cried out. "That's the message! Warren, Rory, we have to go see her again. Now. We've gotta go now."

Heidi opened her mouth to speak. No! That wasn't the message. She wasn't done! She dropped the pen in frustration and confusion. What did they mean, see her again? Was it some kind of prefuneral viewing of her corpse? If that was the case, she wanted to go this time, to see her body and prove this was all really happening, even if it meant Jiminy's soul would spend that much longer unprotected. Maybe she could convince them to bring her along.

She struggled to pick up the pen again, and got it in her mouth the wrong way. The tip stuck out of the right side, and she couldn't muster the coordination she needed to write. She wanted to scream but couldn't, or she'd drop the pen again.

Then everything went to pieces.

In a whirl of activity, her family gathered their car keys and cell phones. They were gone before she even realized what was happening. She'd tried to give them a message and failed. The silence they left behind seeped into her like poison.

She looked up at the angel. "They left. They left before I finished."

"Told you to hurry." He scratched the side of his nose. "Hey, do you have a camera? Video would be best, but in a pinch, point-and-shoot will be fine."

"A camera?"

"Do I stutter?" he said. "I left mine back in my lobby and I'm not going to shoop and leave you alone."

A low growl tickled her throat and leaked out of her mouth. "I thought angels couldn't move physical objects."

"Only the lame ones, only the lame ones. Besides, now that I've seen what you can do with that little dog mouth, you're going to set it up. You can probably even push the AUTO TIMER button."

"I'm not letting you have a camera." She walked into her room, hoping she'd miraculously find Jiminy's soul on her bed. She also hoped to see her artwork one last time but realized her family had probably discovered it and had either tossed it all because they considered it pathetic, or worse — they were attaching the pieces to poster board to use as a decoration at her memorial service. She was surprised to find that she cared little either way. She only wished she'd thought to draw things bigger, to imagine things bigger.

A miniature molded-rubber wing-tip oxford shoe stuck out from under her bed. Vincent Lionheart. She reached for him, ignoring the pain and awkwardness of the effort, and clamped her teeth around him, regretting putting puncture wounds in his perfect flesh. There went his resale value. She worked her way out from beneath the bed and felt the angel's hand dig once more into her back. There was a horrible tug, as though he was trying to rip her soul right out of Jiminy's body.

Then she realized he'd been trying to do that all along.

The Guardian Angel's Handbook:
Soul Rehab Edition

Appendix G: The Ten Commandments for the Living

I. THOU SHALT HAVE COURAGE.

II. THOU SHALT BE LOYAL.

III. THOU SHALT TELL THE TRUTH.

IV. THOU SHALT HAVE FAITH IN THYSELF AND IN OTHERS.

CHAPTER TWENTY-THREE

Jerome

Zero minutes left.

I DIDN'T WANT to go to one of the nine levels, but if I had to, I figured it was better to end things quick, like ripping off a Band-Aid.

I asked Gabe straight off, "Which one?"

Because he is sort of an applemunch, he replied, "Whatever do you mean, Jerome?" Then he clamped down on the toothpick in his mouth and crossed his arms to cover most of his vest. I figured this was maybe a test, so I didn't do what I wanted to do, namely, punch his forehead, but I imagined it making a hollow noise like the sound it makes when you hit a baseball just right. *Pok!*

Gabe and Xavier looked at each other. Then Xavier flattened imaginary wrinkles in his robe and said, "It is interesting, Jerome, that you have chosen this location for our meeting."

"Interesting? If you ask me, this is the boringest room in the place."

"Most boring," Gabe said.

"See," I said. "Even Gabe thinks so."

We were in the confessional, which has no windows, no pictures, no craft tables, and not any color anywhere. It is a white box of nothing. Even the chairs are white, so you sort of look like you're floating in space. Or mayonnaise, because I'm pretty sure space is black.

Xavier made prayer hands. He tilted his head and smiled. "What I meant to say, Jerome, is that it is interesting you chose this place above all others. Particularly your usual spot."

True enough. I usually choose the john. Not that we need one. Spiritual beings are free of that embarrassing kind of stuff, but Heaven has them anyway to make sure we're reminded of our humanity. It's not so much that Earth is a reflection of Heaven. It's the other way around, which is probably disappointing and all to the folks expecting something better in the afterlife. Anyway, it's the perfect meeting space because I can flush the toilet a lot after they get done with their speeches about how much of a flask-up I am. *Sha-boom!* It's like a television laugh track, only wetter.

I waited for somebody to say something, but they sat there like a couple of cows, blinking. I wanted to tip them. They were going to make me do all my own confessing. Why couldn't they lay it all out for me so I could nod like a man and get sent down without crying or puking? It blows to make damnation so hard on a guy.

"Would you like us to use the screens?" Gabe asked.

I nodded quick-like because I was using my throat to hold back tears. Any words that came out would've uncorked the whole thing and I did not want to go below like a wet-faced baby.

He did the finger whammy, and the screen came down and flickered to life. Pretty soon the picture was as clear as anything. Heavenly definition, that's what I'm talking about. That sort of HD isn't available yet to the living, not even in Japan.

I expected the video to start with the thing at the pond, but it didn't.

It started out with me as a kid in my playpen. It was before my mom left, and she was lying on the couch trying to sleep. I knew it was her, because I recognized her face from an envelope of pictures I once found in a closet underneath my dad's ammo when I was looking for something I could use to make a wizard suit one Halloween.

I don't know how old I was in the video, but it was old enough to have thrown all my toys and my blanket and my bottle at her. I guess I wanted her attention, but she was holding her forehead and saying things at me that most moms don't say at their kids. I must've done something to make her sad, because her face was puffy and it had that sticky look you get if you've been crying and you can't find the energy to wash off the salt and snot. I remembered the feeling I saw on my face, where my stomach stretched up around my heart with wanting, and I don't think it was me wanting my toys and blankets back.

I don't know why they showed that to me, though. Or the next video, which was of me and my dad.

I was learning to walk. I didn't have all my teeth yet. Maybe eight little squares in front and you could see them all because my mouth was open wide like my dad's, only he was saying, "One more step, little man. One more step. You can do it."

The carpet looked a whole lot better back then, so I guess my house wasn't always the pit I remembered.

He kept on saying, "One more step," until I had walked all the way into his arms and then he said, "You are going to be a star athlete, little man. Maybe a football player, or a hockey player, or whatever you want and your life will be —"

I couldn't hear what he said next because he was scooping me up and holding me over his head and I was laughing so hard that was all you could hear. He tossed me in the air a couple times and a little bit of spit came out of my mouth and landed on his face but he didn't care.

I wanted to ask why they were showing me this, because it didn't look like I was doing anything wrong in the movie at all. But the words wouldn't come out and I didn't want them to switch to something else. It made my old heart space feel almost full to see my dad and me playing. It was the part of my life where he thought I could be somebody, and I liked living it again, and I didn't care if Gabe and Xavier watched. It felt good for them to know that I wasn't always a screwup.

It ended. I was about to ask for it again when I saw Gabe twiddling with his toothpick. He took a notebook out of his vest pocket and flipped through the pages until he came to one he showed Xavier.

"This?" he said. "We're not really supposed to show these scenes."

Xavier shrugged. "What's the worst that could happen? I mean, at this point?" He held up a finger, like he wanted Gabe to wait a minute. "Let me check on the souls first." He activated his skull phone and dialed one of the guys from rehab, using speakerphone.

"Did you locate Howard?" I heard a little buzzing sound but couldn't make out the words. Xavier's eyes had a sharp sort of worried look. He lowered the volume on his microphone and turned to Gabe.

"He's still out there. Should we activate the soul jack?"

Soul Jack? That sounded like a guy who carried an ax and a black sack perfectly sized for a human head.

"Do it," Gabe said. "Hopefully, he hasn't figured out how to dismantle that feature yet."

"Oh, he won't have found it, not where I put it," Xavier said.

Xavier turned his microphone back up and said, "Thank you for your efforts. Please report back to the group facility. You may have an extra serving of manna and fifteen bonus minutes of free-will time."

Gabe fired up the screen again.

I recognized the scene right away and felt a sharp pain in my forehead. I wondered for a minute whether I'd just been sent down. I breathed all heavy, like someone had turned up the heat, only I felt cold all the way through.

This video was something that wasn't from my life, not the part I was there for anyway. It was the part where Mike ran into my house and got my dad after the arrow thing happened. At first I was expecting Dad to be mad, but that wasn't what happened. That wasn't what happened at all.

The Guardian Angel's Handbook: Soul Rehab Edition

Appendix G: The Ten Commandments for the Living

I. THOU SHALT HAVE COURAGE.

II. THOU SHALT BE LOYAL.

III. THOU SHALT TELL THE TRUTH.

IV. THOU SHALT HAVE FAITH IN THYSELF AND OTHERS.

V. THOU SHALT FORGIVE.

CHAPTER TWENTY-FOUR

Heidi

DURING A FAMILY trip to Disneyland when Heidi was eight and her brother was six, their parents stepped out onto the motel balcony for some fresh air, briefly leaving them alone inside the room. Rory took the small metal key from the minibar and shoved it into the electric socket.

"Zow!" he said. "That felt great. Touch it, Heidi."

She was suspicious. For a little kid, Rory was a sneak. He'd decapitated one of her Barbies a few months earlier, and this was after giving the doll a haircut and melting her hands with a forbidden box of matches. And then he hadn't gotten into trouble for it because he promptly came down with chicken pox, and by the time the scabs healed, (a) Heidi was also infected and (b) their parents had forgotten Barbie Armageddon.

So, while a big part of her was skeptical, another part was hoping he'd meant to make up for the death of Barbie by showing her something really neat. Jerome didn't offer an opinion one way or the other, so she took the risk and grabbed the key.

A surge of electricity raced from her fingertips to her hair. It felt as if someone had stripped out her insides and snapped them like a wet towel. She wanted the feeling to stop, but the current had thoroughly hijacked her hand. She couldn't let go until Jerome shouted "Lean back! Lean back!" Once she finally did, the key slipped out of the socket. She was free.

The angel was hijacking her soul. Only this time, there was no Jerome around to tell her what to do, and no sweet release from letting go. Letting go meant death. Her body — Jiminy's — went rigid as she held on. She felt herself unhooking slowly from Jiminy's flesh and slipping through his cells. She resisted, but it was like trying to squeeze a handful of water. She began to trickle out, Jiminy's body stiffening each time her hold on it slipped.

The angel was relentless, grunting and trembling as he tugged. "Come to Howard," he said. "That's right, come to Howard so we can get this over with and know, once and for all."

She cursed her own stupidity and the brain-numbing effects of the anesthesia. Of course this was Howard. He wasn't helping her or guiding her to Heaven. He meant to do her harm. Whatever he wanted to know — it couldn't be good.

She settled in for the fight of her life. There were no handles to grasp, no poles to seize. She couldn't ask anyone for help, and every second, more strands of the mysterious substance that rooted her inside Jiminy broke. While she'd known before what desire meant in the abstract, while she'd *wanted* things — to be liked by Sully, to be thought of as someone worth respect — she hadn't let herself experience a true desire all the way to her depths. She'd never let go of everything else in pursuit of one. She felt it now, though, a bottomless hunger, a vast wanting that was stronger than fear or reason, a force that would rather fail than be silenced.

In her old life, she'd been protecting herself. Marking time until something outside her changed. And now, that time was up. One by one, she felt her soul's threads snap. They sang inside her like a burning harp, jangling and final. She held on anyway. She clawed at the floor, trying to move Jiminy's suffering body beneath the bed, but it didn't work. She struggled to her desk, trying to wrap her one good paw around it, but it slipped off immediately.

Howard pulled and grunted. Long seconds passed. And then, with one hideous tug, her soul popped free. The room was quiet. She'd failed. Jiminy's body lay on the floor, his eyes open and dull. Vincent Lionheart lay next to him, his torso dented with tooth marks. Howard panted, his hands on his knees. Heidi was spent. The light in the room started to flicker, then fade. Her ears filled with the sound of moving water, and her essence began to crumble.

"You didn't have to make that so difficult, you know," Howard said. "You're part of something important. A major discovery. I'm going to watch what happens when your soul disappears so that we can know, once and for all, what a final ending really is, because death isn't it. A body dies and it rots. It feeds the soil, which grows the plants that feed new creatures. It's an endless, pointless cycle." He stopped to mop his brow with the back of his hand. "But your soul doesn't die. It comes here and gets trapped in another endless cycle. Heaven, Hell. Rehab for a while if you're unlucky. I want to know where the rare lost soul goes when it disappears. I need to know. And it's good for you too. If you disappear, it's proof that life actually matters. Your pathetic little life, once it's gone for good, will finally mean something."

Heidi turned to face Howard. He kept splitting in two and vibrating. She shook her head to see if she could get her eyes to track again. She wanted to launch herself at him the same way she had at Jerome, only with a thousand times more force. Her soul wasn't part of his experiment. It was hers. It did matter. It mattered to her, and that was enough.

She gathered the strength to stand, folding her fingers into fists, struggling to keep her balance, intending to land a punch the size of Alaska on his nose. She never got the chance. A small, pulsing light appeared over Howard's head. It beeped three times, and then shot a glittering web downward. The shining substance closed in on him and collapsed into a pinprick of brightness before it disappeared with a *crack*. A snake of incense reared up from the ground where his soul had stood.

The room dimmed further and her limbs started to hum and lighten. She watched the surface of her soul hands ripple. Their edges blurred and faded to a burnished gold. She dropped to her knees and crawled back toward

Jiminy's body. She reached it and fell upon it, pushing her soul back through his cells. His legs felt harder now, like a leather glove that had been left out in bad weather. She didn't know how much longer she could hang on.

One of her Pigma Microns lay on the floor. She stumbled to it and grabbed it between her teeth. Then she fished a piece of paper out of the recycling bin and scratched out a self-portrait — her first — and a message to her family, trusting that they'd find it someday.

It felt good to do that one simple thing, as though it somehow took away a bit of the pain of everything else she'd never be able to do. That her family would know how she felt, and what she believed, made her death somehow less of a tragedy. As long as they remembered, a part of her would remain alive.

She had almost no hope of finding Jiminy. Maybe Howard was right — he'd already been taken to animal heaven. She let go of her hope of restoring his soul to his body, refusing to think about the hole it left in her heart. On the ground in front of her lay Vincent Lionheart. Her last act would be to deliver him to Megan, along with a similar message to the one she left her family.

Getting out of the house wouldn't be easy. She couldn't reach a doorknob. There was one way she might escape. One way. And it was going to hurt.

She staggered into Rory's room, feeling Jiminy's limbs soften ever so slightly with each step. As usual, Rory's window was wide open, letting in a fat stream of freezing air. She struggled onto Rory's bed, carrying Vincent in her mouth. From there, it was a short leap out the window. A short leap with an awful landing. She breathed in. Breathed out. Inhaled once more.

Then she jumped, landing in a scruffy patch of juniper. She'd always hated those bushes but now appreciated them with new clarity. Something doesn't need to be beautiful to be useful. She'd dropped Vincent when she landed. Good thing he was immortal. She scooped him up with her mouth and headed for the sidewalk. Overhead, the sky rippled with charcoal clouds, and the air carried a sharp, expectant smell. Rain. Lots of it. She put her head down and began to walk, avoiding the puddles of melting snow.

She turned toward Megan's house but made it less than a car length before a pair of thick legs in sensible shoes blocked her way. Mrs. Thorpe, carrying a stack of letters and shiny catalogs.

"Why, you're back from the vet!" she said. "I must not have hit you very hard after all. But we can't have you running around alone, can we?" She advanced toward Heidi, who shrank backward.

"They shouldn't leave you outside when they're away," she said. "You could get run over by another car. I'm going to take you inside and give them a piece of my mind when they get home."

She folded Heidi under her wing, pressing her against the catalogs. It hurt. But not as much as what Mrs. Thorpe did next.

"You can't bring your nasty little chew toy inside," she said. "Open!"

She slipped a finger in Heidi's mouth and plucked Vincent Lionheart out, tossing him on the rough sidewalk.

While there might have been a time in Heidi's life that she'd let that sort of affront pass without comment, that time had passed. She no longer cared about consequences, or the good opinion of others.

She opened her mouth. Her mouth full of sharp canine teeth. And she did exactly what it took to get Mrs. Thorpe's attention.

"Mrs. Thorpe," Heidi said, using the same cadence she and Rory had perfected when telling each other ghost stories before bed. "You have been baaaad . . . so baaaaaaaddd!"

Coming out of Jiminy's throat, the voice sounded truly terrifying: growly, low, full of menace. Heidi almost couldn't believe it.

Mrs. Thorpe yelped and dropped her onto a clump of ferns. She backed away slowly, covering her face with her hands. "What the —"

It might have been a kindness had Heidi merely bitten her.

Heidi stepped toward her cowering neighbor. "I represent the International Order of Mistreated Animals and come bearing a message." She paused for effect and used the moment to gather her energy, as the pain in her belly had reached a new height. "We have been watching you, Mrs. Thorpe. You permit your large dog to bark and terrorize smaller creatures. You ran over the poor animal whose body the IOMA temporarily inhabits, without taking full responsibility for the crime. You are an evil human. Evil."

Mrs. Thorpe dropped her hands to her heart. Her face frilled with red and white blotches, like a giant chrysanthemum. "I'm sorry!" she said. "I'm so sorry! Please don't hurt me!"

Heidi's cheeks curved into a grin. It felt great to smile like a dog, letting her teeth show and tongue hang out. Then she snapped off the happy face. No matter how good it felt, there was too much at stake. Too much, and too little time.

"No harm will come to you, Mrs. Thorpe, if you successfully complete the tasks we have laid out. You must redeem yourself. It is not too late for you — yet." She wished she could do that echo thing that Howard did. That was a good effect.

"I'll do it. Whatever you ask."

"We'll need your car. On the double." Heidi missed her thumbs. It would have been great to offer an emphatic snap.

Mrs. Thorpe nodded. She dropped her mail on the sidewalk and put Heidi in the backseat of the Mercedes. Her hands shook so much, her keys rattled like nickels in a coffee can. It took several tries before she stuck the right one in the ignition.

"Are you sure you don't need me to buckle you in?" Mrs. Thorpe said.

So now she cared about Heidi's safety. Heidi plunked Vincent headfirst into the cup holder so she could talk. "A seat belt is unnecessary at this time."

She gave Mrs. Thorpe Megan's address in the same slow, calm voice. Part of Heidi knew that talking like an NPR announcer was maybe too much. But it was fun — something that had been in distinctly short supply of late. In any case, she was glad for the ride. Huge raindrops launched themselves from the clouds, spiraling down from above, smearing the view through the windshield. The wipers thump-chunked and squeaked at full speed but couldn't come close to keeping up with the rain. Fortunately, the ride was short, and in less than the time it took to listen to one of Mrs. Thorpe's easy-listening tunes, they arrived at Megan's.

"There you go," Mrs. Thorpe said. "Now I'll just be on my way."

"Not so fast." She might want a ride home. Maybe they could even drive around, looking for Jiminy. "Please wait until I return. We have agents watching you, and disastrous things are in store if you should attempt to depart prematurely."

"I wouldn't dream of it," Mrs. Thorpe said. "Oh my goodness, no." She killed the engine and the car grew quiet except for the staccato rain on its roof.

"The door," Heidi said. "The Order expects you to open it and transport me in gentle and humane fashion to the house."

"Oh, of course."

"Please carry the collectible figurine as well. I do not wish to further mar it with my teeth."

"Do you mean the doll?"

Mrs. Thorpe reached into the backseat, her clothes hissing as she retrieved Vincent Lionheart. She dropped him into her purse and lifted Heidi out of the car, more carefully this time, but it still hurt. Terribly.

Heidi tipped her face to the sky and caught a few raindrops on her tongue. They were delicious and wintry:

cold, smoky, wood-drenched. She hadn't realized how thirsty she was.

Mrs. Thorpe carried her across the stepping-stones that led to Megan's house, depositing Heidi on a scratchy coconut-fiber welcome mat that said GO AWAY, one of Mrs. Lin's many sarcastic decorative items. Heidi hesitated. Did she really want to do this? She could always turn around and ask for a ride home, to wait and see what would happen there. Mrs. Thorpe turned to leave.

"Wait," Heidi said. "I need you to ring the doorbell."

"Will I have to go in? I don't even know these people and this —"

"No. Just give me my doll and wait in the car. I won't take long."

"And then what?" Mrs. Thorpe said.

Heidi swallowed. The pain in her belly was intense, as though she'd swallowed steel wool. "I don't know."

None too gently, Mrs. Thorpe inserted Vincent into Heidi's mouth. She rang the bell, spun around, and hustled back to her car with surprising speed. Heidi turned toward the door, realizing another weakness in her plan. If Megan's mother answered, she would take one look at the wet dog standing on her conversation piece and slam the door. Mrs. Lin was more of a cat person, to put it mildly.

Heidi looked back over her shoulder at Mrs. Thorpe, who sat in the front seat of her warm, dry car. Before Heidi could decide whether to stay or flee, the door swung open and the decision was made for her.

CHAPTER TWENTY-FIVE

Jerome

THEY DIDN'T SHOW my actual death in the video because Heaven, and especially the rehab part, has a pretty strict PG-13 policy about violence and sex, which seems majorly hypocritical when you consider all the smiting that goes on in the Bible, not to mention the question of where Cain and Abel's wives came from.

The video started off with a shot of Mike's back. I guess that was the last thing I ever saw. Maybe if I'd been shot in the heart or the liver, I'd remember more. But when you take an arrow in the head, your files get flasked up. It took a while for my mind to work right again. I sometimes wonder if maybe I got permanent brain damage.

Anyways, Mike ran toward the porch. His hair flapped behind him. He had worked himself up to a pretty impressive speed, so it must've hurt when he crashed into the screen door. *Bang!* But he didn't let that stop him. He shook his head a couple of times and took two crooked steps before he got going again. He disappeared into the house and came out a couple seconds later with my dad, who'd been inside dinking with his model train. He had on an undershirt and cutoffs and no shoes.

If it hurt his feet any to run across the gravel to where I was lying, he didn't show it. He ran and skidded down next to me like I was home base. Rocks flew everywhere, sounding like it does when you tear cardboard. He took my cheeks, one in each hand, and looked into my eyes and called my name, but I didn't answer. I was already gone, and even if I hadn't known how my face looked with life in it, I would've known from my eyes that there was nobody home.

He laid my head down like it was an egg and he wiped a trail of blood out of my nose real gentle, without even protecting his finger with a shirt. And then he looked up at the sky like maybe he'd be able to see me up there, but of course he couldn't. He's not the kind of guy who sees souls, even though for a long time when I was little, I thought he saw the Devil under the hood of his car from the way he talked about it.

He sank down next to me and held my hand and opened his mouth wide and shouted "No!" in a way that I don't think I could forget if I tried. It hurt worse than Gabe's reverb.

Mike stood behind him with his face in his hands like he was ashamed, and I felt bad about that because I knew he was a lousy shot and I still let him have a go. I just didn't think he'd miss that bad. He kept kind of walking back and forth saying "I'm sorry I'm sorry I'm sorry I'm sorry," and if I had been my dad, I would've probably popped him because it is maximum annoying when someone says the same thing over and over again even if you aren't looking at your dead kid in the gravel.

But my dad didn't sock him or even yell. He said, "Mike, get the phone."

Mike did, and when he was running toward the house, he stepped on the orange that had rolled off my head and he totally smashed it, which is pretty funny when you think about it. Mike hit the fruit after all. His timing was off. That was always the thing with him.

He came back with the phone, and my dad called for an ambulance, which carried me away, but I didn't get the sirens and stuff because I was already gone.

The video cut away to my funeral.

"How come I didn't get to go to that?" I asked Xavier.

"You were still being processed," he said. "I took the footage for you."

"You went to my funeral?"

"Of course," he said. "That's how we make final decisions about the souls we admit to our rehabilitation program."

There wasn't a whole lot of people in the church, just my dad, Mike and his parents, Mrs. Domino (in her cherry skirt), Darcy Parker (who cried with her mouth open), Trip Wexler and his family, Mr. Moder, and some of Dad's friends from work. I guess I was lucky I got any, considering. But my dad gave a nice speech. At first when I saw him standing up there on the stage part, I was afraid he was going to say everything I'd ever done wrong, because that would pretty much be the only way he could talk about me for more than five seconds.

But he didn't, except for a few funny things like the time we went to a wedding when I was four. I was the ring bearer and I cried because they said we'd have cake after the toast and then they handed out the cake without giving any of us toast, which I liked a whole lot better than cake with fruit in it. I was glad he didn't tell the part about me wetting my pants when I found out before the wedding that I had to wear a suit instead of a bear costume. Darcy Parker didn't need to know that.

Then he said something I won't forget, no matter where they send me.

"My biggest fear was that Jerome would grow up and be a nothing like me." He waited for people to laugh, but they didn't because he isn't a nothing. He served in the Army and can fix everything except tables, and he has visited thirty-seven states and three countries, and my mom never should've left, because she broke his heart. You don't leave the people you love. Not like that.

He took a big swallow and said, "I was hard on him when he screwed up." I couldn't help nodding, even though it made my arrow bounce in kind of a painful way.

"I was real hard on him." His voice got quieter there.

He stopped and sucked in a big breath of air. He also mashed his lips together in a line, and for a second, he looked up into the ceiling of the church like he might see me watching. Then he swallowed again.

"Over time, I forgot to be anything but that, and I regret it. I regret it real deep. I didn't know enough to know what I should really be afraid of, that Jerome wouldn't grow up at all." He stopped talking and folded one arm across his chest, and he used his other hand to hold up his head. He was quiet for a long time, but nobody heckled him or clapped or did anything stupid. People sat there, and the silence wrapped around them like it was something heavy.

"I'd trade places with him if I could," Dad said.

It sounded like he was pushing the words through a screen, because they came out kind of chopped up. I had to listen real hard to hear too. "He wasn't perfect, but he was a good kid. He was my kid. I'm going to miss him every day of my life."

I had to breathe out my mouth when I was watching that. My nose was busy fighting back that pinch that comes with crying, which I wanted to do worse than I ever did over no toast at a wedding.

I spent most of my life feeling ashamed for letting my dad down all the time. I thought there was no way he could've loved me, especially since my mom left on account of me wearing her out. At best, he was letting me crash at his house because we had the same last name and ears. The main reason Mike and me did stupid Chevy was 'cause I figured it didn't matter what I did — there was no hope for me, and life would be a long train of pain until it was over and done. It was like being born with my tail was a sign that I wasn't much different from the Devil, and I didn't try to make things turn out any other way.

I was wrong about there being no hope for anything better, or about the dad loving me part. He did love me.

He did have hope. He was doing his best. It wasn't perfect. But you know what? I wouldn't have known what to do with that anyhow.

A tear worked its way out of my eye and slid down my cheek, warm and slow. I let it hang there for a while before I pushed it away with my thumb.

"I don't get it," I said. "Why'd he say that thing about me to his supervisor? That it took me long enough to get myself killed?"

Gabe answered.

"Sometimes, people say things they don't mean to cover up their true feelings. It's how they cope. It can be the only thing that holds together the pieces of a broken heart."

I sat there for a couple of minutes in the chair, trying to think of something to say. I had been wrong about most everything. Figuring that out tends to take the motor out of a guy's mouth.

In that space of quiet, I felt something change inside me, like a river had gushed over its edges or a wall had broken down, which is probably why Xavier and Gabe had shown me all this. I turned to them, and the braveness came on strong, like I was the soldier in the war movie who was about to volunteer to crawl through a ditch full of rattlesnakes and stuff the grenade right down the enemy's pants.

"I gotta confess something," I said.

And I did.

Starting at the point where Heidi fell through the ice, and ending at the point where she disappeared with her dog.

Xavier and Gabe didn't say a word. Every once in a while they looked at each other's faces, sending secret angel messages probably. But they let me finish without sending any zaps of punishment. Just when I told them Heidi's soul had crumbled into a million bits, probably while Howard watched, there were three little beeps and a funny smell.

Then Howard popped into the room. He was shaking real hard and looked mad. At first I thought his head was on fire, but then I caught a whiff. Incense. Gabe can't get enough of that stuff. I wasn't the only one in trouble, and Howard's hair was going to reek like the inside of a hippie's van for days.

"I was bringing her in, I swear! She's fine, totally fine," Howard said. "It's him you should be punishing, not me! NOT ME!"

He looked back and forth between Xavier and Gabe. But I was glad he was looking at them, because that meant he couldn't see the shock on my face. If Howard was going to bring her in, that meant she wasn't in a bunch of pieces. At least not yet.

Her soul was whole, it was out there, and I was gonna find it. It didn't matter what happened to me. My own life, it was over. I'd flasked up. Even when they gave me a second chance, I'd been a crummy guardian angel, messing with her all the time instead of helping her because I thought it didn't matter, and besides, that's what guys do when they sort of like a girl. I should've followed the commandments. I should've taken care of her like I was supposed to.

But I could make things right. I had a second chance with her. Maybe those horses and men in the rhyme couldn't put Humpty Dumpty together again. But that wasn't how it was going to be for Heidi. There was hope for her. Even after all that, there was still hope.

So yeah. I was going to save her soul and goddammit — OW! — there was nobody who could stop me and no way I was gonna mess this up. I took off running and made it two whole feet before something that felt like the hand of God stopped me in my tracks.

I couldn't move. What the flask!

Xavier was holding my shirt and wouldn't let go. Lucky I didn't listen to my first instinct, because punching is counterproductive when you are about to start a heroic rescue mission. Actually, it's almost always counterproductive because noses are a lot harder to hit than most people realize. They're small and they move around. Like mice.

"Hey, man," I said, calm-like. "Let go already."

"JEROME!"

Gabe used his angel voice, so I stopped trying to get away. Howard laughed, but the sound cut off like he'd been unplugged. I turned around to look. Xavier had done this move on him with the soul-jack thing, and Howard was like an ice mummy, only without the bandages or the ice. He should've remembered that you're not supposed to laugh at someone during disciplinary proceedings. There are consequences to every action. It's all about the ripples.

"THOU SHALT NOT PROCEED WITHOUT A PLAN," Gabe said.

I made my hands go up to my ears, but not fast enough. Stinking reverb. My arrow started to feel weird in my head, like it was the flaming kind instead of this sweet deluxe carbon composite that you can't set on fire even with half a bottle of lighter fluid. It didn't exactly hurt, but it felt weird and urgent, like before a sneeze.

I tried to play cool when I said, "I *do* have a plan," but Xavier and Gabe knew I was dishing a line of Chevy. They had the faces of people with good poker hands. I had the face of a guy who needed another card to make a pair of twos.

We sat on our white chairs and I wished I'd at least picked ones with cushions. But for once, having a tail came in handy because it gave me a sort of an idea. I explained what I wanted to do. Gabe and Xavier had expressions on like they thought my plan sucked apples, and they were probably right since I was making it up as I went.

"It's highly irregular," Gabe said. He ironed his mustache with his fingers. "We'd need to get some waivers from above."

"Waivers?" Xavier said. "Are you sure we can't keep this quiet?"

"What happens when we keep secrets from an all-powerful, all-knowing being?" Gabe said. He took a fresh toothpick from his vest pocket and slipped it into his mouth. That was his tell. He'd won the round.

Xavier brushed something I couldn't see off of his robe. There was a super-awkward pause, like the time my shop teacher found out what I'd been doing with the jigsaw and my driver's ed manual.

"You're right, of course," Xavier said. "Secrets are unacceptable in this realm. But what if we don't get approval?"

"Let's just think about the most important thing here," Gabe said. "Are we really going to let go of these lives? Or is there a more . . . creative solution?"

"Are you thinking what I'm thinking?" Xavier said.

Gabe nodded and went full beaver on the toothpick. "It's all a matter of timing and which forms we fill out."

He pulled a clipboard out of the pocket on his vest, which sounds like it would go against the laws of physics, but up here at least, those are laws we don't have to follow. He checked off boxes on a piece of paper.

"The 1087 is the one we use when we're asking for retroactive permission," he said. "The 1522 could be of use with the canine."

He might as well have been talking about how rockets work, for all I understood. But Xavier nodded and flicked some burnt incense off of Howard, who stood there like a bad statue.

"What happens if we don't get permission?" he said.

"Then we ask for forgiveness," Gabe said.

Xavier stopped dusting and whistled real low.

"I'll have Howard's activity chart in two minutes," Gabe said. "That'll give me enough data to send him down to Level III for a two-week detention for deceiving the girl. He's not going to like the microfiche, but that's sort of the point, isn't it? Then I'll prepare the soul maps so we can see where the dog and girl have gone. Hopefully, there's still enough of them left that we can get a clear readout."

"Sounds about right," Xavier said.

Howard in Hell. It was what I'd always wanted, but instead of feeling happy about it, I felt like someone was folding my stomach into an origami hat, so I tuned my thoughts in to Heidi instead, hoping she was hanging in there.

Gabe fiddled with his portable tracking device and squinted, more out of habit than anything. In Heaven, everyone can see clear. He whammy-fingered a map that showed two sets of lines zigzagging like crazy all around a street I recognized as Heidi's. So that's how they always knew where we were and what we'd been doing. Flask. I had no secrets from these guys. No wonder I hadn't graduated.

"This is where their souls have been roaming," Gabe said. "This one — the one with lots of running back and forth — belongs to the dog. The other one, the really faint one, belongs to the girl. Her tracks have faded almost to nothing, and she's traveling by car, so her soul's not leaving as much residue as it otherwise would.

"The trail will be extremely difficult to follow, even with this uploaded into your head. You'll have to use your best judgment to figure out where it leads. Trust it, though. You'll know when she's near. And be quick. Even with the protection of her dog's body, she doesn't have much time left."

I nodded, but I didn't say anything because my throat felt like it was made out of glass and would crack if I tried to talk.

"Don't be a hero out there," Xavier said. "Just do it one step at a time, like we talked about. You have only one shot at this."

Then Xavier and Gabe started talking about me like I wasn't there.

"That thing in his forehead might get in the way," Xavier said. He stuck his hand in his robe and pulled out an apple, which he polished with his wide sleeve.

"I was hoping it would fall off on its own," Gabe said. "Like a baby's umbilical stump. It was on the checklist."

"I sometimes wonder how reliable the checklist is," Xavier said. He wiped his lips on a little hanky that came from another pocket.

Gabe sighed. "Let's table this discussion until later. Tempus fugit and all."

I wasn't sure what Gabe meant by "table." The room didn't have one. And I had no clue what a tempus fugit was. But I was glad they'd stopped talking about my arrow. It was starting to itch something fierce. If you've ever had a scab get hard and ripe, like a cracker, then you know that feeling. It comes with a voice. A voice that is all, *Pick it! Yank it right off! Probably won't even bleed!*

There was no way I was going to do that. That thing hurt like a motherflasker when anyone touched it. I'd learned to keep my hands away from the goods, like you have to do in the 7-Eleven so they don't accuse you of taking the five-finger discount.

"Um, guys?" I said. "I think I should probably get going. Heidi needs me."

Xavier and Gabe looked at each other. If they weren't angels, I would say it was a sneaky look.

Gabe said, "We're going to bless you, Jerome."

And Xavier said, "Yes, and if you want to close your eyes to receive the blessing, you may."

"What if I don't want to?" When I was alive, anytime someone said, "Close your eyes, Jerome," I usually ended up with my head in the toilet and my underwear yanked up to my shoulders.

"We're not going to give you a wedgie," Xavier said. "Or a swirly."

Have I said he can read minds? It's creepy.

I closed my eyes and waited for Gabe to start the prayer. Then I felt a sandal on my chest and a whomping yank in the middle of my head and then there was a sucking noise and a pop like someone had opened a can of soda, and then a fizzy white explosion of pain.

I said things that made my sensor go off like a box of firecrackers, which made my head feel like it was one of those dinger things on the inside of a huge bell, all smacked and vibrating. For what felt like hours but was probably less time than it takes a halfway decent car to go from zero to 80, I let the pain have its way with my soul. It wasn't like I deserved anything less, considering.

The pain stopped when Gabe put his hand on my forehead. I realized I was lying on the ground and there was slobber coming out of my mouth.

"See," Gabe said. "He was ready."

He took his clipboard and a pen out and made a check mark.

"He's shown selflessness," Xavier said. "And courage. But I admit — I still didn't think it was going to work." He pulled floss out of his pocket and went to town on his teeth.

"Honestly," Gabe said, "neither did I. I thought he was still holding on to too much anger. And a teeny tiny part of me thinks that the tip of the arrow was magnetically attracted to the skull phone. That bit was maybe our fault."

He did this little heh-heh-heh laugh. So did Xavier.

"Bneh," I said.

"Pardon?" Xavier said.

It took a minute for my words to come back. It was all pain carbonation. I wouldn't have been surprised to see it dripping on the floor.

"That hurt," I said. I put my hand on my forehead. I wasn't going to fiddle with the hole or anything, but I was curious about the size of it and whether I was going to have to stick something in there to make people not stare, like maybe a rock or a quarter, depending.

"Why isn't there a hole?" I said.

"Did you want a hole?" Xavier said. "Most people appreciate their improved physical appearance after rehab."

"After rehab? You mean —"

"Yes," Gabe said. "You've graduated, Jerome."

My hands went all numbly-tingly for a second. At first I was thinking that all you had to do to graduate was kill your human. But then I figured it out. I needed to put myself on the line to save her. In being willing to save someone else, I'd saved myself.

"So I get to go to Heaven right now?" I said. All quiet-like, I reached behind me for my tail, the thing that made me think for my whole life I was nothing more than a devil. That was gone too. "But what about Heidi?"

"You could," Gabe said. "It's right through that door."

Great. The first time I didn't need special pants, and I was about to have to wear a robe forever. I looked where he was pointing. Sure enough, a door I'd never seen before was there, twinkling a little bit around the edges, like someone had outlined it with glitter glue. Alls I had to do was cross the room and open it, and I'd be there. It was maybe ten steps away.

Ten steps I couldn't — wouldn't — take.

"That's pretty stupid," I said. Gabe and Xavier looked like they'd swallowed something spicy. "Why would I want to go to Heaven now, you motherflaskers? I gotta go help Heidi before it's too late." There was a little *schloop* sound and the door disappeared. "Hey. Is that coming back?"

"It wasn't really a door to Heaven," Xavier said. "It was one last test. You passed. You don't actually have a choice even though we were required by Heavenly law to give you the illusion of one as a final test of your soul. You have to save this girl."

No one ever tells you this when you're alive, but angels can be real applehats.

"What if I'd gone through that door?" I said. "What would've happened to me? What would've happened to Heidi?"

Gabe stuck a fresh toothpick in the corner of his mouth. "For your sake, it's a good thing you didn't go through the door. Knowing Xavier, he would have stopped you, even if interference of that sort is a code violation."

"But what about Heidi?" I said. "Is this gonna work?"

"We don't want you to get your hopes up, Jerome," Xavier said. "Sometimes, souls are just . . . lost. Nobody likes it, but in the grand scheme of things, considering the billions of souls there are in the universe, the occasional evaporation of one or two still means we have an unparalleled record when it comes to the promotion and endurance of life, human and otherwise."

He put a hand on my shoulder. I shrugged it off.

"Lost?" I didn't like the look on his face or the feeling in my stomach. I had to get going.

"You're going to need my nuts," Xavier said. He reached into his robe and I almost hurled because I didn't want to touch anything that personal. But then he handed me a sack of actual nuts from his lobby and I got his drift. They were bait. And maybe a nice snack afterward. "Whatever you do, don't let the squirrel actually eat one."

Time slowed down as I got myself ready to shoop out of the room. I heard Gabe and Xavier whisper to each other. They sounded weird and slow, like the way people do on TV when a kidnapper is trying to disguise his voice. But it did help me pick up most of what they were saying.

"Should we tell him all the details of her condition?" Xavier said.

"No," Gabe said. "He has to discover that on his own."

"If he does succeed," Xavier said, "what's going to happen to *him*?"

"We'll invoke the Easter clause," Gabe said, which made me think he was mixing up Santa and the Easter Bunny. Maybe my head was still fizzing from the arrow yank. "It's what Jerome really wants anyway. More than all this."

"Won't that be dangerous?" Xavier said. "I mean —"

I tried to slow down my shoop a minute so I could keep listening, but once you've started, it's hard to change gears. Their words kept fading out, like an AM radio in the rain.

"He's broken every commandment. So has the girl."

"Those are the commandments for the *dead*, Xavier," Gabe said. "For the —"

Then my shoop was done and time speeded up and I couldn't hear them anymore and even if I could, I didn't get what they were talking about. But I didn't care about it any more than a rat cares about roller skates. I'd lived. I'd died. I'd seen the borders of Heaven and Hell. The truth was, I didn't fit in anywhere, and the one person in the world who needed me had only a little time left before her soul turned into dust. If there was any way I could stop that from happening, I would.

I hoped the squirrel would understand.

THE GUARDIAN ANGEL'S HANDBOOK: SOUL REHAB EDITION

Appendix G: The Ten Commandments for the Living

I. THOU SHALT HAVE COURAGE.

II. THOU SHALT BE LOYAL.

III. THOU SHALT TELL THE TRUTH.

IV. THOU SHALT HAVE FAITH IN THYSELF AND OTHERS.

V. THOU SHALT FORGIVE.

VI. THOU SHALT BE HUMBLE.

CHAPTER TWENTY-SIX

Heidi

MEGAN STOOD AT the door, damp-haired, wearing her favorite striped shirt.

"Oh my God! Jiminy! What are you doing here? Good thing my mom's at her psychic ladies' circle or you'd be halfway home, courtesy of a swift kick from one of her Birkenstocks."

She took a closer look at the doll sticking out of Heidi's mouth. "Oh no! Bad dog, Jiminy! Drop!" Heidi dropped Vincent on Mrs. Lin's Tibetan rug. "How did you get this? Was it Heidi's? She never told me she —" Her gaze traveled to the cast and she changed her tone. "Hey, buddy. Aw, what happened to your leg?"

Without waiting for an answer, because who would, from a dog, Megan carried Heidi down the hall. The pain was overwhelming, but Heidi knew she wouldn't have to hang on that much longer. She'd already exceeded her soul's time limit, and Jiminy's body was fading fast. Megan laid her on the bed, and Heidi sank into the soft, clean blankets. The scent of geranium laundry soap glazed the aching parts of Heidi, taking the sharp bits off the pain, infusing her soul with the illusion that it was still a thing of substance.

Heidi looked up. Megan was wiping Vincent Lionheart down with a tissue. Two tears raced each other down the sides of her nose. A plaintive sound escaped her mouth, and Heidi covered her nose with her paw.

"What's wrong, boy? Are you hurting?" Megan sat lightly on the bed next to Heidi, scratching behind her ears. "You miss her too, don't you?" she said. "Is that why you came to visit? This is hard, really hard. But it probably won't be all that much longer."

Heidi's ears pricked up. How could Megan know that? Was it that obvious that Jiminy was dying, or were Megan's psychic powers actually developing? Heidi felt a powerful urge to tell her everything that had happened so they could sift the mystery together the way they used to examine and polish every facet of the daily school dramas.

Words expanded in her throat, threatening to rise out of her mouth. But the sound of her voice was so awful and the truth so upsetting, Heidi couldn't let herself do it. Megan didn't need to know what had happened. She needed to know she'd been a good friend, sometimes goofy and embarrassing, but always loyal, always beloved.

Heidi lifted her head — Jiminy's head — and rested it in Megan's lap, staring into her eyes and into that part of Megan that had seen something worth caring about in her. She sent a message of love and felt her heart shift, like the final piece of a puzzle snapping into place, and a sad and sweet sensation overwhelmed her, the feeling she got when she turned the last page of a good book.

The phone rang. Megan glanced at it over her shoulder. She sighed and slipped Heidi's head gently off her lap.

"Hello?" Then came a brief silence. Her face blanched as she whispered into the phone. "Okay. Can't — I'll — I'll be here."

She returned to the bed, curling around Jiminy's body.

"That was the call, Jiminy." She buried her face in Jiminy's fur. "Heidi . . . she's brain-dead. They're taking her off life support in half an hour. They told me I could be there, but I don't think I can handle it. I'm not that strong. I'm going to send her psychic messages instead." She sat up, closed her eyes, and pressed her fingers to her temples.

For a moment, Heidi was in such shock she couldn't feel her legs, let alone move them. She wasn't dead. She hadn't drowned for good. They must have revived her body after her soul came loose, and now, because she'd been roaming with Jerome, sniffing cookie essence, riding trains, and trying to keep Jiminy's corpse alive, her own real self was about to be unplugged from the machines sustaining it.

She'd been stupid. So stupid. She felt the way she did when she was playing a board game with Rory at the moment she'd taken her hand from the piece she'd just moved and instantaneously realized she'd made a terrible, unfixable mistake.

Her ears filled with a strange, limping thump, like the sound of a basketball on a court. It was a heartbeat. Jiminy's. Meanwhile, her own was beating its last somewhere halfway across town. She'd be there for her final moment, or she'd die trying. She had no hope that her soul was strong enough to reenter her body so that the two parts of her could leave the world together; she prayed only that Jiminy's body was strong enough to carry her the last few steps. The pain alone made it obvious to her he had only a little time left.

"Megan." She spoke her friend's name, regretting how her growly voice broke it into ugly pieces. "We need to get to the hospital."

Megan jumped off the bed, knocking Vincent Lionheart on the floor. She pointed at Heidi. "Holy cow."

"Hey," Heidi said.

"Not cow," Megan said. She paced alongside the bed, grabbing the hair on top of her head with both hands. "You know what I mean, though. You're not Jiminy, are you? You're Heidi in there. Whoa. The psychic messages worked. Just wait till my mom finds out. She kept telling me you wouldn't die and she was right. And do you know what the best part is, Heidi?"

"There's a best part to this?"

"We are so getting on *The View.*"

"Megan," she said. "Sit down. Be quiet. There isn't time to talk about your Whoopi Goldberg dreams. We have to get to the hospital. Quickly."

"Gotcha. Whoopi can wait. And I definitely don't mind going to the hospital if we can go together. I'm strong enough for that." She ran a brush through her hair and poked her head in her closet door. "Can I tell you, this reminds me *exactly* of an episode of *Ghost Whisperer*? It was the one where Jim died and he couldn't stand being away from Melinda and as soon as he found a dead guy who was young enough and not an old janitor with a bad prostate, he —"

"Megan," Heidi said. "Hospital. We can do the episode recap on the way."

"Yeah, of course. I was just getting a coat." She slipped on the green one made of Muppet fur. "Can I say I am very glad that I'm open to mystical experiences? Otherwise, this would be freaking me out."

Then she gasped. "Oh, Vincent Lionheart!" Megan scooped him off the floor. "I get it now. You brought Vincent as your last grand gesture. You wanted to give me my heart's desire." She clutched him to her chest. "That is so sweet. I don't even mind the tooth marks."

Heidi barked. "Megan! My parents are going to pull the plug on my body in less than thirty minutes. I don't want to die without being there."

"Oh! I'm sorry! Geeesh! I don't want you to die at all. But how are we going to get there? My mom has the car."

"I have a ride lined up. For me anyway. But I'm sure she won't mind if you come along."

⣿

Mrs. Thorpe, still sitting in her slightly steamed up car, wasn't wild about the idea of taking Megan to the hospital. She crossed her arms and swiveled so that she could better glare at Megan through the rolled-down passenger window.

"Shouldn't I have permission from your mother? I don't want to be accused of kidnapping."

"But you're taking *Heidi*," Megan whined.

"Shhh!" She hadn't had time to explain the ruse to Megan.

"No," Mrs. Thorpe said. "Heidi is the girl, the one in the hospital. This is her dog. Jim Beam or something. The one that was hit by a car."

"You didn't tell me you got hit by a car," Megan whispered. "You just said you were injured. Wow, Heidi. You are like a hero or something."

"Shh." Megan had no future as a secret agent. Fortunately, Mrs. Thorpe was rummaging in her purse and didn't seem to hear. She pulled out an emery board and whisked it back and forth across her pinky nail.

Water dripped in Heidi's eyes and poked its fingers through her fur. She was cold and weak. There couldn't be more than twenty minutes left before her parents ended things, if Jiminy's body could even hold out that long. Her soul was now hours past its expiration point. She could feel it crackle inside Jiminy's body like a dead leaf. She had an overwhelming urge to curl up under a bush with her paw over her eyes but knew it would only make her feel worse. She gave it everything she had.

"You will take the girl as your passenger, and you will drive us to the hospital."

The air thickened while Heidi waited for an answer, blinking away the raindrops. Mrs. Thorpe put away the nail file. "All right, get in. Mr. Thorpe can make himself a sandwich for once in thirty-nine years."

Megan opened the door and placed Heidi on the backseat. She slid in and clicked her seat belt. The engine rumbled to life.

"You doin' okay, Heidi?" Megan asked.

"Shhh. She thinks I'm Jiminy."

"That's ridiculous," Megan whispered. "Dogs can't talk."

"Ahem!" Mrs. Thorpe said. "There will be none of that hissy-sissy whispering. I don't like it."

She sniffed and turned her attention to the road, flicking on her headlights. The windshield wipers swatted the rain at top speed, in contrast to the car, which glided along like a giant metal snail. Mrs. Thorpe *would* choose this moment to learn to drive with caution.

Heidi couldn't see over the seat to read the dashboard clock, but it was just as well. To watch the minutes slip by would only make things worse. She felt like she was on death row, counting down the minutes until her end, only she didn't get to choose her final meal or say a few last words without anyone interrupting.

Her last words. She tried to plan some, but Megan kept talking. She didn't believe in the concept of comfortable silence.

"God, how I adore Vincent Lionheart." Megan held him close to her chest and sniffed his molded plastic hair. "I mean, if he's really for me. I won't judge if you decide you want to chew on him or anything."

"Of course," Heidi whimpered. "Sorry he came out of the box. Now he's not worth anything anymore."

"That only matters if you plan on selling it. I'm keeping him forever. I love him. What else matters when you have love?"

Then, suddenly:

"OHMYGODOHMYGODBRAKEBRAKEBRAKE!" Megan shrieked.

"What?" Mrs. Thorpe said, scanning the road. "What?"

"Squirrel!"

THE GUARDIAN ANGEL'S HANDBOOK: SOUL REHAB EDITION

Appendix G: The Ten Commandments for the Living

  I. THOU SHALT HAVE COURAGE.

 II. THOU SHALT BE LOYAL.

III. THOU SHALT TELL THE TRUTH.

IV. THOU SHALT HAVE FAITH IN THYSELF AND OTHERS.

 V. THOU SHALT FORGIVE.

VI. THOU SHALT BE HUMBLE.

VII. THOU SHALT RESPECT ALL LIVING THINGS.

CHAPTER TWENTY-SEVEN

Jerome

HERE'S THE THING with squirrels: Sometimes when you're walking down the sidewalk minding your own business, one will run straight at you, and it freaks you out because for a second you think maybe it has rabies and is coming in for the kill, but then at the last moment it zips off in a crazy direction and you can breathe again.

There's a reason for that. Squirrels can see souls. But unlike dogs, they go out of their way to avoid them. Maybe it's because there's not that much separating squirrels from death. Maybe they think death is like tag and if a soul touches you, *bam!* You're it!

Here's another thing with squirrels: They are usually not very smart, which makes them way hard to catch. You can't chase them and think, "Okay, what's that little dude going to do next?" because that would mean they are using their brains to figure out which way they're going to skitter. Whatever part they're using, it's not brains. But there's maybe some stomach involved, because when I showed the first squirrel I saw the sack of nuts, he stopped panicking and started creeping toward me with his tail fluffed out like a toilet brush.

"Come on, little dude. Come and get the nut. Nut, nut, nut."

I said this and made these smacky little kissing noises and prayed no one would see me enacting my piece-of-Chevy plan, which was to lure him to me using the nuts as bait. Then I'd use the squirrel as bait for Jiminy's soul, do the switcheroo with him and Heidi, then shoop her right quick to Gabe and Xavier and straighten everything out.

Hopefully the squirrel wouldn't be too mad when he figured out they were celestial nuts, because I don't think those are edible for the living.

Once I had the squirrel's attention, I zeroed in on the soul map, which worked a little bit like the Terminator's evil robot eyeball, giving me an extra layer of information on top of everything else I was seeing. Jiminy was nearby, even if I couldn't quite make him out through the rain. Heidi's soul wasn't visible, but I couldn't worry about that. One thing at a time.

I walked backward down the sidewalk in the direction of Jiminy, saying, "Nut, nut, nut." The squirrel followed, stopping every so often to sniff the wind and flick the rain off his whiskers. At that point, it was really coming down. We were in a rhythm with the nuts and whiskers thing, so I checked the map again. Jiminy was so close, it felt like someone was tapping a finger in my head.

Before long, I spotted him in real life. As soon as that

happened, the map started dinging too. That was the good news. The bad news was that Jiminy'd seen us first. He bore down on the squirrel like someone had shot him out of a cannon. Or maybe a .177-caliber Beeman rifle, which kind of would've served me right. I was so surprised I jumped backward through a tree and lost sight of the squirrel for a second — enough time for his little pea brain to forget about the nuts I was offering.

By the time I saw the squirrel again, he was smoothing his whiskers, and Jiminy was coming in for the kill. That's when the squirrel noticed he was under attack. He did this little sideways sort of hop into the street, which wouldn't have been all that bad except for he chose to hit the pavement the very moment a car was zooming by, an old diesel Mercedes.

Brakes squealed. Rubber burned. It was the sound and smell of Hell, and I wanted to close my eyes but knew I had to stay in the game and make sure the little dude didn't get turned into a fuzzy hood ornament. I stuffed the nut sack in my pocket, took a flying leap, and used every bit of screaming emotion I felt to scoot him onto the bumper. Then I prayed to the Creator that he'd hold on as the car plowed through me.

As my soul was run through with two thousand pounds of swerving metal, the map in my head started flashing and dinging like the slots at the reservation casino. Heidi. She was near. Not only near but also inside the car, and I couldn't do a darned thing about it. After the car drove through me, I got so dizzy I took a header on the pavement. The car stopped, but only for a second. It picked up speed, kicking up clouds of misty rain that fuzzed the edges of the road.

Jiminy zipped up to where I was lying on my back. He gave me a quick sniff and took off after the Benz. I rolled onto my stomach. Rain splattered through my soul like someone had dumped a bucket of it on me, and I wished I still had my field jacket. It wouldn't have kept me dry, but somehow, I would've felt better wearing it as I lay there in the middle of the road watching the car's taillights disappear into a red smear. The soul map faded back to almost nothingness.

I was about two seconds from giving up when I realized something important about all that nothingness. The road. It was empty. There wasn't any squirrel on it. No carcass, no ripped-up tufts of fur. And right that second, I got a little dose of something I hadn't tasted in so long, I'd almost forgotten what it was.

Hope.

Maybe I'd been lucky. Maybe he'd been lucky, and he'd stuck himself to that bumper like he was corn and it was teeth. There was only one way for me to find out if he'd made it. I picked myself up and started running down the road after all of them.

In the distance was a big white building full of lit-up windows looking down on me like eyes. When I was close enough, I figured out what it was. The hospital. That's where Heidi was going. I knew it as sure as shorts, as sure as I knew the truth about me and my pop and everything that had happened in my life. What's more, I could beat them there if I shooped.

THE GUARDIAN ANGEL'S HANDBOOK:
SOUL REHAB EDITION

Appendix G: The Ten Commandments for the Living

I. THOU SHALT HAVE COURAGE.

II. THOU SHALT BE LOYAL.

III. THOU SHALT TELL THE TRUTH.

IV. THOU SHALT HAVE FAITH IN THYSELF AND OTHERS.

V. THOU SHALT FORGIVE.

VI. THOU SHALT BE HUMBLE.

VII. THOU SHALT RESPECT ALL LIVING THINGS.

VIII. THOU SHALT HAVE GRATITUDE.

CHAPTER TWENTY-EIGHT

Heidi

Seven minutes to go.

"DID WE HIT it?" Megan asked. "I don't see a body, but the windows are pretty fogged up so it's hard to tell."

"Oh, one can tell when one has hit something with one's car," Mrs. Thorpe said. "Or so I've been told. No doubt that squirrel scampered right back onto the sidewalk where he belongs."

She glided into the hospital parking lot, pulling to a stop by the emergency entrance.

"Is that close enough for you two?"

"It's fine," Heidi said. She stole a glance at the dashboard clock. Seven minutes. "Megan, help me out of the car. And hurry."

Maybe there was such a thing as being fashionably late when it came to terminating life support, but Heidi doubted it. She'd read about organ donation and had come away with the distinct impression that doctors liked to be prompt about these things.

She tried not to dwell on that, or the pain in her body as Megan carried her through the rain toward the hospital. She wondered which of the windows overhead was hers. Most glowed with light — so many sick and dying people in there.

A thought struck. Maybe they could call. Ask for a stay of execution. "Did you bring your cell phone?"

"No," Megan said. "Why would I be making phone calls when you were dying? Sheesh."

They stood in front of the double glass doors.

"Oh no," Megan said. "The sign. It says no pets." It also had a picture of the international NO symbol stamped over silhouettes of a cat, a dog, a baby chick, and a coiled snake. Heidi was about to curse her impossibly bad luck when she remembered something.

"You're wearing the shirt," she said. "The one with the stripes."

It took Megan less than a second to understand her point. "And the contractions are coming every two minutes. The baby's not quite crowning, but —"

"Megan. Enough detail. Be careful. I'm still injured."

Megan unbuttoned her hairy coat and arranged Heidi under her shirt, holding the dog's body in place with both hands.

"Coming through!" she said. "Pregnant teen coming through!"

She waddled up to the information desk, even using a Southern accent for the performance: "Now don't you worry your pretty little head, sugar," she said. "I'm not due for another, oh, twelve hours or so. But you can be darned tootin' I'll holler if my water breaks."

The nurse didn't buy it. She didn't even rent it for a second. "Do you have an animal underneath your shirt? I saw you through the window, holding a dog."

"No," Megan answered, the Southern accent disappearing. "That was someone else."

"Megan," Heidi hissed. "Run!"

She ran. The receptionist paged security in a voice loud enough to make the hospital intercom system erupt in static. Behind them thudded the heavy footsteps of the security guy. Every bounce was agony.

"Heidi," Megan panted. "I'm running, just like you asked. But it would probably be better if we were actually running somewhere specific."

"Stop!" a man's voice yelled.

"Should I stop?" Megan said. "Are we going to get arrested? I don't want to get arrested."

"Don't stop. Lift up your shirt instead."

"I don't think that's going to work. The good part of me is up front and if I turn around —"

"It's not that. I think I caught the scent of my family. They're on the fourth floor. The fourth floor!"

"The fourth floor?" Megan repeated. "Are you sure?"

Heidi hoped her mind wasn't playing tricks. But it was true. Over the stronger scents of Megan's bath gel and perspiration, she picked up the sharp smell of Rory's cinnamon gum. She smelled her mother's lotion and her father's dandruff shampoo. And she smelled something else — despair. She also caught sight of a clock. Three and a half minutes left.

"Should we take the elevator?" Megan said.

"Stairs. That jerkbox might catch us before the doors even open."

Megan dashed to the stairs. Heidi peered around her and caught sight of the security guard, who'd opted for the elevator. He jabbed the button repeatedly and glared at Megan. He held four fingers up and nodded slowly. He'd heard their exchange. The only thing they could do was get there faster.

Heidi whipped her face back around, and Megan pressed through the door and ran, her sneakers ringing against the metal stair treads. Unit names were printed on the walls of the floors they were passing: SURGERY, X-RAY LABS, CHILDBIRTH CENTER, and finally, INTENSIVE CARE.

Megan set Heidi gently on the ground. "Sorry," she panted. "I can't open the door and hold you at the same time." She scratched Heidi behind the ears and leaned in to give her a kiss on the forehead. "Are you going to be okay? You don't look so good."

"Just hurry and open the door."

Megan pushed. She grunted and pushed harder. "It's locked! I can't open it."

"They never lock hospital doors. It's impossible."

The last of Heidi's hope drained away. Surely her time was up. She wondered what her soul would feel like once the body it belonged to was gone, and resolved to face the moment with her eyes open, absorbing every last detail as if she could bring the world around her inside her soul. She took in the scuffed, white walls of the stairwell and found the beauty in their imperfection. She smelled soap and sweat on Megan's skin and it filled her heart. The sound of Megan beating the door rocked her ears like thunder. She was no longer at the edges of things. She was at their very center. And then, as quickly as it started, it stopped.

"Oh, it's a pull door," Megan said. "Sometimes I can be such a silly."

Megan whipped it open. There, in front of them, stood the security guard.

"I'm going to have to ask you and your dog to come with me," he said. He slid his flashlight out of his holster and tapped it against the meat of his hand as if to show he wasn't afraid to brain a girl and her terrier in the name of hospital security.

Heidi trembled beside Megan and spoke. "We surrender."

Megan looked down at her as if she'd gone bonkers. She pulled off her jacket and threw it at the guard, who dropped his flashlight and pawed at his covered face. Megan lifted Heidi across her chest and ran.

"Which way?"

Heidi sniffed. A riot of scents — flowers, sickness, Tic Tacs, tears. She pushed aside a split-second bout of despair. She could do this. She took one last whiff and panted, "Cinnamon gum. To the left. Halfway down the hall."

Megan's shoes squeaked as she turned. Heidi hoped she was right. Even more, she hoped she'd have just a minute left to see her family and her body before she disappeared.

They ran.

"Stop!" The guard was after them again.

They reached the door. Megan held Heidi to the window and she saw her mom. Her dad. Rory. They'd gathered around the bed that held her, and while it was a terrible thing to see herself pale and still, with an octopus of tubes curving out of her nose and mouth, she felt something more powerful than fear. In her separation from her body — her gross, giant, hesitant body that was a laughingstock on at least two continents — it had turned into something different in her mind.

Something, she realized with a pang, that she loved.

THE GUARDIAN ANGEL'S HANDBOOK: SOUL REHAB EDITION

Appendix G: The Ten Commandments for the Living

I. THOU SHALT HAVE COURAGE.

II. THOU SHALT BE LOYAL.

III. THOU SHALT TELL THE TRUTH.

IV. THOU SHALT HAVE FAITH IN THYSELF AND OTHERS.

V. THOU SHALT FORGIVE.

VI. THOU SHALT BE HUMBLE.

VII. THOU SHALT RESPECT ALL LIVING THINGS.

VIII. THOU SHALT FEEL GRATITUDE.

IX. THOU SHALT BE KIND.

CHAPTER TWENTY-NINE

Jerome

I BEAT THE car to the hospital and watched it drive up. When it got close enough, I could see the squirrel hanging on to its bumper. The car stopped in front of the hospital entrance and the squirrel slid off, shook the water from his coat, and crawled into a shrub. I got that. If there was a shrub big enough to shield me from everything that was happening, I'd dive in too.

Heidi and Megan got out. They walked to the hospital's sliding doors and stopped. Perfect. Alls I needed was Jiminy's soul and I could get this show back on the road.

"Don't move!" I told them, even though they were too far away to hear.

The car drove off, clearing the view of the sidewalk. Sure enough, there was Jiminy, still running at us like crazy. Gotta give credit to that mutt. His legs might be little, but they don't quit. For a second, I hoped he'd see Heidi there, or at least his body, and decide he wanted back in. But then Megan picked Heidi up, stuffed her in her coat, and took her inside.

"Come here! Come here, boy!" I said. I was gonna stick with the plan, see it through.

Jiminy obeyed. I couldn't believe how easy this was. Like it was meant to be.

"Sit."

He sat.

"Stay," I said.

He did.

Then I walked all calm-like over to the shrub and took the sack of nuts out of my pocket. I hadn't even cracked it open when Jiminy stopped sitting and staying and started jumping up against my hand like he was starving. Which he probably was. He knocked the nuts out of my hand and they flew all over the parking lot. He started snorfing them up. He was eating my last chance. His too, actually.

I scrabbled on the ground for them, but I couldn't keep up. That's when I spotted the one last nut. I dove for it and got it. Then I went over to the bush, holding it out to the squirrel. He sniffed the air, rubbed his whiskers, and crept forward.

But he'd wised up to me. This time, he shot forward and snatched the nut. But that wasn't the worst thing that happened. He shoved it in his mouth and swallowed it, and when I made a grab for him, I felt this huge kind of pulling on my soul, worse than the time Mike stuck a toilet plunger on my head, which was shaved down on account of lice.

The pulling felt like the shoop on acid, all these flying colors and crazy music that filled my insides so much the soul map fizzled out. Then the spinning stopped and I was surrounded by leaves, looking up through them at Jiminy's tongue and teeth. I was inside the squirrel.

I said something that gave me a shock so big the squirrel felt it too. He shot out of the bush. Jiminy followed. I tried to steer the squirrel's body toward the hospital door, but he wasn't having any of that business. I can't say I blamed him.

I tried to hop out of his body, but my soul was stuck inside, held there by that nut, surrounded by a hundred-percent squirrel. I could feel the rain in his fur and the puddles on his feet. I could feel his lungs breathe in and out. I could feel the blood whooshing through his veins. I could feel his heart thumping in his chest. It was like a whole separate animal at the very center of him and me, and it made me hurt all over from remembering what it was like to have something like that living inside of me.

The soul map was completely busted, so we had to turn our head to see where Jiminy was. In a word, close. So when the squirrel skittered up the nearest tree, I didn't complain. There was a chance that mouthful of celestial nut or the body full of me might mean Jiminy could do us some real damage, and I didn't want to take any chances of that, not with Heidi so close and all.

The squirrel climbed like nobody's business, but every so often he turned his head to look down through the branches. The parking lot was full of wet cars. The warm ones steamed in the rain. A parked ambulance had its lights on, looping shadows all over everything. We were up pretty high. Jiminy watched and barked from below. My fear of heights was making an alarm of death ring full blast.

I tried talking with the squirrel, explaining that we needed to go inside the hospital, preferably through the door. But here's another fact: Squirrels aren't much for conversation.

We climbed higher up the trunk of the tree, winding around the thinner and thinner branches, stopping every so often to check on Jiminy. The situation wasn't good. Each time he barked, all four of his paws lifted into the air a bit. That's probably how he figured out he didn't have to keep his feet on the ground. His face was all, "Look at me! Dudes! Look at me!" as he rose in the air toward us, like someone had him on strings.

Pretty soon, there was no more tree left to climb. So the squirrel took a flying leap over to the side of the building. When he got to a windowsill, I was hoping he planned to knock and ask to come in. But no, he just looked. That's when his little heart started pounding even harder. I looked past his reflection in the window, hoping he'd maybe read my mind and seen Heidi.

But it wasn't Heidi's family in the room. It was a woman having a baby. That was like the last thing I wanted to see, what with her face all sweaty and red and her hair sticking out in all sorts of directions and . . . let me just say it was so gross that it made me glad I was going to die as a virgin for the second time. From the look on her husband's face, I think he would've agreed that was a better way to go.

With our eyes full of that mess, we started climbing. The side of the building wasn't as easy to go up as the tree, so he stopped again for a breather at the next window and that's when I saw her. Heidi.

Alive, but not for much longer. I could tell.

She lay in bed with all sorts of tubes coming out her nose and arms and her forehead. Her mom sat by her, leaning in, holding Heidi's hand. Her little brother's nose was red from crying and maybe also from chewing his weird, spicy gum. Maybe the saddest was her dad, who only had one hand to wipe his tears because he was holding her mom's free hand with his other.

I know I'm not an expert in much of anything, but I know what a dad feels when his kid is gone. It isn't something I'd wish on anyone. Not only was I trapped outside, I was too late.

A nurse was in the room with them, pointing at all the plugs and showing how he was going to take them out of Heidi. I was thinking that he'd unplug one thing and be done, but that wasn't how it went. He unhooked the tubes and machines one at a time, starting with the one that fed Heidi. He moved all slow, like a stoned panda. It was killing me. I started pulling on my soul, trying to get it out of the squirrel.

Below me, Jiminy was getting closer. I could hear his breath and practically feel it on the squirrel's feet. But I couldn't take my eyes off the room, even if I hadn't been afraid to look down. Heidi looked like she was sleeping. That was the only time I felt like a good guardian angel, when I watched her catch Zs. She looked so sweet and peaceful. Would her face change when she died? I was scared to find out. But I wasn't going to let her die alone, no matter what.

I didn't notice right away that Megan and Jiminy had arrived. The door swung open and Heidi's soul started leaking out of Jiminy's body and she looked terrible — cracked and fuzzy, like an old mirror. As soon as she was all the way out, Jiminy's body dropped.

Behind me, I could hear his soul panting. He'd almost made it to the window. The squirrel said a string of things that would have fried my brain, and I guess I was maybe scared that was going to happen, or maybe my soul wanted to be with Heidi's and finish this thing more than it wanted to be wrapped around a beating heart, because I managed to launch myself out of his body and right through the glass.

Jiminy took a flying leap, not realizing his soul would pass through the squirrel and the window too. He busted into the room right after me.

The Guardian Angel's Handbook: Soul Rehab Edition

Appendix G: The Ten Commandments for the Living

I. THOU SHALT HAVE COURAGE.

II. THOU SHALT BE LOYAL.

III. THOU SHALT TELL THE TRUTH.

IV. THOU SHALT HAVE FAITH IN THYSELF AND OTHERS.

V. THOU SHALT FORGIVE.

VI. THOU SHALT BE HUMBLE.

VII. THOU SHALT RESPECT ALL LIVING THINGS.

VIII. THOU SHALT FEEL GRATITUDE.

IX. THOU SHALT BE KIND.

X. **THOU SHALT LOVE, THOU SHALT LOVE, THOU SHALT LOVE.**

CHAPTER THIRTY

Heidi & Jerome

HEIDI'S SOUL ROSE out of Jiminy's body. She stopped fighting it. He couldn't have much more time left, she ached to realize. More, though, she didn't want anyone else's flesh — even as beloved as her dog's — between her soul and her body during its last moments. Jerome's handbook hit the floor with a slap. Too late for that now.

Only a few steps separated her from her physical self, but the distance seemed vast, unmanageable. Her vision was hazy, which might have accounted for the glow she perceived around her motionless body. Her toes, her fingertips, her hands, her throat, her cheekbones, her forehead . . . the edges of each were lit. She traced them with her eyes.

Separated from Jiminy, her soul seemed to expand and absorb everything. She felt sadness ooze from her family, a humble sense of purpose from the nurse who'd slipped the feeding tube out of her nose and then turned off the whooshing respirator. And then, in the clean silence of the room, Heidi first felt, then saw, Jerome, followed by Jiminy's bounding spirit.

Jerome. He'd brought Jiminy. The one thing she'd wished for, besides her own life back. Somehow, Jerome had known. And he'd known where to find her, even if it was too late to save her. It was all right, Heidi realized. Really, it was. It meant everything for her to be understood that well by another soul.

Jerome looked different somehow. It took her a moment to understand why. The green canvas jacket was gone. She followed the squared edges of his shoulders up past his neck, to his face. The arrow. It was gone too. On his unshadowed face, she noticed his lips and his nose and his eyes. They were brown, the color of chocolate and spring mud. Without that arrow, he looked — he looked exactly as he was meant to look, like someone she knew well enough to draw by heart.

Jerome said something, and she said his name, and without stopping to consider that he might reject her, or that she might be embarrassed, she moved toward him and wrapped her arms around him, every bit of anger she'd felt replaced with a greater share of love. She held him and gasped to feel her soul and his, together. She knew what she felt, and it was deeper than words.

All around her was the feeling of music, not made by any person or being but rather the vibration of their two souls that for one perfect moment had become one. Jerome looked into her eyes and she knew he was going to kiss her, and even though she wasn't sure that was necessary or even something she particularly wanted, it seemed like a good way to spend a last moment. He pressed his warm lips to hers, and before she could figure out how to respond, there was a *whoosh*, as though he'd fallen through a skin of ice on a pond.

And then he was gone.

※※※

At first I thought he was chasing me — but no, he'd seen his body on the floor and was sniffing it. He whined a little bit and I think he understood what had happened.

"Hey, little buddy, it's dinnertime in dog heaven," I said. "Go."

But he didn't. He slipped back inside his quiet little self and wagged his tail — *thump, thump* — and I couldn't take looking at anything that hopeless. When I was standing there, Heidi's family looked up and I swear they saw me, because of the shock on their faces, but maybe they were watching the security guard drag Megan off, or looking at the nurse, who said, "And now, I'm going to unhook the ventilator. This will be quiet and peaceful."

Shows what that applehat knew.

He unplugged it and it stopped its hissing and Heidi and I saw each other, and like we were thinking the same thing, we both turned our heads and looked at her body.

Her chest stopped going up and down and she had this look on her face and I don't care who knows, but it was beautiful. And I could swear her soul was made of music because I could hardly hear anything over the sound of the stupid angels singing.

I looked at her soul and I said, "I'm sorry I didn't take better care of you. I'm sorry I didn't help you see who you really are," and I closed my eyes because I thought she was probably going to hit me again, but she didn't. She shooped up to me and called my name, Jerome, like I was someone who mattered.

And then we stood together with no space between us. I felt her soul and my soul mix together like you'd put them in a blender, and that's when I knew something sort of huge. We might get born alone, and we might die all by ourselves, sometimes with some help from our cousins, but the best part of life is when you find someone you can be with, and you're good enough and they're good enough and no part of you wants anything else. I knew what the feeling was, and the word *happiness* didn't do it justice. Not even close.

I looked in her eyes and did the one thing I'd been thinking about since I pulled her out of that pond. Only in my imagination, I slipped in some tongue.

But there wasn't enough time before I felt a horrible pulling, like the kind you feel on those spinning amusement park rides that slam you up against a wall and press your cheeks into your ears. It was like gravity times ten, ripping my soul down like the Destroyer himself had grabbed ahold of my ankles. I felt my essence tear from Heidi's, and the sound was terrible and I knew that I was headed down to the lowest level of Hell — maybe a whole new level created just for me — and there was a part of me that was glad to feel her heart break as I left.

I thought about telling her something I'd only just figured out because I am slow even when I'm paying attention, which was this: I loved her. But instead, I called out something that would maybe be more useful.

And anyway, I got the feeling that she knew.

❧

His last words to Heidi weren't the ones she would have expected or hoped for. But they were the ones she needed to hear.

"Don't miss," he said.

She took one final look at her body, the body she'd come to love all the more for its flaws and its vulnerability. Without the ventilator, her chest was still. The heart monitor beeped, growing slower by the moment, a mechanical echo of the sound of a person bouncing a basketball.

Don't miss.

This time, she wouldn't.

CHAPTER THIRTY-ONE

Jerome

THE BOTTOM LEVEL of Hell wasn't what I expected. It was loud. Dark. Wet. And kind of pink, like maybe it had been decorated by the love child of Elton John and a mermaid. But it was punishing, all right. I wasn't sure I could take an eternity of the kind of abuse I was getting, which I can only describe as what a chicken probably feels like when a farmer is wringing its neck.

I used to think it was worse to kill chickens with an ax because of the way they would sometimes run around without their heads. Me and Mike were once talking with this friend of my dad's who told me that he knew of a headless chicken they kept alive for a week by squirting water down its throat with an eyedropper. Fact: There was no way a chicken could live for a week getting the kind of squeeze I was getting.

It was so bad I couldn't say anything. I couldn't have sworn if I tried, which was fine because my brain was having a hard time remembering any words, good or bad. I could hardly remember anything besides Heidi, Xavier, Gabe, and the taste of corn dogs.

For the longest time, I thought this was the Destroyer's way of making me suffer, giving me nothing to think about but the sensation of being crushed to death every sixty seconds or so.

And just when I thought things couldn't get worse, they did.

The crushing let up and my eyes were slammed with the brightest light — way brighter than the flashlight the security guard at the mall used, and that one had a setting meant to give people seizures. It was a killer light and I was cold and naked and someone was fiddling with my belly button and whipping me through the air and putting me in a cold, metal basket.

"It's a boy," a voice said. "A perfectly healthy boy."

I looked around to see who they were talking about, but my eyes were still melting with light. I couldn't make out anything farther away than my nose.

"Whoa! Nine pounds, fourteen ounces," the voice said. "Let's hope this is the most trouble he ever gives you."

Someone wrapped me in a soft blanket, and I stopped looking around to see who they were talking about. I was surrounded by people. And some of them were crying.

That's when I figured out they were talking about me. Me. Maybe if my head hadn't been squeezed so hard, I would've picked up what had happened sooner. I tried to explain that there had been some sort of mistake, that I wasn't where I was supposed to be, that I was someone else, but the words came out all messed up.

My arms and legs pushed against the blanket they'd wrapped around me, but there was no way out and after a while I stopped struggling because I got this urge, a stronger one than I'd ever felt in all my weird, messed-up life. I didn't even know these people, but I wanted to tell them what I knew about life and chances and the nine levels and the mistakes you don't have to make. I kept trying to say it, but it came out all wrong, like a crying cat or something, and the more I talked, the more I realized I was starting to forget. With each sound I made, what I knew, what I'd learned . . . it was slipping away.

I felt something struggling in my chest, this wild wiggling that hurt and made me gasp until I figured out what it was. A heart. After all those years, I had one again and I couldn't tell if the darned thing was beating or breaking. Maybe a little bit of both. I hoped with all of it that Heidi had made it, or I didn't know how I'd hang on to this new life. I imagined her face and I locked the memory of it inside me as best I could, and after a while, my crying turned into squeaky hiccups and it almost felt like things were going to be okay.

"Oh," a woman's voice said. "I think he's hungry. And just look at those beautiful brown eyes. Doesn't he look like an old soul?"

The memory of Heidi grew stronger inside of me, strong enough that I'd know her always, even if I never saw her again. And I felt the strangest thing in the air, something better than the smell of movie theater pop-corn. I felt it, and I knew what it was, even if I couldn't speak the word.

In that moment, I knew there was nothing else I had to say.

CHAPTER THIRTY-TWO

Heidi

HEIDI HEARD THE doctor's voice before she was fully awake.

"This is a very unusual case," the doctor said. "Ordinarily, patients who show no brain activity don't wake up, particularly when life-support measures have been terminated. They certainly don't wake up with all of their faculties intact."

Heidi opened her eyes. It was the morning after. The sky had finished with its business of raining, and it had wrapped startling blue arms around the world, lighting everything with a silvery glow: the clock, the sink, the old television that hung from the wall, silently broadcasting the news. On the wall across from her bed were her drawings. Someone had fastened each of them, one by one, to the bulletin board–covered wall, using tiny pins that shone like stars in the sunlight. Together, the images were huge.

Her parents, Rory, and Megan sat by her bed while the doctor stood at her feet, discussing the mystery of what had happened.

"Would you say it's a miracle?" Heidi's mother asked.

Megan, now fully dressed, opened her mouth but stopped herself when she saw that Heidi was awake. Heidi shook her head and Megan nodded. There was an instant understanding between the friends that they wouldn't speak of this.

The doctor slipped the clipboard under her arm. "The lawyers would have a heart attack if they heard me say it, but we're going to have all the equipment checked out to make sure it's working properly. That seems the most likely thing to me. But you can look at this however you want."

When they realized she was awake, the doctor departed. Heidi's family turned their full attention to her. Rory ran off to buy her some gum from a vending machine. Her dad ran a comb gently through her tangled hair, and her mother rubbed her feet, attention that would have mortified her before any of this had happened. Now, though, she didn't mind, not even when she couldn't tell whether it was her father's tears or her own sliding down her cheeks.

They did have some bad news about Jiminy. He'd been hit by a car. There was a chance he wouldn't make it. But the vet was hopeful.

Heidi didn't have to fake the look of shock she felt. He might live? After all of that?

"When I find the person who hit him," Rory said, handing her a stick of gum, "I'm going to go Uncharted 2 on his —"

"Don't use that word, Rory," Heidi's mother said.

"His apple?" Heidi said. She tucked the piece of gum in her mouth, savoring the cinnamon burn.

"Yeah," Rory said. "He'll have a sorry apple."

Heidi never told Rory whose apple he should pound into sauce. Mrs. Thorpe had done what Heidi needed her to do, and Jiminy was going to get better. She'd see to it.

She spent another day in the hospital, during which she was visited by many of her classmates, including Tammy Frohlich, who told her all about how Sully had broken his elbow and was sporting a cast that ran from his wrist to his armpit. He'd taken a spill at the mall while skateboarding in the food court. Apparently, he'd hit a patch of ice cubes.

"I'm totally going to be taking notes for Sully," Tammy said. "Do you want me to take them for you too?"

Heidi felt the slightest twinge of envy until she noticed Tammy had a cluster of poppy seeds between her top teeth. Her heart expanded; she recognized Tammy's offer as kindness in a clumsy package. As for Sully, well, his broken elbow was funny. She wished she'd seen it happen. It seemed his guardian angel hadn't been watching. Again.

"Your drawings are awesome, Heidi," Tammy said. "Can we print some of them in the yearbook? We'd planned to set aside a memorial page for you — no offense or anything. We could use that page for your art instead."

Did Heidi want the world to see her tiny cities? She looked at the wall and considered her work. From a distance, you couldn't see the detail in each drawing. Together, though, what she'd created looked interesting. Maybe even spectacular. The lights and darks made complicated patterns, and if you looked at them just so, you could imagine the many lives bubbling in the depths of the paper. So many lives, so many dreams, so much love.

"Sure," Heidi said. "Use your favorites. I'd like that. I'd like it a lot."

⊗⊗⊗

The day she left the hospital, she was alone in her room, missing the noise of Jerome in her head. A couple of times, she'd opened her mouth to point something out to him before she remembered he wasn't there — that he wouldn't ever be again. She couldn't keep the tears from filling her eyes, slipping down her cheeks. Her face was sticky with them and she imagined what he'd say to her. *Get up. Get out of bed. Get on with it. Whoosh!* He'd wanted her to live, even when it cost him everything he had. He'd wanted to live himself, and it was the least she could do to reenter the world.

So Heidi stood and dressed herself and, as she did, marveled in the feeling of being inside the body that belonged to her. She pulled a new shirt overhead, a gift from her mother, the sort of thing she'd never have had the guts to wear before because it fit her shape exactly. She stepped into her pants, appreciating the way her legs worked and they way they felt when covered in the soft denim of her jeans. As she slipped a pair of cotton socks over her feet, she admired the vamp toenail polish Megan had applied when Heidi was first admitted to the hospital, back before they knew she'd ever walk out again. It looked

292

good. Really good. Last came her favorite shoes, a pair of boots that had molded to her feet and felt like perfection to the very bottom of her soles.

She sat on the edge of the bed, looking through the window that Jerome had burst through, and she missed him fiercely. It was quiet inside her head without him, a silence that seemed to span the width of the universe, a silence nothing could ever fill. She wouldn't let herself imagine his fate, couldn't believe that he wouldn't, somehow, get one more chance. And part of her desperately wanted more time with him, time to see where that kiss might have led.

But, having tasted it just for a moment, she was beginning to understand a hard truth about what can happen when two people find each other in life. In a way, it was a lot like art. To draw someone, you have to see their edges and all the space around them. To even start to love someone, you have to know where you start and where you end. Where you are, and where you aren't, the shape you make in the world.

❈

Heidi left the hospital in a wheelchair. Though she could walk and felt surprisingly good, it was a hospital rule. She planned to ditch the wheels as soon as the nurses stopped looking. The elevator stopped on the third floor, the maternity ward. The doors slid open and Heidi's family moved to the side so that another family had room to board. Heidi looked at them. The mother cradled a brand-new baby. A boy, judging by his snug blue hat. The mother too was in a wheelchair. She gently stroked the back of her baby's tiny neck. From where she sat, Heidi had a good view of his face.

"What the —" Heidi whispered.

When the baby heard Heidi's voice, he turned to look in her direction. Those eyes. She'd know them anywhere. She wanted to reach for him, touch his tiny nose, hold his little hand, run a finger down his cheek, just marvel at him. While everyone around her practiced good elevator etiquette, staring forward, taking care to space themselves evenly, Heidi gaped, hoping for another look into the baby's eyes. A couple of times, she opened her mouth to speak. But the words wouldn't come. What could she even say? It was impossible anyway. She was probably still messed up from the drowning. But the idea filled her with a seed of hope, nonetheless.

The elevator touched down and the doors whooshed open. The air smelled of wet earth and sunshine. The baby's father pushed the mother's wheelchair up to the glass doors in the lobby. He hurried outside to get the car while the mother waited, holding the child. Heidi eased herself out of her wheelchair. Her legs still felt a bit wobbly, like she hadn't been inside them for ages. She filled her lungs, found her center, and walked slowly toward the woman, who was straining to reach the button that would open the door.

"Heidi," her mother said. "What are you doing?" But Heidi was listening to a different voice now. Her own.

"Let me help," she said.

The woman looked surprised and Heidi almost instantly

regretted making the offer. She'd embarrassed herself. The woman was a stranger, after all.

"Thank you," the woman said. "You're an angel. With perfect timing. And here's our ride now."

Heidi blushed, and though the tips of her ears turned red, she didn't mind. She took the handles of the wheelchair and helped the woman and her baby through the door. It was so bright she could hardly see anything but what was right in front of her. The wheelchair grew light as the woman eased herself out of it and walked away with the baby. Heidi felt her heart in her chest, the sun on her skin, the light in her eyes, and the earth beneath her feet, and she extended her soul out to the edges of her body, and even a bit beyond, as she took a strong, steady step into the world.

ACKNOWLEDGMENTS

WHEN THEY GIVE out Academy Awards there are always those recipients who rush to the stage, fan their teary faces, and then bore the audience to death by thanking everyone they've ever met, including their lawyers.

Seriously, the lawyers? You paid those people $500 an hour. That's a good thank-you note. It even included your signature, unless your accountant signed it, and the only thing duller than thanking a lawyer is thanking an accountant. Thank a speechwriter next time. Please.

On the other hand are the winners who deliver polished speeches that knit the theme of the movie with a vivid philosophy of life. These actors are inevitably British, which is why you're meant to read the following in a crisp accent.

I had a dream once when I was still in my teens. In it, I died.

This is not supposed to happen in dreams, but I was most certainly dead. I knew this because my soul was sitting atop the refrigerator, something I never could have managed were I still among the living.

As I looked down on the people I loved, I felt this terrible sadness. My grief wasn't that I was dead. Rather, it was that I would no longer be able to walk and talk with the people dearest to me. Anything I'd left unsaid would stay that way forever. It wasn't my life I'd miss; it was the people who gave it beauty and meaning.

From the metaphorical fridge-top where I now do my deepest thinking, I can see quite a collection of beloveds today: family and friends and people who believed in my work and dreams as I believed in theirs. I'm eternally grateful to you, and you know who you are, and in a way, this book says what I wish were true, that we could go on knowing and loving each other for all time.

This book was designed by Phil Falco and Becky Terhune. The text was set in Sabon, a typeface designed by Jan Tschichold. The book was printed and bound at R. R. Donnelley in Crawfordsville, Indiana. Production was supervised by Cheryl Weisman, and manufacturing was supervised by Adam Cruz.